WHAT CAN'T BE TRUE

JAKE HOUSER CRIME SERIES #1

BO THUNBOE

WESTON PRESS, LLC

Published in 2018 by Weston Press, LLC

Cover Design by Jeroen ten Berge (jeroentenberge.com)
Interior Design by Kevin G. Summers (kevingsummers.com)

ISBN: 978-1-949632-00-2 (trade paperback)
ISBN: 978-1-949632-01-9 (ebook)

Weston Press, LLC
Naperville, IL
www.thunboe.com

For Diane

PROLOGUE

He pushed his hand into his pocket and rubbed the rosary, the cool stone beads rolling over each other with a muffled *chack-ing*. There was nothing to think about; he'd done what needed doing. This was just the cleanup. He squeezed the rosary tight, then released it.

Sticking his head inside the car, he looked out through the windshield to check his aim one last time. The car's front end pointed across the picnic grove, straight at the old concrete footing, all that remained of the pedestrian bridge that had once spanned the waters. Beyond the footing the Paget River rushed, the full moon's light glinting off its rain-swelled waters. He would drop the rock on the gas pedal, force the car into gear, and get out of the way. The Buick would speed across the grass, launch off the bridge footing, and disappear into the river forever.

A harsh *skritch*ing to his left. He flinched and dropped into a crouch, scanning the parking lot and the long curve of road entering the forest preserve. His heart pounded, his ears hot with pumping blood. Again. A scraping this time. Maybe a deer working its antlers against a tree. Or a skunk rooting around in the garbage cans. Nothing to worry about. The gate closed at dark, so the park had been empty for hours.

He picked up the rock he'd pried from the mud along the riverbank. It was heavy, flat, and cold in his hands. A breeze puffed, then held steady, the cool fall air chilling his sweat.

A bulbous white shape sprang up, startling him so much he nearly dropped the rock. The shape bounded across the picnic grove and snagged on a clump of grass. The breeze dropped, and it deflated, a plastic bag turned ghostly by the full moon.

"Get a grip."

But the bag and the clump that had snagged it had his attention now. A mound capped with a stout tuft of grass. His gaze went to the dozens more such mounds that stood between the car and the river. He ground his teeth. If he didn't tie the steering wheel in place, any one of them could throw the car off target.

He dropped the rock and searched the passenger compartment, avoiding the body, but found nothing to use to tie the steering wheel.

He reached for the trunk release lever, then snatched his hand back. The trunk was staying closed.

Remembering the rosary, he fished it from his pocket. He gathered up the body's wrists, pinned them to the top of the steering wheel, and tried to wrap the rosary around them. But it was an awkward job in the tight space, and the arms kept slipping before he could get them tied. He settled his hip on the seat's edge and squeezed the wrists tighter to the wheel before trying again.

He felt a throb against his thumb.

Another.

He jerked up out of the car, bile rising in his throat.

The body looked dead, pale and limp, dark blood crusted on its face. But its lips parted, and it sucked in a long whistle of air. He took a step backwards, and another, then stopped on shaky knees. He pulled in a deep breath, rolled his shoulders, and ducked back into the car.

The body shuddered, gulped air, and arched back against the seat. He threw his weight against it, but the body convulsed so hard it flung him back onto the grass.

The body moaned, a deep vibrato that broke into gasping breaths.

He lunged back into the car, trapped the head in the crook of his right elbow, and forced it down. The body fought him, but he cranked harder, a scream escaping him. Then he heard a quick string of pops and a *crack*, and the body went limp.

He pushed away and slid out of the car, sucking in big slugs of air, slick with sweat and trembling with adrenaline. A hot gush rose in his throat and he puked, the sour spew fouling his mouth and burning his sinuses. He wiped his chin, blew his nose into his hand, and rubbed the filth onto the grass.

He took long slow breaths until the pounding in his head subsided. Then he got back on his feet, fished the rosary off the floor, pushed the body up straight, and got its wrists tied to the steering wheel. He lowered all the windows and started the car.

He was ready.

He set the rock on the gas pedal, and the engine rushed to a high-pitched whine. Then he put the car in gear.

The Buick leapt away, the door brushing against his hair as it swung shut. The car's back end bobbed as it bounced across the grass, but its course stayed true. Sparks sprayed when the front bumper hit the concrete bridge footing.

Then the car was airborne.

He chased after it and saw the splash. As he arrived at the riverbank, the car was floating, its momentum carrying it away from him across the dark waters. The engine coughed, then fell silent. The current turned the car, which was sinking slowly, its front end low under the engine's weight.

The silence was broken by a muffled shout. From the trunk. Then banging. A film of water was flung off the trunk with each blow.

"God damn it!" He clenched his fists and stepped forward. The riverbank crumbled beneath him, and he fell backward, his hands grabbing at air, and hit hard. A short squeal of pain escaped from him before he bit it off.

A gunshot cracked, shaking more water off the trunk. Another shot.

The water reached the open windows and flooded into the passenger compartment. The car dropped abruptly, leaving only the trunk above water.

Four more shots punched through the trunk before the car slid beneath the surface with a bubbling rush.

Now the deed was done.

CHAPTER ONE
Five Years Later

Detective Jake Houser scanned the crime scene from the shade at the edge of the parking lot. The Buick had been pulled from the water trunk first, and a muck-spackled smear across the grass led to where it now slumped on flat tires in the sunbaked picnic area. The mud slathering the car's faded blue paint was drying and starting to crack, the windows gaped empty, and the trunk lid stood open. The body was there, in the trunk. A person committing suicide couldn't drive his car into the lagoon from the trunk.

So this was a murder. Weston's second murder this year.

His phone buzzed with a text message. Detective Callie Diggs, asking if Jake wanted help with the case. The text he'd sent her the day before was visible at the top of the screen, and his chest tightened when he saw it. It had felt right when he sent it, but her deafening silence in response told him it had been wrong.

He put the phone away and turned back toward the car. The dead came first.

Stepping into the sun, he backtracked along the mud trail, his feet crunching the browned-out grass, to the gap in the weeds where the car had been dragged up over the riverbank.

The sun was so strong he had to squint through his Aviators, his face slick with sweat.

His gaze followed the car's path across forty feet of mud-flat. Bootprints pocked the mud, left by the Boy Scouts who had discovered the car while cleaning up the lagoon. Ripe decay filled the air.

Officer Grady, the responding uniform, stepped up beside him. "I grabbed a handout from the information box, and it shows that spot as the deepest point in the lagoon. Nineteen feet." Grady offered Jake a tri-folded piece of paper. "Probably only ten or twelve feet deep right now, thanks to the drought, or the Scouts wouldn't have spotted it."

Jake gave the map a quick look, then pushed it into his front pocket. He'd spent a lot of time in this park as a teenager and knew it well. Back then a walking bridge spanned the lagoon and led to the narrow island that shielded it from the Paget River's main flow. Jake would often cast down from the bridge to that deep spot, hoping to land one of the monster flathead catfish rumored to live there. He never did. It felt strange to be here now, investigating a murder, in the same spot where his memories were full of the clean energy and hopefulness of youth. He'd never had that feeling while working in Chicago, but had experienced it often since returning to Weston.

There was nothing left of the old walking bridge now, other than a concrete footing on both banks. But even when the bridge existed it had been too narrow for a car, and any car driven out onto that mud bottom would bog down before the rear tires got wet.

Sweat ran into his eye, and he blinked the sting away. He glanced at Grady, who had an excited sheen on his face.

Youth.

Grady bobbed his head toward the Buick. "The body's still in the car."

"Lead the way."

Beyond the car, a horde of boys in Boy Scout khaki, green, and red swarmed along the shade at the wood's edge. A half dozen men dressed in similar uniforms held them in check, and a scattering of other adults lingered back under the trees, swatting at the mosquitos bombing them from the underbrush. It was a big crowd, but cleaning out the lagoon was a massive project. The boys had already filled a big Dumpster that squatted in the parking lot.

Grady went straight to the Buick's trunk, but Jake always examined a scene from the outside and worked his way in. He knew that once he saw the victim, anger would shift his focus from the scene to the killer—and he needed to learn what the scene could tell him before allowing the shift.

He stepped to the front of the car and scraped away the muck clinging to the front bumper with the bottom of his shoe. He found a pair of holes where the license plate should be mounted and rusty scrapes down the chrome. He dragged his shoe against the grass to wipe off the mud, then called out to Grady. "Is there a plate back there?"

Grady shook his head as he came around the side of the car. "No, but I got the VIN off the dashboard and called it in. It's owned by a Pearl Cassano. Last registered in December of 2011." He ripped a sheet from his notebook and handed it to Jake. "Here's her info."

"Nice work." The registration date gave Jake the beginning of a timeline, and the owner's name gave him a person to question. Questioning people was Jake's specialty. But the crime scene always came first. He had limited time to get what he could from it; after he released it, anything found would be useless in court.

He stepped over a clump of muck to the driver's door. He could see where Grady had rubbed through the mud on the windshield and scooped mud off the dashboard to get at the Buick's vehicle identification number. Bending down, Jake peered into the passenger compartment. The cloth seat covers hung in tatters from rusty springs. The rear bench seat had been dislodged and lay twisted across the space; light shone through from the open trunk. Mud, sculpted into smooth swirls by the current, filled the compartment halfway to window level. A tangle of riverweed hung from the steering wheel, with something caught in it. Probably a fishing lure. A whiff of organic dampness reminded him more of a compost pile than death.

"How do you think they killed him, Detective?" Grady's voice reverberated through the car from where he stood behind the trunk.

Jake pulled back. "Let's take a look."

He stepped around to the rear of the car and examined the shadowy space. A skull stared back at him from the mud-filled trunk. A handprint was pressed into the sludge on a jaw stained nearly as dark as the muck around it.

"Run it for me while I look it over." Jake pulled latex gloves from his pocket and tugged them on.

"One of the Scouts picked up the skull and waved it around before a dad stopped him," Grady said. "Kid thought it was a Halloween prop."

Jake removed his sunglasses, folded them into his shirt pocket, and ducked his head into the trunk. The organic stench was so dense in the tight space he tasted it. Sweat dripped off his nose into the mud.

He reached in and rolled the skull back with a knuckle. The lower jaw gaped open to reveal crooked teeth, stark white against the stained bone, the molars crammed with amalgam. In the upper jaw, a gold central incisor glowed dully. Dental work. Which meant x-rays existed to confirm an identity—when he had one to compare to.

He caught the shine of slick nylon against the back of the passenger seat, with a skeletonized hand sticking out of it. The hand looked too big for the skull, but the comparison was hard to make when all the flesh was gone. Jake shifted to get a better look, and a tight shaft of sunlight blinded him.

He straightened up and found its source. A hole in the trunk lid. Six of them. *Christ!* Jake burped up a mouthful of bile and swallowed it back down with a grimace.

"Grady." Jake gestured at the holes. "Take a look."

Grady eyeballed the open lid, then walked around the side of the car and rubbed a hand over it. "Are those what I think they are?"

"Bullet holes."

"When do you think that happened? Do you think he was still alive when the car went in the water?"

"I do."

That's exactly how it had gone down. A man locked in a trunk with a loaded gun would shoot the latch, but these bullet holes were scattered across the trunk lid, which meant the shooter had been in a panic. The panic of someone locked in the trunk of a car with water pouring in. Someone who was drowning, and knew it. Had the killer stood here on the bank and listened to the shots and the screams that must have gone with them? Did he laugh? What kind of monster killed this way?

Jake sent Grady to take down the names and contact information of all the Boy Scouts and their families before sending them home. Then he called for a forensic team and an assistant coroner. Between the two of them, maybe he'd get an identity.

Then he would find the bastard who'd done this.

And make him pay.

CHAPTER TWO

Bull Warren stared out the hospice window, nothing to do but endure. Clouds drifted across the sky, thinning into wisps that passed from view, leaving behind an empty blue expanse. He flopped his head to look out his door, but the hallway was empty.

The air concentrator thumping away in the corner and the airy hiss from the cannula under his nose wormed back into his consciousness. Again. Bull gritted molars worn smooth by decades of teeth grinding, and turned on the bedside radio just as "traffic and weather together on the eights" began. As useless as that information was for a guy in a hospice bed, even traffic reports beat listening to the constant reminder that there wasn't enough man left of him to even breathe for himself.

He straightened the cannula under his nose—his COPD tether—and turned back to the window. He imagined that beautiful sun warming him. Maybe Bev would come by and push his wheelchair over to the baseball fields—just a girl taking her dad for a walk like a damn pet.

He closed his eyes, mind drifting, memories pulsing in and fading out. He had always lived with an eye on the future, but now that he didn't have one his focus kept drifting to the past. The hospice social worker said this was normal. Father John said it would help him make a full confession so he would be ready to join Jesus in Heaven. The confession wasn't going to happen. No offense to Father John, but Bull would be his own best advocate in front of the Almighty. The Big Guy would cut him some slack—almost everything he'd ever done had served a greater good.

So Bull worried less about the afterlife, and more about what he might be leaving behind. The possibility that one of his old deals might rise up against his daughter after he was gone... it twisted his insides worse than the damn stomach cancer. She deserved better, and he hoped his past would stay as dead and buried as he would soon be.

He barked out a laugh at his weak joke. It shook his stomach, sending out a flick of intestinal fire. He rubbed his gut and searched for a pleasant memory to distract from the pain. He found several. Bev pitching her team to the city championship when she was twelve. That was a good one. And their road trip to the Grand Canyon. And that trip to Canada with Ernie and his boy. Seeing those two together always made Bull think of his own son and what might have been if—

"Mr. Warren! How are you today?" A pink-clad nurse bustled into the room.

"Fine, Nancy." Bull pushed himself up straighter in the bed. Eleven different nurses rotated shifts without a pattern he could identify. He knew each nurse's name and as much about her and her family as she was willing to share. Knowing about people and what they did and who they did it with was how he had been so successful for so long. "But call me Bull, okay?" He'd gotten the nickname during high school football. It suited his thick body and blunt style so much better than his given name—Grant—that it had stuck.

Nancy merely nodded. She wasn't a talker.

"How're your White Sox doing?" Bull asked. Like most west-suburbanites he was a Cubs fan, but he could talk about the Sox if he had to.

"Not a World Series year." Nancy turned away and fussed about the room, filling his water pitcher and checking his machines.

"I don't think the boys in blue will be heading back this year, either." The Cubbies could string together a couple hits for a win if the bullpen didn't implode, but they weren't the force they'd been last year. He was damn glad he'd lived long enough to see the Cubs beat the Billy Goat curse and end the hundred and eight year drought. "But you never know."

Nancy ignored him, and Bull went back to staring out the window at the day passing him by. Three boys with baseball gloves and a bat jostled each other on the sidewalk along West Street. Above them, a giant bird—some kind of hawk or maybe even an eagle—swooped down and landed on the light pole. Bull had always wanted to be able to identify birds, especially the raptors, but now he was out of time.

A rattling buzz sounded from the table that spanned his bed. His cell phone. He picked it up and checked the screen. He didn't recognize the number, but that wasn't unusual. He had traded a lot of favors over the decades and was still collecting.

He pulled in a big breath. "Bull Warren here."

"It's Rick Miller." A tight, hoarse voice. "From the Secretary of State's office? IT department? You helped me with my—"

"I remember. It's my body giving me trouble, not my brain." Bull put a little truth in all his lies. Sometimes his mind lagged like it was pushing through a fog. But the painkillers caused that, not the cancer. The fog would only get worse when he finally agreed to the morphine Doctor Death kept pushing on him.

"I... uh."

"What is it?" Now Bull remembered the little weasel. Miller's son had been picked up for possession, and Bull had fixed it. "Spit it out."

"Someone ran a search on the Buick."

"Hold on." Bull pressed the phone to his stomach, his pulse accelerating. "We done, Nancy?"

"I still need to—"

"I have to take this." Bull gave her his nice-guy smile, and when she didn't respond, he threw in a head tilt and a pout. "Please. Just a… few minutes." He ran out of air, and the last words were an effort.

"Of course." She picked up the water pitcher and left the room.

Bull drew two more breaths in through the cannula, his head lifting with each effort. "Who ran it?"

"I got that right here, but this is it." Miller's voice wavered with tension. "I do this, and we're square."

Bull didn't have wind to waste arguing about a future he wouldn't see, so he kept quiet and let Miller stew.

"Hello?"

"You done weaseling?" Bull pulled in a big breath. "Spit it out."

"Okay. Officer Sean Grady with the Weston Police Department ran the search at eleven thirty-six this morning."

Bull knew of Grady. Second-generation officer. Bright bulb in a dim force.

"That it?" he asked.

"Yeah, but I wa—"

Bull ended the call. His heart hammered, and darkness edged into his vision as his open-mouthed gasping bypassed the air supply pumping to his nose.

The Buick.

He clamped his mouth shut and concentrated on long even breaths through his nose. Eventually his vision cleared, his pulse slowed, and the pounding faded away.

He could do this. He wasn't helpless. He knew people and owned favors.

He scrolled through his contacts to the numbers for his many relatives. He found the one he wanted and hit dial.

"Margie? I need to know"—he sniffed in a lungful—"what Officer Grady is working on right now."

"He was first on the scene out at Radar Grove." Margie's voice hovered above a whisper. "Some kids found a dead body in a car they pulled out of the lagoon."

He almost asked her if she had the body count right, but his synapses fired just fast enough to stop him. He needed to focus and fix this, or it would destroy him before the cancer and COPD finished fighting over the job. "Which detective?"

"Deputy Chief Braff sent Jake out to handle it."

"Thanks, Margie. I owe you one."

Of course Braff had sent Houser. The DC thought Jake Houser was God's gift to detection.

"You don't owe me anything. You just focus on getting better."

She hung up without a goodbye, and Bull smiled. Margie understood family. Claire Warren had, too, but then she'd married Frank Houser, a nobody from nowhere with nothing.

Bull had pegged Frank as bad news from the very beginning. And Jake looked so much like his dad that seeing him always put Frank in Bull's mind.

He still had his family contacts open on his phone, and he caught himself about to call Houser. Damn pain medication! He pushed the NURSE CALL button. Time to back off the drugs. He deleted Houser from his contact list so he couldn't make that mistake again. If only it were so easy in real life.

He lay back to wait for Nurse Nancy's return, his pain-muddled mind clearing as he focused on the Buick. He would need help with the car—and with Houser. And he'd get it. Radar Grove was a county forest preserve, and his county ties were still strong. Bev didn't yet understand the full scope of her power as sheriff, but even playing it straight, she had a lot of influence. And they both had Hogan. Ernie's boy was working out great as Bev's right hand. She appreciated his loyalty, and Bull liked having someone he could trust looking out for his daughter. Besides, the kid had deserved a break after that mess back in Newark.

Maybe the Buick turning up now was for the best.

While he was here to handle it.

And to take the heat, if he failed.

CHAPTER THREE

Paget County Sheriff Bev Warren clicked from one spreadsheet to another and back again. According to her source, the county board chairman planned to cut her department's budget by another five percent this year. Five percent probably didn't sound like much to the chairman, but *he* didn't have to find where to make the cuts. Bev had already cut the department's fixed costs to the absolute bone with last year's budget, which left her with—

Her desk phone rang. She stared daggers at it. She had told her secretary to hold all calls.

After three rings it went silent.

She stabbed another forkful of salad and stuffed it in her mouth, the raspberry vinaigrette tangy on her tongue. A droplet of dressing landed on her notepad, and she wiped it off with her thumb, leaving a purple smear. *What ever happened to going out to lunch? This job, that's what.* It chained her to this desk fourteen hours a day. But here, sitting behind this desk, was where she did her best work. She had risen through the administration division, and the things a sheriff did from behind a desk—crunching numbers and planning and scheduling—were her strengths.

Her dad always said to focus on your strengths.

She clicked through the spreadsheets again, but there was no getting around the obvious. The only line items big enough to handle a five percent cut were fuel and deputy salaries. If she cut those, she'd have fewer deputies on the street, and they'd be covering less ground when they were out there. Reducing deputy visibility *always* resulted in more street crime. That couldn't be the solution.

She rolled the problem around, looking for an angle of attack, and smiled when she found it. Her department received eighty-nine percent of its budget from the county fund, and the other eleven percent from fees it charged for its services. Simple math said she could make up for the funding cut by raising all her department's fees by fifty percent. She didn't want to raise those fees, but if she played it right, she wouldn't have to. Most fees were charged to lawyers—to serve court papers and evict tenants—and lawyers were a vocal group. If she leaked the potential fee increases to a friendly reporter—with a finger pointed at the county board chairman, where the blame belonged—she might be able to kill the budget cut before it happened.

A sharp knock sounded on her door as it swung open. Deputy Hogan stepped into her office and closed the door behind him.

"Why don't you just come right on in, Deputy?"

Hogan's aftershave wafted across the space, a leathery citrus like Bev's dad always wore. Hell, it was probably the same brand. She hadn't realized how tight those two were until her dad went into hospice and she saw how often Hogan was there. He even brought her dad the Eucharist on Sunday afternoons, in a shiny container that looked like a brass coin purse.

Hogan leaned against the wall by the door and crossed his thick arms, stretching his suit jacket to the limits of its flexibility. His eyes drilled into hers, but he stayed silent. His intensity—and the rumors that had followed him from Newark—unsettled some people. But he was loyal, and a deal was a deal. She'd made Hogan her assistant and her dad had gotten her the Republican nomination for sheriff. Which meant he'd gotten her the job. The Republican nominee always won the election in Paget County politics.

"Did I forget an appointment?" She pawed through the papers on her desk, found her planner, and confirmed she had the afternoon wide open. She pushed back from the desk and was about to ask Hogan what he wanted when her cell phone rang from the depths of her purse. She fumbled through the big bag and finally found the phone. Her dad. She pulled on a smile and fought back the sadness she felt every time she talked to him. His voice had been reduced to a trembling shadow of its former strength.

"Hey, Dad." She swiveled her chair to hide the tear threatening to spill from the corner of her eye. Her mom and brother had both died when Bev was nine—leaving her alone with her dad—and knowing she would soon lose him, too, hurt through to her core. "How are you?"

"Hogan with you?"

Her dad's voice held some of its old vigor. Oxygen hissed into the phone, and the machine pumping it thumped away in the background.

"He just walked in." She wiped the tear away.

"You're going to need him."

Sweat broke across her forehead. After her dad went into hospice, he'd tried to tell her about some of his old "deals"—in case something came up after he was gone. Some might look bad if taken out of context, he'd said. But halfway through his first story, about how he'd convinced a key councilman to vote in favor a new youth center, she'd stopped him. She didn't want to know. He'd accepted that, eventually, and told her he'd left her the tools to deal with things—whatever the hell that meant—and to work with Hogan if something came up.

She shot a look at Hogan then turned back to the window. "What is it?"

"Remember when the Bears looked at building a new stadium in Paget County?"

"Vaguely."

Thirty years ago, maybe more, the Chicago Bears had talked about relocating to a large piece of then-empty land just outside Weston in unincorporated Paget County. The county went crazy with excitement, but instead of moving out to the suburbs, the Bears rebuilt Soldier Field into something that looked like a UFO landing on the lakeshore.

"I worked that hard. Behind the scenes." He wheezed and his machine hissed. "Would have meant a lot of jobs for Paget County."

"And?"

Bev's mind cartwheeled through what he might have left out. His involvement in the stadium deal was news to her, but it wasn't surprising. He had always been working one deal or another.

"Some of what I did wasn't completely on the straight and narrow."

Hiss.

Bev gulped and turned her chair back toward her desk, a hand reaching out and flicking the corner of a stack of manpower reports.

"Five years ago a guy found a document that would have dredged it up." Her dad coughed. "We set up a meet so I could... buy it. He showed up, but something spooked him and he took off..."—*hiss*—"... before the exchange. I never heard from him again."

"And?"

"The car he was in that night just turned up on the bottom of Radar Grove Lagoon."

Shit! The skeleton in the trunk.

Bev's face flushed, and sweat beaded on her arms. "For Christ's sake, Dad." She took a few seconds to gather herself. "You sure this is the same car?"

"I'm sure. We—*you*—need to get ahead of it." *Hiss.* "Right now."

"Who was the guy?"

"A nobody named Donald Silva. He's been missing since then."

"But if he had the document when he went into the water, it would be dissolved by now, right?"

"We can't be sure of that. He could have had it in something."

Bev said nothing.

"I didn't do this, Bev."

Of course not. Her dad swapped favors and pulled strings. He didn't kill people.

His machine hissed and thumped in the silence.

"But Bev, see how it might…"—*hiss*—"… look if that document is found in that car?"

It would look like you killed a blackmailer. But that couldn't be true.

Bev glanced at Hogan, stoic against the wall. "Hogan knows the story?"

"Everything."

Her dad's tone stretched Hogan's knowledge far beyond hers.

She heard him suck a tight breath between his teeth; it was the sound he made when the cancer was stabbing fire through his gut. "You need to take over the investigation so you can find the document and not Houser."

"Jake got the case?"

"He can't be the one to find it."

Her dad ended the call as abruptly as ever, leaving her with the phone still pressed to her cheek. She put it back in her purse and spun her chair to look out into the glare of another hot day. She closed her eyes against the brightness, then squeezed them tight as the pain of her dad's approaching death spread through her. Putting her dad in hospice was supposed to have allowed them both time to prepare for his death, but that had turned out to be bullshit. It had been three months, and nothing about it was easier.

She forced her mind back to the problem her dad had dumped on her. There was a document that would reveal some effort he'd made to acquire the stadium for Paget County that—out of context and with the twenty-twenty vision of hindsight—would look bad. Even if all it did was link her dad to the body… that was bad enough. It would spur his enemies, and he'd made plenty over the years, to try to score a few headlines before his death took away their opportunity, to hell with the truth.

Whatever her dad had done with the stadium deal, he didn't deserve that.

Her eyes sought the photo on her credenza. She and her dad at a Cubs game, the bright green field behind them. They went to one game every year. Even during her teens, when their relationship was rocky. Even when the Cubbies were terrible. She took a moment to let the memories of that day—it had been her birthday, and the Cubbies had won—fill her. She could handle this. She *would* handle this. But she'd do it her way, using the tools her job and the law gave her.

"Jansen owes us," she said to Hogan. "I'll send him out to the scene personally."

"Good. Controlling the cause of death is half the battle."

She picked up her desk phone and dialed the number.

"Coroner Jansen here."

"Did you get the call out to Radar Grove?"

"Sheriff? I did, but I'm golfing with Mayor Dietz. We're on the twelfth hole."

"I need you—"

"One of my deputies will handle it. Skeletonized remains in the trunk of a car. The body has obviously been in the water for many years."

Bev changed tactics. "My dad thought you were the man for this job. I'll call him back and—"

"Hold on a minute now, Sheriff. There's no need for that." Jansen's voice now had that whine she hated. "I'll head down there as soon as we're done."

"Now," she said, with more bite in her voice than she'd intended. Having to invoke her dad always pissed her off.

Silence.

Then Jansen's voice came faintly through. "I've been called to a crime scene, Mr. Mayor. We'll have to play again another time."

He came back on the line. "What do you want me to do?"

"I want you to tell me about every piece of paper in that car—every McDonald's wrapper, gas receipt, and scrap you find—before any of it goes in a report. Got it?" She needed that damn document, whatever it was.

"I understand."

She warned him Jake had the case, then she ended the call and swiveled her chair around to face Hogan.

"What is in this document?" she asked bluntly.

"Bull said not to tell you."

Of course he did. She considered *ordering* Hogan to tell her, but what if he didn't?

She'd leave it alone.

For now.

Hogan pushed off the wall with a bounce of his shoulders. "What about Houser?"

With Jansen, Bev controlled the determination of *what* caused the death, but the investigator—Jake—would decide *who* caused it. Could she trust him? Jake had always been a straight shooter growing up, but he'd spent ten years with the Chicago PD, a notorious cesspool of corruption, before coming back to Weston. And even if he played it straight, he wasn't the boss in Weston—that was Chief Arvind, who was as political as they came.

She couldn't risk it. She needed to take over the case.

She stepped over to the county map covering her wall. It had more than a dozen colors splashed across it, each marking the jurisdiction of a different law enforcement agency. A couple quirks in intergovernmental relations had caused Radar Grove to be hatched with three colors: County Forest Preserve Police blue because it handled patrol, Weston PD green because it had investigative responsibility, and her department's red because it was a county park. She had an obvious argument to make, and several ways to make it.

She considered her options. At a recent law enforcement event, Jake had chided her about loving media attention, and a trunk murder like this one would generate lots of it. So he would be expecting her to want the case. She would meet Jake's expectation with one hand while working the power silos in the rear with the other.

"Send the zone car out there with instructions to take control of the scene directly from Detective Houser. The park is within county jurisdiction."

"And?"

Bev turned away from the map and faced the big man. "And remember you work for me. We'll do this my way."

Hogan grunted and reached for the door. She opened her mouth to warn him against doing anything more than what she'd told him to do, but stopped. No matter what the real truth was back in Newark, here in Paget County Hogan had earned the benefit of the doubt.

After he left she picked up her desk phone and dialed County Board Chairman Borgeson. He was new to the job, and with his inflated sense of county government power, it would be easy to convince him her office should run this investigation. And when he was convinced, he'd convince others. As the top Republican in county government, he could apply pressure to people even her dad could no longer reach.

While she waited for him to come on the line, her thoughts turned to her dad's answer to a question she hadn't asked him.

I didn't do this, he'd said.

She believed him.

Didn't she?

CHAPTER FOUR

Jake wanted to dive into the trunk and identify the victim—the first step in any murder investigation—but protocol required him to wait for the deputy coroner's permission. And she wouldn't give it until after the forensic team had finished documenting the scene.

So he paced the grove.

He glanced into the trunk on each pass, but he'd put his sunglasses back on, and all he saw through their tint was a faint gleam from the skull's teeth.

He rubbed the back of his neck, his skin tight and sore from the sun. He stepped under the shade at the edge of the woods and pulled at the front of his shirt to fan some air under the sweat-dampened fabric. With the noisy Scout group gone, the silence was disturbed only by the distant hum of traffic on the East-West Tollway and the twitter and click of birds and bugs.

His phone buzzed. Callie again. A call this time.

He answered, working hard to keep his tone light, free of emotion. "I'm not sharing."

"Can you at least run it for me?"

It didn't take long, because he didn't know much. When he finished, silence stretched between them. It had never been like that before they started... whatever it was they had started.

"So…" she said.

"I'm waiting for a deputy coroner and a forensics team."

"Waiting isn't one of your strong suits."

"No."

"Doctor Deception needs someone to question."

Jake laughed in spite of himself. "That's a new one." She usually called him "The Truth Whisperer." A patrol officer had overheard her say that one, and the nickname had spread around the department.

Silence again.

"Jake. Look. I'm sorry about not responding to your text. It took me by surprise. I'm just not sure about… this."

"You mean us."

"I mean about whether there *is* an 'us.' I thought we had agreed to keep our, uh… friendship… casual. And secret."

Not secret. That implied there was something wrong with them being together. He'd just wanted to keep it private. It was his first relationship since his wife's murder, and it had taken him a long time, and some serious soul searching, to work through what it meant: to his present, to his future… and to his past with Mary. But he *had* worked through it, and now he was ready to move forward and go public—which was why he'd sent Callie the text inviting her to go with him to the United Way charity dinner.

A thought pushed into his mind, and he blurted it out before he could stop himself. "Is it because I'm white?"

Callie said nothing, but her silence was an answer in itself.

"That's why you kept it secret," he said.

"We all have families and their expectations."

I don't, he thought. He was too disconnected from the Warren family to feel any expectations from them, and on the other side there was only his dad, Frank Houser, the least judgmental man he had ever known. "I need to get back to this."

"Sure. I know." Her voice was soft. Then it gained energy, and a playful tone. "Vengeance is yours, sayeth the Jake."

He almost smiled. "Bye."

He ended the call, stared at his phone for a minute, then stuffed it in his pocket. Callie was right about two things: he would avenge the dead man, and he needed someone to question.

He considered leaving the scene in Grady's charge and heading up to see the car's owner. The body probably wasn't hers—the hand was too big, and few women had gold incisors—but she might be able to tell him who was in the trunk. Unless the car was stolen. Then he would have to solve that crime before the car could help him.

He waved Grady over. "Did you check for a stolen vehicle report?"

"No report."

So the car hadn't been stolen. Or at least, if it had, it was never reported. And Pearl Cassano hadn't registered it since 2011. She might have stopped driving it... but that would put the car in her garage or sitting on flat tires in her driveway, not in the lagoon. Or, a third possibility, Pearl Cassano had sold the car and the buyer ended up in the trunk before he sent in the title transfer paperwork.

"Is the owner—Cassano—still alive?" Jake asked.

"I didn't check that." Grady pulled out his smartphone. "Want me to find out?"

"No thanks."

Jake would wait. Without knowing the dead man's identity, he might fail to spot any lies Pearl Cassano tried to sell him. The forensic team could find a wallet stuffed with identification in the trunk.

The wail of a siren pierced his thoughts. A sheriff's department patrol car cruised slowly into the parking lot.

"Grady, didn't you post a patrol unit at the bridge?"

"I did, Detective." Grady's voice rumbled with anger. "I'll get rid of this guy."

"No. I'll talk to him while you call over and tighten it up at the bridge."

Jake strode to the car. Bracing both hands on the door, the metal hot on his palms, he leaned down to the half-open driver's window. The aromas of coffee and a spicy body spray flowed from the cruiser on a wave of cool air.

"What can I do for you, Deputy?" he said.

"I've been ordered to take over this crime scene from Detective Houser, because this is county land." The deputy looked up at Jake through giant wrap-around sunglasses. He put his car in park and started to push his door open.

Jake held it closed. "No need to get out, Deputy."

"You're Detective Houser, right? I'm supposed to tell you it's the sheriff's orders." The deputy gave the door another push.

Jake leaned into it and kept it closed. "The sheriff herself ordered you to take this case?"

"Well, not herself, but it's her order."

Jake could understand his cousin wanting to take the case—and milk it for publicity—but sending this fresh-faced newbie? That lacked either of her normal signatures: being blunt and being political. Jake shook the thoughts from his head. Sheriff Bev Warren was more politician than cop, and worrying about a politician's motives had never gotten him anywhere but deeper into whatever mess was being shoveled.

"Deputy," he said, "Weston PD has investigated crime in this park for as long as I can remember. Are you telling me the sheriff wants to take over this responsibility from now on? Is that what you're saying?"

"From now on?" The deputy reached for his radio. "I don't know about that, but I was ordered to tell you Sheriff Warren is taking over *this* case. I wasn't told anything about from now on. I need to call in."

"Do it from the other side of the bridge." Jake straightened up and pointed back the way the deputy had come. "Tell her I said hello."

As the deputy backed his car in a tight half-circle and drove slowly away, the deputy's words ran through Jake's head: *Take the case from Detective Houser.* It sounded so personal. And that wasn't like Bev. It was more like her father, Bull. When Jake first moved home from Chicago, he had hoped to reconnect with the Warrens, but fixing the rift between him and Bull had proven impossible. The old bastard wouldn't let go of some problem he'd had with Jake's dad dating back to the early eighties. Bev was different, but... who knows. Maybe with her dad dying she was falling in line with him.

He stepped back into the shade, swatting away the few mosquitos tough enough to survive the drought. A weak breeze kicked up and wicked away the moisture in his shirt. But he was antsy to do something and barely a minute passed before he was headed back out into the sun to look at the Buick again.

As he stood gazing into the trunk, a high-performance engine revved behind him, and a gleaming BMW shot into the lot and stopped next to the Dumpster. The driver's door sprang open and the coroner himself climbed out. Jake's mouth dropped open, and a mosquito flew in, making him gag. He coughed the bug out, wondering what the hell Coroner Jansen was doing here. He was neither a doctor nor a cop—in Illinois, a coroner didn't have to be either one. He owned a men's clothing store, treated the job like an honorary position, and didn't come to crime scenes. Which was fine. No one wanted him there, and he added nothing.

"Detective Houser!" Jansen shouted from the parking lot, swinging his car door shut. "I hope you're not disturbing my crime scene."

This was the first time the coroner had ever remembered Jake's name.

"I'm not," Jake said. He met Jansen halfway between the parking lot and the Buick. The man wore orange and red plaid pants and a white polo. "Golfing?"

"Yes, Detective. With the mayor." Jansen pulled himself erect. "But when duty calls…"

Jake waited for more. When it didn't come, he asked directly, "Why are you here?"

Jansen shot Jake a poisonous look. "I *am* the coroner."

"I'm used to working with your deputies."

"Well, today you get to work with me."

"In the trunk." Jake didn't bother to brief Jansen; the man couldn't use the information to any purpose.

Jansen glided across the grass with his strange delicate walk. He leaned into the trunk, then recoiled and covered his mouth with one hand. He swallowed, his giant Adam's apple running up and down his neck, and drew in a long ragged breath. "This is a suspicious death and must be investigated." He pulled a cream-colored handkerchief from his back pocket and wiped his mouth. "Where is the forensic team?"

"Not here yet," Jake said.

He stepped back under the shade and watched Jansen circle the car, dabbing at his giant dome with the hanky. Jansen had the authority to root through the trunk for identification, but there was no way that was going to happen—he would get dirty.

Jake checked his watch. 12:41. It had barely moved since the last time he looked at it.

As the minutes passed. Jake managed to keep his eyes off his watch, but he couldn't help glancing at the parking lot. Finally, the forensic team's van rolled in, parking behind Jansen's car and boxing him in. Three techs piled out behind Duke Fanning, the county's best forensic investigator in charge, or FIC. He and Jake had worked a lot of scenes together, and Jake nodded a greeting. When Fanning spotted Jansen, he raised an eyebrow at Jake, but Jake could only shrug in response. He had no idea why Jansen was there.

"FIC Fanning!" Jansen shouted, quick-stepping back to the parking lot. He gave Jake a sharp glance as he led Fanning a few steps farther away and into the shade.

While they talked, the three techs got to work. One had a video camera and started recording, while the other two began measuring and drawing a map of the clearing, the car, and the lagoon. The car only sat where it was because the tow truck had dropped it there, but Fanning and his team were doing the job by the book, the way it should be done.

Jake took a long stride toward the Buick, then stopped. He needed to stay clear and let them do their jobs. So instead he stepped out into the sun and walked along the car's trail, across the burned-out grass, to the lagoon. The deep spot where the scouts had found the Buick was at least forty feet of mud flat away from the riverbank. The Buick hadn't driven out there.

Jake walked along the bank to the remnant of the bridge he had fished from as a boy. The footing would make a hell of a ramp, he thought. Its top edge was eight feet above normal water level, with about a twenty-degree launch angle. The concrete was scarred and chipped, and a long gouge up its face was discolored by dirt and lichens. The Buick could have done that. And if it went into the lagoon when it was filled with the spring or fall rains, the car could have made it out to that deep spot. Not on the fly, but floating, nose down under the engine's weight, until the open windows and the holes in the trunk lid let enough water in to flood it.

He scrambled up to the top of the footing and looked back across the clearing. A wide gravel path led away from the ramp, but it bled into the grass and disappeared within thirty feet. Two hundred feet beyond that, the woods rose up in a dark green wall. Was that enough distance to get the car up to launch speed? He didn't have the skills to answer that question mathematically, but the obvious answer was that it must have been. It was the only way for the car to have gotten out there.

Jake wiped sweat from his forehead and onto his gray pants. The delay in getting the victim's identity was a tick-tock against his skull, and he allowed himself a look at the techs bustling around the car. Then he pulled in a deep breath and let it out long and slow, trying to channel his energy back to the scene and what it might tell him.

A body in the trunk… that looked like mob work. East Coast cops called it "trunk music." But closing the trunk on a guy with a gun and enough life left in him to use it was too sloppy for a mob hit. And this was the suburbs, not the city. And a mob hitter from the city wouldn't know the one spot in the lagoon deep enough to hide the car.

So no, this wasn't a mob hit. It was something local, and probably personal.

That brought Jake back to the victim and his identity. He headed back toward the parking lot.

The registration lapse gave him at least a rough idea of when the vehicle had gone in the water. Cassano had registered the Buick for the last time in 2011, so the car had most likely gone into the water before that registration expired in 2012. Five years ago. Because of the flowing water and the voracious life it contained, forensics probably wouldn't come up with a date for the murder any closer than that.

He leaned against his Crown Vic and watched the techs, his mind working.

When he knew who had died here, he was confident he would be able to figure out the how and the who-done-it. That was all he needed for a conviction according to Illinois law. But juries always wanted to also know *why*. The motive. That last fact that rounded out the story and made sense of all the rest of it.

To the jury, to the survivors, and to him.

CHAPTER FIVE

Jake's thoughts had turned to Callie again when he was interrupted.

"Detective?" Grady stood a few feet away, holding out his cell phone. "My uncle says to ask you about the Halloween case."

All the young guys wanted to hear that story, but Jake never told it. Only he and Callie knew the truth, and it would stay that way.

"I've got nothing to tell you that's not in the report." Jake added a wink, to give Grady something to talk about.

Grady got back on his phone but returned a minute later, laughing. "He says I should ask you about the Jeep full of pig piss."

Jake smiled and shook his head. Only a few people knew about the prank he and his best friend, Bill Coogan, had pulled in sixth grade. Grady's uncle was one of them. "The guy who drove that Jeep deserved it, and that's all I'm saying about it."

"My uncle says if you don't tell me that one, he'll tell me about the time you got suspended in eighth grade." Grady's smile suggested he already knew the story.

A voice from the clearing saved Jake from having to get into either one.

"Coroner Jansen?" It was Fanning, standing by the trunk with one of his techs. "We're ready to go in if it's okay with you."

Jansen waved agreement from next to his car, still blotting his bald skull with his hanky.

Fanning pointed, and the tech reached into the muck-filled trunk with gloved hands and came out with the skull.

"Your uncle will have to tell you those stories," Jake said to Grady. "I want to keep my eye on this."

Grady backed away, talking into his phone.

Jake watched the tech. With a little luck he would have the victim's identity within minutes. And then he could get moving.

"Hold it!"

Jansen's yell froze the action. He had his cell phone pressed to his face with one hand, and the other hand was raised, waving his hanky.

What now? Jake started toward the coroner, but thought better of it. He went back and leaned against his car, arms crossed.

The coroner hunched over his phone, his head bobbing along to whatever he was being told. He shot a look over his shoulder and skewered Jake with a glare, then turned away again.

What the hell?

When the call finally ended, Jansen straightened up and strode out into the sun. "Inspector Fanning! Convey the entire vehicle to the garage at the county morgue. Once you arrive, extract the human matter from the nonhuman, and secure all of it—no matter how insignificant *you* might think it is."

Damn it. Taking it to the garage would delay identification by hours. Jake couldn't wait that long. But there was no point arguing with Jansen about it. He couldn't change a decision he hadn't even made. Whoever had been on the other end of that phone call had called this shot.

Politics!

He went back to his Crown Vic, opened both front doors to let the light breeze waft through, and sat in the driver's seat. He called his civilian investigator to get her working on the vehicle's owner.

"Did you ever run into this in Chicago?" Erin asked when she picked up. Her phone etiquette didn't include greetings or goodbyes. "Disposing of a body that isn't dead yet."

"You heard about the bullet holes in the trunk lid already?" He'd never been able to figure out who her sources were, but they were always right on. "Can you tell Braff what's going on?"

Jake's boss, Deputy Chief Braff, didn't like getting information third-hand or, God forbid, from the media. So far, Jake had seen no local news presence and no TV choppers thumping overhead, but better safe than sorry.

"Can do." Computer keys clacked as Erin shot out the email. The deputy chief loved email. "You have anything on the victim or the car you want me to work?"

"Grady ran the VIN." Jake opened his notebook and read it off. "Vehicle last registered to Pearl Cassano in 2011. That's all I have to work with. Grady already checked the stolen vehicle database, but can you recheck it? And see if Pearl Cassano is missing or if she has a criminal record." He didn't have to tell Erin to jump right on it. She understood the ticking clock.

"I'll call when I have something. Probably a half hour."

"I want to run something else past you," Jake added. Erin had a better grasp on politics than he did. He told her about the deputy showing up with the sheriff's explicit instruction to take the case away "from Detective Houser," and about the coroner himself showing up instead of one of his deputies. "*And* someone told Jansen to take the car to the garage," he finished. Only the sheriff or the county board chairman could order Jansen to do anything.

Erin paused. "Bev isn't like her dad, you know."

"You think Bull's behind it?"

"What's the *it* you think he's behind?"

"Taking over the investigation so she can milk it for publicity."

"No, I don't think so. I don't think Bull is up to much of anything. Cancer and COPD is a powerful double whammy."

Jake didn't buy that. Bull liked political games too much to let illness sideline him. He would play until he was dead. "Call me as soon as you finish with Cassano and her car."

"A-sap it is."

With time to kill, Jake pulled out the park brochure Grady had given him. It had a simple map of the grove, including the parking lot and the trails. He sketched in the bridge abutment and the gravel leading away from it, and drew an *X* where the car had rested on the river bottom.

A rhythmic beeping drew Jake's attention to a flatbed tow truck backing up behind him. It bumped over the asphalt mound at the edge of the parking lot and crunched its way across the brown grass to the Buick. The evidence techs had stretched a black tarp over the car and secured it with rubber cords.

With a sigh, Jake admitted there was no more he could do here. Nothing more he could do at all until Erin got back to him. He may as well grab lunch; once the investigation got moving he would be eating energy bars from his glove compartment. So with a wave to FIC Fanning, he cranked up the AC and headed out.

At the park entrance, a reporter from the *Weston Sun* shouted a question, but the closed window and blasting air conditioner muffled it, and Jake rolled on. Bev would have pulled over and given the guy a half hour of her time—but only cops using the job as a rung on the ladder to elected office wanted media attention.

* * *

Jake followed Ogden around the curve to Genaro's Wood Pit Barbecue. Genaro's was a cop favorite, but it was too late for lunch and too early for dinner, so Jake was the only cop there. In fact, the only customers were seven mechanics from the BMW dealership, seated at the big table in the middle of the room. They were loud with some story about a Fourth of July party one of them had apparently missed.

Jake had been planning on a gyro, but when he smelled the barbecue sauce he changed his mind and ordered a pulled pork sandwich with a bottle of water to wash it down. When the counter guy shouted Jake's number in his thick Albanian accent, Jake collected his meal and sat at a window table. The barbecue tang cut through the river decay clogging his sinuses and made his nose run. He worked his way through half a stack of napkins just from wiping his mouth and nose.

When he was done, Erin still hadn't called. The mechanics had finished and hustled off, and Jake sat alone. He considered going in to the station, but decided against it. The station ran on politics, and Jake always tried to stay away from the place once he started an investigation.

He cleared his thoughts to let the case fill it, but Callie came to mind instead. Their miscommunication was his fault. He'd been so focused on himself—on keeping the relationship private while he worried about disrespecting Mary's memory—he had missed that Callie had wanted to keep the relationship secret. If he'd been more tuned in to what she'd wanted, he never would have asked her to attend the charity dinner with him.

But where did all that leave them now?

Alone again. That was the likely answer. He felt an ache in his chest and rubbed at it, but it was deeper than his probing fingers could reach.

Quit wallowing, Houser. The man in the trunk deserves your full attention.

He pulled the park map out of his pocket and ran his finger over the prominent features: the river, the picnic grove, the trails cutting north and south along the river. Another line ran east from the picnic grove and cut through the woods to end at the park's edge. Back in high school, Coogan had forced his Ford Pinto down that overgrown trail, and they'd popped out between two houses onto Cress Creek Circle. Jake had seen no hint of this trail today.

His stared at the X he'd put on the car's lagoon-bottom resting place. Only a local could know about that deep spot. And only an amateur would put an armed man in the trunk while he was still alive. That was good: amateur killings tended to involve perpetrators and victims with strong relationships—which meant they were solvable. And when the amateur heard the news that the car had been found, he would panic. A panicked killer might do something stupid. Something revealing.

Jake's cell phone rang.

He answered it immediately. "What do you have?" Erin didn't need a hello.

"Officer Grady was right. The car belonged to Pearl Cassano. She stopped renewing the registration, and it expired in December of 2012."

Nothing new there. "Did Cassano report the car stolen?" Erin's database skills were better than Grady's.

"Nope, and her driver's license expired in 2013. She'd be eighty-six now. There's a phone listing for her at the same address where the car was registered. The old bird doesn't have a criminal record. And no obituary either, in case you were wondering."

Jake wrote down the phone number as Erin read it off. The address Grady had given him put Cassano in the Bends, a north-side working class neighborhood that had become separated from the rest of Weston when the tollway went through back in the fifties.

"She might have sold the car and the buyer left the title open," Erin said.

This idea agreed with Jake's own. He doubted the car was stolen. Insurance companies didn't pay claims without reports. "Great minds," he said. "Thanks, Erin. Check with forensics. See if you can push them along. I'm heading up to talk to Cassano."

"Have fun."

Jake slipped the phone back into his pocket. It wasn't fun, but his work—avenging the dead—mattered. And since Mary's murder, it had been his singular focus.

Until the thing with Callie. Whatever it was… or had been.

* * *

Bev snatched up her cell phone on the first ring.

It was Hogan. She told him to hang on as she hopped up and closed her door against the outer-office hubbub and prying ears.

"Okay, what is it?"

"Houser ran the deputy off so fast the kid never even got out of his car."

"He did it himself?"

"Yep. Told the kid to tell you he says hello."

Bev smiled. Now that she'd made the expected play for the case, Jake wouldn't give her a second thought and she could maneuver without his interference.

"You want maybe I should run things by Bull just—"

"Absolutely not," she said. "I want you to follow Jake." Until she had control, she needed eyes on him. "Keep track of where he goes and who he talks to. Can you do that without him spotting you?"

"Houser's not a real go-getter. He went straight out for lunch when he left the park."

"You're already following him?"

"Don't worry. Guy has no idea I'm on him."

"*I'm* running this, Hogan. Don't do anything without my okay. Follow and report. That's it." The Newark stories niggled at her once more, but she shook them off.

"What if he—"

"I make the call on *all* what-ifs. Got it?"

"I got it." Hogan sighed. "What about the car? We need eyes on what they pull out of it."

"Jansen will stay on the car."

"Then I'll stay on Houser."

"And that's it." It was worth saying twice. "Follow and report."

Bev ended the call and swiveled her chair to stare out her window at the clear sky. She wanted to be out there handling this herself instead of trusting it to Hogan, but that would raise eyebrows. Hogan would have to be her eyes and ears.

And... her dad probably wanted Hogan involved because Hogan was capable of doing things she couldn't—and wouldn't. Capable and willing.

She wasn't going to let it get that far. Not if she could help it. But...

But what?

Her lips pulled into a tight grimace.

The what-ifs, that's what.

CHAPTER SIX

Jake planned his interview with the Buick's owner during his drive. She was his only lead, and he needed to leave her house with a place to go, a person to interview next. He decided to focus on the car and leave out the body. If Cassano had already heard about the recovery of a body, he would change his strategy—but that happened a lot less with the media in Weston than it had in Chicago.

He also had to consider the possibility the body was Cassano's. A son or nephew might have killed her and taken over her house, telling neighbors she was out of town, and all the while cashing in her Social Security benefits. But the huge hand and gold incisor made that unlikely.

His leading theory was that Cassano had sold the car, and the buyer hadn't transferred the title before ending up in the trunk. And if that was the case, Cassano *might* have prepared a bill of sale and kept a completed copy for her records. In which case, Jake would have the victim's identity, or a solid lead on it, within minutes.

He crossed up and over the tollway, enjoying the energy the hunt pumped through him as he dropped down into the Bends, named for its location near a wide curve in the Paget River. It was a neighborhood of narrow lots and small houses. Cassano lived two blocks north of St. Theresa's Catholic Church, on a street lined with giant oaks that cast deep shade. Jake slowed and checked the addresses along a string of Chicago-style bungalows separated by concrete driveways that ran to garages in the back.

When he found the house, he pulled up at the curb. The lawn was clipped short and edged along the walk, and the bushes were trimmed neatly. That told him Pearl Cassano was alive. No squatter would maintain that level of gardening perfection.

He leveraged himself out of the cruiser, reached back in for his black blazer, and pulled it on. Older people liked formality, and in the deep shade of the oaks he could handle the extra layer without sweating through it. Plus, it covered the gun. It was a necessary tool of his trade, but it made anyone who didn't belong to the NRA uneasy.

As he headed across the lawn, a light breeze jingled a collection of wind chimes on the screened-in front porch.

"She don't like people walking on her grass."

The deep voice caught Jake midstride. A gray-haired head peered at him from the neighboring house's front porch.

"If I were you, I'd back off of there."

Jake nodded and stepped off the lawn. He walked along the sidewalk and driveway until only a low hedge stood between him and the neighbor's porch. The old man bobbed his head in greeting, then set his porch swing moving in a steady rhythm.

"Is Mrs. Cassano particular about her lawn?" Jake asked. Cops loved nosy neighbors.

The old man held a book of Sudoku puzzles in knobby hands sprouting from ropy-muscled forearms. His striped golf shirt hung loose on his shoulders. "She sure is. Waters the hell out of it and pays a kid to mow it with her old combine-style mower."

"I haven't seen one of those in years. Does she keep it in the garage with her car?"

"It's in the garage." The old man squinted, then cast a glance up the street.

"With her car?" It was an awkward question, but the old man wasn't Jake's subject, so it couldn't do any harm. A weak breeze moved the tail of Jake's blazer and the wind chimes jingled behind him.

The old man started swinging again and jabbed his ballpoint pen at Jake's car. "I don't mind telling you what you want to know because she's not—"

"Mr. Simari?" A high, smooth voice came from between the houses.

The old man smiled and cocked his head toward the back yard. "Here she comes. Put in a good word for me if you can slip it in. I've been working this for a full decade."

A tall woman with a head-forward posture and a mild shoulder hump appeared at the back corner of the Cassano house. She wore beige pants and a white cardigan over a shirt in that green that was suddenly so popular. "I can entertain my own visitors, Mr. Simari."

Jake thanked the old man and walked up the driveway to the woman. "Mrs. Cassano?"

"Yes, young man. Come around back and you can tell me why you're here."

She led him behind the house to a concrete patio. An immense honey locust tree sheltered a white metal table, and the breeze ruffled its tiny leaves, dappling the shade. The air was much cooler here, and thick with the sweet scent of a flowering bush pushing over the top of the fence from a neighbor's yard.

Mrs. Cassano eased down onto a scallop-backed metal chair painted bright red, and Jake sat across the table from her in a blue one. The metal felt cool through his thin pants. A hardback mystery novel sat closed on the table, with a tasseled bookmark near the end.

"Can I pour you a glass, Mister…?" Mrs. Cassano gestured to a pitcher of water on a cart next to the table, with lemon slices floating among the ice cubes. The pitcher was speckled with condensation, and an extra glass stood beside it.

"Detective Jake Houser." He wasn't thirsty, but accepting her offer would enforce the social obligation of host to guest—with all that it implied. "I would like a drink, but please let me pour it myself."

She smiled, her hands in her lap. He got up and stirred the pitcher, the glass rod ringing against the sides, then poured. He sat back down and sipped the drink. It was cold and tart from the lemons, without the sweetness of lemonade. He smacked his lips. "Very refreshing."

Mrs. Cassano smiled again, her face crinkling in a web of tiny wrinkles. Time to hit her with it.

"I'm here about your car," Jake said.

Her smile drooped, but she pulled it right back up. "Oh, how I used to love to drive, Detective." She touched her cheeks then held out her hands, her fingers trembling. "But now, as you can see, driving would be a bad idea."

"I'm sorry to hear that, Mrs. Cassano." Two indicators of deception—avoidance and touching her face—told him she was hiding something. He decided to follow up with an open-ended question to draw her out—and to avoid revealing the limits of his knowledge. "Please tell me about the Buick you last registered in 2011."

Her smile held for a moment, then faded. Jake waited, still and quiet, letting his question percolate inside her. She looked away, her fingers walking up and down the buttons on her cardigan. She was going to spill it, he was sure.

But then she squared her shoulders and lifted her chin. "I shouldn't have reported it."

Report it? She *hadn't* reported the car as stolen—but Jake didn't want to contradict her so early in the interview. He let the silence build, hoping her old-time manners would move her to keep talking.

They didn't.

"Please tell me what happened to the car."

"I don't know, exactly." She drew herself up straighter and pursed her lips, aging her face ten years. "Given that you're here, it seems you know more than I do. So please, would you stop with your *policing* and tell me?"

A trio of deception indicators this time: refusal to answer, the qualifier—she didn't know *exactly*—and the attack on his behavior. She definitely had a story to tell him... if he could find the right prod to get her started.

Maybe a bit of truth from him would pull some truth from her. "Some Boy Scouts found your car at the bottom of the Paget River this morning."

Her lower lip trembled, and her shoulders slumped a fraction. "Just... the car?"

Bingo. Jake fought the urge to lean forward. He turned her question around on her. "What else are you missing?"

Her eyes slid away from his. He didn't push her. Instead he drank from his glass, giving her time to find words.

"I didn't use the car much." She held up her quivering hands. "These were already giving me trouble." She laid her hands back in her lap and finally looked at Jake. "So I'm not sure when it disappeared. One evening I went out to the garage to drive to St. Theresa's annual Living Rosary performance, and it wasn't there. Have you ever been, Detective?"

Jake was so focused on the car that it took him a beat to realize she was asking about the rosary event, not her garage. "Not in a long time, Mrs. Cassano." He'd gone once, many years before, and found it ridiculous. A long string of people circled around the inside of the church, with each person representing a rosary bead and reciting the applicable prayer. Each voice jarringly different. Two teenagers giggling through their parts. He never went back.

"A parish praying together is powerful, Detective Houser." Mrs. Cassano gave Jake the old-lady eye, as if daring him to disagree and be damned to hell, but he was decades past that look having an effect on him.

"That was in, what, September?"

"The fourth Tuesday in October." She gestured at the house next door. "Mr. Simari gave me a ride, so I didn't miss it. Never have, truth be told. Not once in as long as I can remember."

"This was in 2012?"

"Yes, that sounds right."

Nothing but the truth from Cassano now. "Do you know who took the car?"

"Anyone could have taken it." She nodded. "At the risk of sounding the old fool, I confess I took to leaving the keys in it. I kept misplacing them."

Anyone could have. A half-assed denial if he'd ever heard one. And she nodded when she said it: a disconnect between her words and her non-verbal communication. Deception.

"*Could* have?"

"Anybody could have, Detective. But I know who did."

CHAPTER SEVEN

Jake waited silently as Pearl Cassano stared into her past. He wanted to pull the memory from her, but once a subject started talking, it was best to get out of the way. From the agitation creasing her face, it was clear that telling him who took the car would hurt her… but she'd do it.

He drained his glass, then got up and stirred the pitcher. He stepped around the table and topped off her glass before refilling his own.

The courtesy jump-started her. "Thank you, Detective." She picked up her glass and sipped, then set it on the table and held it with both hands. "My husband died eleven years ago this September. The good Lord didn't bless us with children, but otherwise we had a very traditional marriage. When he died… well, I didn't even know we *had* a mortgage. Then the young man my husband had taken into his carpet business came by to see how I was doing, and he took those things over for me. He figured out the bills, paid them, collected rent on the shop building, all of that. You see?"

She stopped talking again, her eyes losing focus.

Jake pulled his notebook and pen from the inside pocket of his blazer and set the notebook on the table where she could see it. He held his pen poised to write—a little prod that sometimes got people talking.

She looked at the notebook. "Donald Silva." Her chin trembled, and she looked away.

Jake wrote down the name and waited for the rest of the story, but nothing else came. "Donald Silva took your car?"

She released the glass and waved a finger. "I will not say he stole my car. I never meant to say that. I knew he sometimes borrowed it. I saw him leave in it once, and he explained his van wasn't running and he hadn't wanted to wake me up. So I knew he borrowed it. But he always brought it back."

The long speech to forgive Donald Silva for taking the car kicked Jake's pulse up a notch. "When Donald Silva took your car one night in October five years ago…" A nudge to get her started. He wrote *October 2012* in his notepad and kept the pen pressed to the page.

She sighed. "Donny disappeared at that same time."

Jake's mind spun forward to who had put Donald Silva in the trunk and why.

"Poor Victoria has been on her own ever since."

"Victoria is…?"

"His wife."

"Is it possible Donald moved away and didn't tell you?" Jake asked. "Maybe to get away from Victoria?"

Cassano's face, gone loose and jowly with heartache, tightened as she shook her head. "He wouldn't have left Victoria." Her head pulled back in a little snit. "Not alone with their little boy."

"Do you have Victoria's phone number and address?"

"She lives over on Rogers, a couple blocks west of the river. I'll get her address and number for you."

Mrs. Cassano pushed herself out of her chair, shuffled across the patio, and used the wood handrail to pull herself up the three steps to the back door. Jake wrote *Wife, Victoria* in his notebook and looked over what he had. It didn't cover a lot of paper, but it had been a good interview. He had a possible identity for the victim—or the killer; he had a date to work;

and he had the next person to interview. He wanted to get moving and ride this momentum as far as it could take him.

Mrs. Cassano returned and handed him a yellow slip of paper with Victoria's address and phone number.

"Thank you, Mrs. Cassano." Jake closed his notebook around the paper. "For the ice water, and for taking the time to talk with me."

"Should I call Victoria?" Mrs. Cassano gripped the back of the chair and looked up at him.

"It's better if you don't." That was the last thing he wanted. People revealed a lot more when surprised. "I have a lot of experience talking to spouses of missing people. It'll be okay." People liked to hear that hollow old saying; they pulled whatever comfort from it they needed.

"Well, all right then." The old woman's smile was unsure, but her manners kicked in, and she straightened up. "I don't get that many visitors anymore. It was nice to share the pitcher."

"I'm sure Mr. Simari would be happy to drink a glass with you anytime."

Mrs. Cassano's eyes brightened. "Did Richard enlist you, too, Detective?"

"Guilty."

* * *

Bev shot a look at the clock—it was already four thirty. She'd made it crystal clear to Jansen that he needed to keep her informed, but it had been two hours since he'd followed the Buick to the garage, and she hadn't heard a peep.

She pulled out her cell phone and called him.

"This is Paget County Coroner Jansen." A mechanical whirring almost drowned out his voice.

"Tell me what they've found."

"One moment, please."

The background noise faded, and a door thumped closed against the sounds. "I had to find a quiet room," Jansen said. "So they don't know to whom I'm talking."

To whom. Christ. She held her tongue and waited for Jansen to get to it.

"I was about to call you. FIC Fanning found a second body buried in the mud in the trunk."

"What?" Nothing in her dad's story had involved a second man.

"Not a whole one, but enough extra pieces to know there are two bodies. Both men."

Bev's stomach churned, and sweat broke out on her forehead. A double murder would make the powers that be in Weston crap their pants. It would also bring out the media. Normally, she liked their attention, but not with her dad in the backstory.

"Any identification?" she asked. One of them had to be Silva, but who was the other guy?

"None so far."

"So far? What do they have left to do?"

"The mud's making for slow going."

"Two things, Jansen. One, I want you to stay there until they're done. Two—"

"I have plans tonight, Sheriff, I can't—"

"My dad's counting on you."

She waited. Jansen kept his mouth shut. She took that as agreement.

"And two," she continued, "I want you to tell me everything they've pulled out of the car so far that isn't a bone."

Jansen ran down the list, but it didn't include any documents.

"Thanks, Jansen. Call me when there's news."

A second body. What else had her dad left out of his story?

CHAPTER EIGHT

After Jake started the car and got the air conditioning pumping, he checked his phone. One missed call from Erin. He called her back.

"*Two* bodies," Erin said when she answered, jumping right into it. "FIC Fanning says the interior's so rotted away the bones moved all through the car. Both are males. Both about thirty, judging by their teeth."

Jake's stomach clenched. A double murder right here in suburban Shangri-La. Maybe it was a mob hit exported from the city after all. He let his mind run with that for a few seconds before shutting it down. The second body didn't change his earlier conclusions: the murderer—*double* murderer—had to be a local.

"Did you tell Deputy Chief Braff?" Jake asked.

"He wasn't happy."

Weston was averaging less than one murder a year, and they'd already had one in March—the result of a drug skirmish in neighboring Kirwin leaking into Weston. And now a double murder… It might even draw out the Chicago media.

"Did FIC Fanning find identification on either body?"

"Not yet."

"You get descriptions?"

"Just his first impressions. One guy is bigger and thick-boned with a fake knee. The other is shorter and slight and had a gold tooth."

The hand had looked too big for the head because they belonged to different men.

"Who's doing the autopsies?"

"Dr. Franklin is already working on them."

"Did Fanning find the gun?"

"Still looking."

Jake pulled his notebook out of his blazer pocket and wrote down the information, using his knee as a desk, the phone trapped against his shoulder. "Check for missing persons reports consistent with those descriptions. Focus on October and November of 2012."

"Cassano gave you a date?" Computer keys clacked in the background.

"She first realized the car was missing on the night of St. Theresa's Living Rosary recitation in October of 2012. She also gave me a name. Donald Silva. He sometimes borrowed her car, and he disappeared when it did. I'm heading over to see his wife—or widow."

"I wonder if Donald Silva had a bionic knee or a gold tooth."

"Or enemies with those features."

Erin's fingers clacked across her keyboard. "Silva doesn't have an arrest record. And there's no missing persons report on him."

"Okay. Well let me know when Doc Franklin has something solid."

"Sure." Erin hung up.

Jake pulled out the yellow slip Cassano had given him and checked the address. Victoria Silva lived less than a mile away. He'd prefer to know whether her husband was one of the victims before he talked to her, but decided to keep moving. He would be careful with her, again focusing on the car and not the bodies.

As he headed east, he turned on news radio and listened for any mention of the case. A block before he got to Silva's he heard a short report that played up the Boy Scout angle before speculating that the death was a suicide.

So far, so good.

Until the Chicago media heard about the second body.

CHAPTER NINE

Jake found Victoria Silva's house in the grid of streets between the Paget River and the Bends shopping district. With its mold-stained roof and cracked concrete driveway, it fit right in with its tired neighbors. Just past the house's back corner, the driveway spread out in front of a building that was more barn than garage. Its large rolling door was open, showing the shaded interior. But there were no cars parked on the driveway or on the concrete expanse; Victoria Silva might not be home from work. Jake checked his watch: 5:15. He'd give it a shot, and wait if he had to.

He started to get out of the car, then stopped. Donald Silva was a suspect as much as he was a potential victim, and even though Cassano *said* Silva had been gone for five years, that didn't mean it was true. Jake needed to proceed with caution. He leaned back, yanked his gun out of its holster, and thumbed the indicator to confirm there was one in the chamber. Then he re-holstered the gun. He grimaced, fighting off a painful memory. The gun was simply a tool.

Jake strode past a large ash tree that had peppered the sparse lawn with fallen branches and cast shade over the stoop. At the top of the front steps he met his reflection in the glass storm door. He straightened his blazer and bloused it over the gun before pushing the doorbell. He waited, but heard no movement. He aimed an ear toward the door and pushed the button again, but still nothing after the bell.

He walked around to the side of the house. A metal clang sounded from the barn, then a muffled curse. Someone was home after all.

Jake took off his sunglasses as he stepped through the barn's open door, then paused to let his eyes adjust to the relative darkness. The air was cooler in here, and rich with the complex odors of grease and gasoline. A radio played in the back, acoustic guitar in a pulsing strum. Spanish, maybe.

"Who are you?"

The voice belonged to a man sitting on a short stool next to a motorcycle, wrenching on the horizontal cylinder of an R Series BMW from the early eighties. He wore black jeans and a T-shirt with the sleeves cut off. A cross was tattooed on his left deltoid, and there was an elaborate tribal design around his right forearm. He was on the young side of thirty, with wide shoulders and thick, veiny muscles rippling his arms.

"Detective Jake Houser, Weston PD."

The man stood, his gaze running up and down Jake before settling on his face. He set his long-handled torque wrench on the motorcycle's seat, then pulled a blue rag from his back pocket and started wiping his hands. "I only buy bikes with clean titles."

"I'm here to see Victoria Silva."

"She isn't home."

Jake scanned the space. To his left was a double row of motorcycles in various stages of disassembly—all from the seventies, by the look of them. A long workbench spanned the back wall, a tool-laden pegboard above it, and to the right stood a stout rack filled with wheel rims, a metal table, and a tall tool chest on wheels. A large fan hummed with mechanical precision on a stand in the far corner, sweeping back and forth. A Honda nearly identical to one Jake had ridden in college stood on a lift table, parts taken from it laid out on the floor around it.

"These are some great old bikes," Jake said, shooting to establish some rapport.

"Why do you want Vicky? She's as straight as they come."

"I'm afraid I can't say."

The man continued wiping his hands, shoulders and arms flexing, veins popping into stark relief.

Jake circled around the bike. "A BMW R series."

"You ride?"

"Dirt bikes when I was a kid. A CB360 like the one on the table when I was in college."

"Those are hot right now. Make 'em into bobbers and cafes and brats."

"Is the BMW your ride?"

"No. A guy bought it out of an estate sale and asked me to give it a going over. Carbs and brakes. New tires and tubes. Make sure everything works and it's safe to ride. Had to put in new valve seals, but it's a solid bike."

"I've always like these because of the horizontal cylinders," Jake said. "What's your name?"

"Lace."

Every serious biker had a nickname. "This what you do? Fix bikes?"

"Some, but mostly I flip 'em." He gestured at the rows of bikes, then to the storage rack. "And I do wheels. That's where the name comes from."

"What do you mean?"

"I build custom spoke wheels for motorcycles. It's called lacing. So, Lace."

"What's your real name?"

"Craig Morgan." Lace stuffed the rag back in his pocket and picked up the wrench again. "Vicky's good people, you know. I can vouch for that."

"How well do you know her?"

"She rents me the space here."

"How about her husband?"

Lace's eyes narrowed. "You're here about him."

"When did you see him last?"

Lace lowered the wrench until it dangled next to his leg. "It's been almost five years, I'd say."

"How long have you been working here in the barn?"

"Since I got—"

He was interrupted by a woman's voice from the driveway. "How about some help with these groceries." It wasn't a question. Assent was implied in the tone.

"That's Vicky," Lace said.

"I'll help her with the groceries," Jake said.

As he stepped outside, the sun was so bright he immediately put his sunglasses back on. A dark green Volvo station wagon had pulled up near the house, and the back passenger door was open, a woman bent inside. She stood up and stretched her neck to look at him over the car's roof.

"Who are you?"

Jake rounded the car. The woman was taller than the vehicle made her look—only a few inches shorter than him, maybe five-eight.

"Well? Cat got your tongue?" She reached up and adjusted a band that held a mass of jet-black curls off her freckled face. Faint crow's-feet pinched the corners of her eyes as she squinted against the sun.

"Sorry, Mrs. Silva." Sweat began to film Jake's face and fog his sunglasses. The sun burned his neck. "I'm Jake Houser."

"Call me Vicky." She looked him up and down, her mouth pulling into a hard line, then started hauling out groceries. She pushed two bags at him, and he took them. She kept the third bag and hooked two fingers through the handles of a pair of gallon milk jugs before bumping the door shut with her hip. "I need to get these groceries inside before I go pick up Donny."

"Donny?" Had both Lace and Cassano lied about Silva being gone?

"My son. He's nine." She started toward the house, calling back over her shoulder, "Help me out with those, then you can ask me your questions, officer."

The back door led straight into a kitchen that was brightly lit by windows overlooking the back yard. It was air-conditioned to a chilly level and smelled of toast, coffee, and burned popcorn. A large wood table held a neat stack of newspapers and a pile of blank paper topped with a flat metal tin of colored pencils. Drawings of superheroes and spaceships covered the cabinets. They looked too good for a nine year-old to produce, Jake thought, but he had zero experience with children and what they could do.

Vicky set her load on the Formica counter between the sink and the fridge. Jake set his two bags next to hers, then pulled out a chair and sat down at the table, establishing himself before she could change her mind and send him away. He took off his sunglasses and poked them into his shirt pocket. While she unpacked her groceries, he scanned the room. He found no trace of Donald Silva, or of any man—not among the coats on the hooks behind the door, nor among the jumble of shoes on the rubber tray beside it.

Vicky folded the paper bags and slipped them into a cabinet under the sink. "I only have a few minutes and then I need to get going." She sat down across from him and folded her hands on the table.

Her confident look wavered, and he realized she'd seen something on his face.

"I'll be quick." As he focused on her face and her hands—the most expressive parts of the human anatomy, and the hardest to control—she went still. She was going to be a tough subject. "I'm a detective with the Weston Police Department." She didn't change expression. Her attention was so fully on him it was like the tables had turned and *she* was examining *him*. "But you called me 'officer' before I introduced myself. How did you know?"

She held his eyes for a few seconds, then smiled. "You look like a cop."

He smiled back. "What gives me away?"

"You're not trying to be undercover, are you? If you are, the car has to go."

"So it was the car?"

"And the way you stand. Your feet were farther apart than normal and your weight was forward, ready to move. And only cops wear Aviator sunglasses anymore. Plus, I saw a gun when your blazer flapped open."

It always came back to the gun. "Aren't Aviators back in style?"

"Not even close." She shook her head, the mass of curls moving together.

"I want to talk with you about your husband."

She frowned. "Cut to it."

"Vicky, Pearl Cassano told me Donald borrowed her car the night it disappeared five years ago." Mrs. Cassano had only *assumed* this, but converting theories into fact during an investigation was standard operating procedure.

Vicky's head tilted, and her mouth stretched in a scowl. "That's not a question."

She was right, but most people just needed a little push and off they went without Jake having to ask a question that might give away what he didn't know.

"Did Donald borrow Mrs. Cassano's car often?"

Vicky pushed back into her chair, her hands falling to her lap. Her eyes widened. "It was the car on the news."

Jake said nothing.

She stood up, her arms crossed and her face wrinkled with pain. "If you're here to tell me Donald's body was in the car, just do it. Was it Donald?"

"We don't know yet."

"But you think it's him. That's why you're here." She sat back down and squeezed her hands together in front of her on the table.

"Why didn't you file a missing persons report when Donald disappeared?"

"And have the cops poking around in Donald's life? Forget it."

Jake fought off a frown. "I do have some information I can share with you. There were two bodies in the car."

Vicky lifted her chin, eyebrows raised.

"Both are males in their thirties. One a heavily boned man with an artificial knee. The other man was smaller and had a gold tooth."

She blinked, then stood and turned away. A shudder ran through her.

Then she fled down the hall. A door slammed.

Every time Jake performed a notification, he felt like he'd done it wrong. He pulled out his notebook and wrote *Smaller victim: Donald Silva*, then closed it around his pen and laid it on the table, waiting.

A faucet ran in a distant bathroom. A few minutes later Vicky reappeared in the doorway.

"Tree and Shotgun. That's who you found, Detective." She wiped under each eye with a white towel. "The big one is Tree."

More nicknames. "Your husband went by Shotgun?"

"Neither one is Donald." She breathed deeply. "The men in the car were Robert Graves and Nicholas Lange. Donald's friends since childhood. My friends too, I guess, but I wasn't crying for them. I was crying for me, and for my boy." She stepped into the kitchen but didn't sit.

Jake wrote down the names, putting a question mark after each. He needed more than her say so before he could cross off the question marks.

Vicky paced, then stopped across from him, twisting the towel in her hands. "It's been five years and… well, I've worked through a million scenarios in my head, but I always come back to only two real possibilities. Either Donny's dead, or he ran out on us. I didn't realize it until now, but… I guess I'd rather he was dead."

CHAPTER TEN

Hogan was parked in the deep shade of an oak tree a few houses down and across the street from Silva's. As the minutes passed, the air inside the car got stale. He turned the key and powered down the windows. Fresh air swirled in, hot and dry and smelling of dirt and lawn clippings.

He called Bull and told him where Houser was.

"Houser's good at what he does." Bull gave a sharp gasp, and his voice got reedy. "Fanning found another body in the car, but"—*hiss*—"they haven't figured out who they are yet."

"Houser will push harder," Hogan said.

"Houser only has the one speed. Full ahead." The air machine drowned out whatever he said next. Then his voice came through again. "… got nothing to worry about. Bev'll come through on her jurisdictional thing. Take the"—*hiss*— "bury it."

"Even if that works, won't it take too long? We need to slow Houser down. Maybe I could—"

"Call Bev," Bull wheezed. "It's her future." *Hiss.* "Her call."

"She doesn't know enough to make the right call," Hogan said. "We should tell her the rest."

"No." Bull sucked in a fast lungful. "Trust her. She can do this."

The line went dead.

Hogan called Bev and dumped his news. "Houser's in Silva's house right now talking to the wife. Been in there for twenty minutes. Came straight here from the old lady's house. She must have told him it was Silva who took her car. He's moving fast."

"FIC Fanning found a second body in the trunk."

"Does Houser know about the second body?"

"Of course he does. It's his case."

"I could do something to slow him down," Hogan said.

"Absolutely not. You follow and report and that's it."

Hogan squeezed his phone until the plastic creaked, but he kept his mouth shut.

"You hear what I said?"

He paused. "I'll stay on him."

He ended the call and stuffed his phone back in his shirt pocket.

"Follow and report," he said. "What bullshit."

CHAPTER ELEVEN

Jake wasn't shocked by Vicky's admission, but she had apparently shocked herself by saying it to him. He gave her a minute to recover. He hoped to get a few more questions in before she made her way to the obvious conclusion: her husband had run away because he was the killer.

She paced the kitchen for a few minutes before retaking her seat, still twisting the towel in her hands.

"Why do you think the bodies are these two men?" Jake asked. "Lange and Graves."

"Robert had a knee replacement. Football. And Nicky had a gold tooth."

"When did Donald disappear?"

"October twenty-second, twenty-twelve. He just went out that night and never came home."

"With Graves and Lange?"

"I didn't think so. We hadn't seen either of them in years. We were living the family life, and they didn't fit in. Donald was supposed to be laying carpet. He was always laying carpet."

"Maybe he took the two along on a job? To help haul a roll or lay it out?"

Vicky shook her head. "He only needed help when he landed a commercial job with big rooms that needed exacting seam work. And then he just hired day laborers. Cheap." She blinked, and twin lines of tears streamed down her face. She dabbed them away with the towel.

"Can you—"

"I'm sorry, Detective. I just… I need to pick up Donny and think about what I'm going to do now. What I'm going to tell him."

"I understand. I'll call you tomorrow to follow up."

She waved a hand toward the door, and Jake left without another word.

As he stepped outside, he heard a rhythmic slapping from the barn. Lace stood in the doorway, slapping the big wrench into his palm.

Jake walked over, putting his Aviators back on against the bright sun. "Do you know Robert Graves and Nicholas Lange?"

Slap. "No."

"Did you grow up in Kirwin?"

"No. Right down the street." Lace pointed the wrench to the west. "My mom moved down to Florida, so it's just me in the old homestead."

"But you and Donald were buddies?" Jake wiped sweat from his forehead.

Lace gestured behind him with the big wrench. "Saw him on his bike one time. The CB450 under the tarp back there. Struck up a conversation and started hanging out. Worked on our bikes together right here."

Jake stepped around the big man and into the shadowy interior. "Which one's yours?"

Slap. "Whichever one I'm trying to sell. Right now it's that Yamaha XS650." He nodded at a stripped-down bike with a solo seat and no fenders.

"Where do you think Donald went?"

Jake took off the sunglasses and watched Lace closely. The man had answered everything straight, but now his eyes darted away and he licked his lips and scratched his jaw.

"I honestly don't know," Lace said, widening his stance.

Four indicators clustered together: the lips, the claim of honesty, the face touching, and the anchor point movement with his feet. Deception.

"Guess."

Lace was silent for a minute, then his gaze shot around the garage before coming back to Jake. "Some guys can't handle the reality the rest of us pray for. Having your own business, the wife, the kid."

"Was Donald Silva one of them?"

Lace shrugged. "After he... was gone... Vicky asked me what I knew about it, about him. Like you're doing. And I realized me and Don didn't *really* talk, you know. We mostly stuck to motorcycles and sports. And I didn't notice it before—I wasn't paying attention—but he was always either working or he was out here."

"Not inside with his wife and child."

Lace nodded.

Jake gave him a business card, told him to call if he thought of anything helpful, and left the man there, the big wrench hanging loose along his leg.

* * *

Jake drove back toward the station. He needed to confirm the identities Vicky Silva had provided before he could visit next of kin. On the way, on impulse, he stopped at a Walgreen's and bought a pair of wraparound sunglasses that looked nothing like the Aviators that, apparently, announced he was a cop. They probably made him look like a sales rep. He wondered if sales reps carried guns and made women cry. Probably not.

His cell phone vibrated a block before he got to the station. He pulled into the parking lot at the bowling alley to answer it.

"This is Houser."

"I've got some news: bad and good," Erin said.

"Start with the bad."

"Dr. Franklin says cause of death isn't in the bone record they've found so far. The smaller man did have a trauma mark on his skull that happened near the time of death, but it wasn't enough to kill him."

"What do you mean by 'so far'?"

"They didn't find two complete skeletons laid out in the trunk. Loose bones are scattered all through the car."

"The good news?"

"FIC Fanning found two wallets in the trunk, and Dr. Franklin confirmed both identities. The big one because his fake knee had a serial number he could trace. The little one because his teeth matched the dental records of a missing persons report, which I'll send you. Got your pen ready?"

"Robert Graves and Nicholas Lange." Jake smiled for beating her to it.

"Victoria Silva knew them?"

"Her husband's friends. She confirmed Donald's been missing since the car disappeared, like Cassano said. She was sure of the date. October twenty-second."

"Both dead men have records. Graves for strong-arm robbery and bar fights. In and out of Joliet since high school. Lange was a petty thief. Never made it past county lockup, but he had an open felony case against him that would have sent him to Joliet. There's a warrant out on him for failure to appear from November of 2012."

"A great pair of guys for a family man to hang out with."

"What did Mrs. Silva have to say about her husband?"

Jake summarized the conversation.

"Why no missing persons report?" Erin asked.

"She and her husband don't like cops. Can you look up another guy for me? Craig Morgan. Lives on Rogers in the Bends. He's a shade tree mechanic working out of Silva's barn."

"Will do."

"How about last-known addresses and next of kin for Graves and Lange?" He checked his watch: a few minutes to six. Nine-to-fivers should be home from work.

Erin read off the addresses and gave him the name of the person who'd filed the missing persons report on Lange; he had no next of kin. Jake wrote it all into his notebook, then headed west.

CHAPTER TWELVE

Robert Graves's last known address was a tidy yellow four-square in neighboring Kirwin. A pair of massive maple trees shaded the yard so deeply that Jake took off his new sunglasses as he started up the front walk. He straightened his blazer and passed both hands down the front of his shirt to smooth the wrinkles, as if his appearance might soften the news he was about to deliver. He hated notification visits, but they were both a duty and an opportunity. People whose minds were muddled by grief sometimes talked very freely.

As he crossed the wide front porch, the sound of creaking wood came from inside the house. The front door opened before he could ring the doorbell.

"Yes?" A tall woman stood in the doorway, her housedress hanging in loose folds, the neck gaping to reveal the hard angles of her clavicles pushing against rough skin. She looked down at him through dark eyes sunk deep in the wide planes of her face. No welcoming smile or hostile frown, and nothing in between.

"Mrs. Graves?"

"Is it about Robert?" Her hands came together under her chin, massive knuckles on thin fingers making them looked skeletal. "It *is* about Robert, isn't it?"

"I'm Detective Jake Houser of the—"

Her eyes rolled to white, and she collapsed like her spine had dissolved. Jake stepped forward and caught her around the shoulders, dropping to one knee under her weight, his shin smacking sharply against the concrete threshold. Her head bounced off his shoulder and flopped against his neck.

He got his feet under him and walked her back into the front room, her legs trailing along the floor. Easing her over to a floral-print sofa, he stretched her out, placing her arms by her sides and propping her sock-clad feet on the sofa's arm. He checked her pulse at her neck. It ran fast, but strong and steady.

He closed the front door, sat on the coffee table, picked up a celebrity gossip magazine, and fanned her face. Within a minute, her eyelids fluttered, then opened, searching for focus. Her gaze landed on his face and stayed there. He smiled in a way he hoped was reassuring and kept fanning.

After another minute she sat up, her face pale and shiny with sweat.

Jake put the magazine down. "Can I get you a glass of water? Or do you want me to call a neighbor or your doctor?"

She shook her head. "I'm fine." Then her memory caught up, and tears welled in her tired eyes and drained down her cheeks. She wiped them away. "He's been gone for five years, so I'm ready."

Jake delivered the news directly, simply. "Your son's body was found this morning in the Paget River."

Mrs. Graves nodded, the tears coming faster now. She pulled a wrinkled handkerchief from a pocket of her house-dress and wiped the tears away, leaving wet smears on the dry skin. "He's still my best boy." A smile, then it broke into a sob.

He told her most of the rest of it. He didn't tell her that her son might have been alive when he went into the river, or that his bones had been picked clean by whatever river creatures scavenged dead flesh. When he told her that her son had been with Nicholas Lange, and that Donald Silva was also missing, her face relaxed slightly.

"Robert always did better when he was with Donald and Nicky. They were good boys, together. I was so glad they got past... I'm glad they got back together."

"Did the boys have a falling out?"

Mrs. Graves lowered her head and squeezed her eyes shut. A trickle of tears started again from the inside corner of each eye. After a moment she looked up and dabbed the moisture away. "I suppose you'll want to see his room? Like on the TV shows? To look for clues as to who killed him?" Her voice rose to a hopeful note. "I haven't touched his room since he's been... gone."

"Mrs. Graves, may I ask why you didn't file a missing persons report?"

"Well, I tried to. I did. But the policeman said Robert was an adult and unless it looked like bad had been done to him, it was a waste of time."

A practical response, but not a professional one.

"Before you show me his room, can you tell me a little about Robert?"

Mrs. Graves smiled and launched into a set of stories from her son's childhood and teen years. Stories she had clearly told many times, and told well. Jake pushed her to talk about the grown-up Robert—to learn what he did and who he spent time with—but her knowledge of her son's adult life was thin, and that clearly embarrassed her. He assured her it was the same for all parents of adult children. Twice more she dodged the question when he asked her about a falling out among the boys, and the best he could do was narrow it down to an issue between her boy and Silva.

When he said he was ready to see Robert's room, she led him past the kitchen and up the stairs. She opened the bedroom door and left him there.

He stood in the doorway for a minute before going in. Dust motes floated through shafts of sunlight coming in the window. NFL posters covered the walls, and an army of trophies crowded a shelf above the bed. Footballs and goalposts and helmets decorated the bedspread. Jake recognized the balsam scent of a plug-in air freshener.

He went through the room carefully, but found nothing out of the ordinary: sports magazines, football cards, T-shirts. Athletic clothing and jeans and model cars. He sat down on the bed and checked his watch. 6:42. He could still talk with the person who had filed the report on Lange before it got too late.

It hit him as he stepped through the doorway to go back downstairs. The room was ordinary for a child or a teen, but nothing in it hinted of adulthood. No paycheck stubs or unpaid bills. No checkbook or bank statements.

Mrs. Graves stood at the end of the hall, her hands clasped at her chest, the fingers fretting together.

"Where was Robert living when he disappeared?" Jake asked.

She looked away, then brought her gaze back to Jake. "You'll find who killed my son?"

"I'll find him, Mrs. Graves." He could promise that, but nothing more. The other three arms of the justice system—the state's attorney, the judge, and the jury—were too tainted by politics, ego, and prejudice for him to promise someone would actually go to jail.

She motioned for him to follow her, and he did, all the way to the basement door.

"In high school he moved down here. I didn't want him to, but my husband had passed by then, and Robert... well, he didn't listen to me anymore." She pushed the door open.

"Why did you show me his old room?" Jake asked.

"Robert had two boys in him—two sides to him." Her eyes pierced Jake's. "Everybody else has forgotten that first side, but I haven't. And I wanted you to see it."

Jake gave her a soft smile. "I understand."

"When he lived down there he didn't allow me in his space, so I didn't know about all of that. Not until after he didn't come home."

Jake took the creaking wooden stairs down to a bare concrete floor. The area to his left held a Ping-Pong table, loaded with cardboard boxes and stacks of pop culture magazines on one side, clean laundry on the other. A washer, dryer, and sink were lined up under a window well, the dryer *whump-whump*ing away. The head-clearing scents of detergent and bleach filled the air. To the right of the stairs, bed sheets hung from nails in the joists overhead. Jake pushed through them and found where the adult Robert Graves had lived.

It was a large space, set up like a studio apartment, with a pair of sagging couches flanking a scarred coffee table stacked with magazines and a tall bong. An old console TV sat across from the couches with a DVD player and a stack of videos on top of it. Centerfolds papered the concrete wall behind the TV. A bare twin-size mattress on a metal frame and a chrome-and-red vinyl dinette were set up in the area behind the couch. Cardboard boxes were lined up on the floor along the back wall.

Jake picked through every box, flipped through every magazine, and dug under every cushion and between the mattress and box spring. Robert clearly liked trucks and sports and marijuana and naked women—though the pornography that apparently shamed Mrs. Graves was mundane compared to what was available on the Internet. The only interesting thing Jake found was a half-empty box of .38 Special shells on a tray scattered with marijuana seeds under the couch. The .38 Special was the most popular revolver round in the world. Maybe Graves had been the one still alive when the trunk lid closed, the .38 in his pocket or wedged into his waistband? Jake considered taking the box for evidence, but it wasn't evidence of anything. He doubted the revolver killed either man—a revolver held six shots, and there were six shots in the trunk lid.

And Dr. Franklin had found no bullet impacts on the bones he'd examined so far.

Jake sat down at the dinette. A niggling in his head told him something was off. He cast his eyes across the worn-out furniture, but couldn't bring it to the surface. It wasn't the pornography, or the pot, or the shells. It was something else.

Then he had it. The place was clean. With Graves five years gone and his dad long dead, Mrs. Graves kept house for her sweet boy, dusting the centerfolds and porn videos that disgusted her.

Jake shook his head.

A mother's love for her child was beyond measure.

* * *

Bev tried to concentrate on her department's budget, but the Buick kept pushing its way into the front of her mind. And the bodies. How were Nicholas Lange and Robert Graves connected to her dad's story about Donald Silva?

As she forced her focus back to her spreadsheet and its columns and rows and numbers and totals, her cell phone rang. It was Jansen.

"What have they found?"

"The only thing new is from the glove box. What's left of the owner's manual. It was in a plastic case."

"That's everything, then? They're done, and you've told me everything they've found?"

"They aren't done, but they're shutting it down for the night. Kicking everybody out except a deputy to guard it."

Damn it! She could throw her weight around, but that would only bring attention she didn't want. "How far from done are they?"

"I think they're getting pretty close. They've flushed out the inside and sifted through the muck. Nothing left but rotting seats and the like."

What if Silva had hidden the document inside the car? Was there some little place inside a car's structure that could preserve a document?

"Tomorrow, have Fanning strip the inside of the car to bare metal. Tell him you need to be sure you have every last little bone."

"But I don't need all—"

"Tell him. The families deserve it. Lay it on, and make sure he does it."

"But I can leave now?"

"As long as you're back there first thing in the morning."

Bev smiled as she ended the call. That was the first time Jansen had agreed to do what she asked without her having to reference her dad. The man was coming around.

She tried to get back to work, but the bodies pushed their way into her thoughts again. Her dad's story didn't account for these two men. He was holding back to protect her—but she could protect herself better if she knew the whole truth.

However bad it was.

CHAPTER THIRTEEN

Jake drove to the address on east New York Street where Sheila Murphy—the person who had filed the missing persons report on Nicholas Lange—had lived at the time of the report.

It was a two-story concrete block building in a string of run-down businesses. The first floor held the Get Ripped Gym on the right and Wade's Small Engine Repair on the left. Wooden staircases on either end of the building led up to small landings.

Murphy's address said Apartment A, so Jake parked in front of the clustered Toros and Lawn Boys. Before getting out of the car, Jake scanned the missing persons report Erin had sent him. It contained little more than Lange's name and Sheila Murphy's assertion that he wouldn't have run off on her. Shoddy police work, at best.

A wiry old guy wheeling a mower into the building gave Jake a hard look as Jake checked a dented mailbox screwed to the wall at the foot of the staircase. It held a peeling italic *A*; this was the right place.

Jake climbed the wobbly steps and rang the bell.

A short, doughy-faced woman answered the door with a baby on her hip. She was barefoot and wore a pair of drawstring sweats cut off at the knee and a stained Bears T-shirt. Behind her, a toddler ran naked in circles, swinging a fly swatter at an immense bug buzzing just out of reach. Both children and their mother had blond hair hanging stiff with dirt and oil. The reek of soiled diapers spilled out around the woman, and Jake had to force himself to hold his ground as his nose wrinkled against the stench.

The woman was not Murphy but had heard of her. "Wade'll tell you where she's at. He's chasing her for back rent."

Wade was the wiry old man at the repair shop below. He was happy to talk after Jake showed his badge.

"You can't lock up that Murphy broad. She still owes me fourteen hun'erd." He pointed at Jake with a grease-stained hand. "I got a judgment against her, and I'm adding nine percent to what she owes me. Every single month. If you lock her up I got no chance of seeing my money."

"I'm not locking her up, sir. I just need to talk with her about someone else. You know where she lives?"

"*He-ell*, yes." Wade wiped his hands on his pants. "What I *don't* know is where she works at. I need *that* to go after her pay."

"Do you remember Nicholas Lange? Lived here with Murphy."

"You're after Nicky? I ain't seen him in years." The old man scratched his jaw. "Lazy as hell, but a good kid. He sure never took a hand to her. Not like the beast she's with now."

"Who's that?"

"She moved in with one of them amped-up steroid freaks from the gym." Wade jabbed a thumb over his shoulder. "Don't know his name, but hold on and I'll get you the address."

* * *

The address led to a small duplex ranch a mile west of the Wolf Valley Mall. The entire area had the run-down look of cheap rental housing: torn window screens and plastic bags blown into ratty hedges and beater cars choking the driveways.

As Jake strode up the walk, he gave his Glock a tug to loosen it in the holster. The reflex brought him to a stop. Was his subconscious preparing to use the gun to handle the steroid freak? He pushed the gun back into the holster and swore to keep his hand off it.

He knocked on the door, the metal skin of it loose and rattling against the wood core. Within a few seconds it creaked slowly open. A thin woman stepped into the narrow gap and leaned on the jamb, dull brown hair draping her face.

"What?"

"I'm Detective Jake Houser. Are you Sheila Murphy?"

The woman nodded and started to open the door, but it struck hard against something. A droning murmur came from behind the door. Her eyes darted behind it, then had trouble finding their way back to him. She was on something.

"What do you want?" she asked.

Jake raised his voice so the beast behind the door would hear him. "I'm here about the missing persons report you filed on Nicholas Lange in 2012."

A muffled laugh behind the door.

"Nicky." She pushed hair out of her face. "That was a long time ago."

Makeup caked her eye but didn't hide the swelling around it. A handprint was bruised into the pale flesh of her upper arm. Wade had been right about the beast. An angry heat bubbled in Jake's chest. His hand moved toward the holster, but he stopped it.

"Are you okay?" Jake asked, though the bruises made the answer obvious. "Do you need help?"

More mumbling behind the door.

"No." Murphy shook her head. "I mean, I'm fine."

That was the beast's answer, not hers.

Jake swept Murphy's hand off the door with his arm and drove his foot into the door next to the knob. It flew back a few inches and struck something solid with a deep *thunk* that vibrated up Jake's leg. He sidestepped through the opening, brushing past Murphy, with his hands up and ready, adrenaline pumping, sweat popping from every pore.

But there was no need for the adrenaline. The muscle-head was out cold, blood welling from split flesh on his orbital socket.

"*Jesus.*" Murphy stepped back and wrapped her arms around herself.

Jake took a few long breaths before checking the man's pulse. It was strong. The man was barefoot, wore a tight tank top and loose jeans, and needed a shower.

"Is… is he dead?"

"He's fine." Jake grabbed the man's wrist and pulled, straining against the bulk, until the man flopped onto his stomach. Jake took two sets of zip cuffs out of his blazer pocket, knelt on the man's back, folded his thick arms behind him, and cuffed him. He used the other cuff on the man's skinny ankles. "He will have a headache."

"He's bleeding on the carpet."

Once it dried, it would blend right in. "What's his name?" Jake asked.

"Tim." She uncrossed and then re-crossed her arms, turning away. "Tim Woodling. He's gonna be super pissed."

Jake led her away from Woodling, into a kitchen with a sticky vinyl floor. He sat her at a wood table, its top covered in magazines and crumbs. The air was dense with the stench of food and garbage. Dirty dishes and bowls filled the sink, and big plastic jars of protein supplements crowded the countertop. The garbage can overflowed with banana peels and eggshells, and a cloud of tiny flies hovered around it.

"Sheila," Jake asked, sitting down beside her, "are you okay?"

"I was going to move out anyways." She wiped her eyes with the heels of her hands. "I'll call my sister to come get me. Will you stay until Angela comes?"

"Of course."

He went back into the front room while she made the call. The air conditioning kicked on with a loud rush, and Jake closed the front door to hold the cold inside.

Woodling came to while Jake waited. The man flopped onto his side, cursing and struggling against the cuffs. "What the hell?"

Jake straddled him to check the wound.

"Who the hell are you?"

"Cop. Shut up."

The flesh around the cut on Woodling's face had swelled enough to squeeze off the bleeding, but it was still an ugly wound. Ugly enough for a civil rights lawsuit or a brutality complaint to Professional Standards. Or both.

But every time a cop acted, he ran such risks. And Jake had a good defense even if Murphy flipped on him. He had the lawnmower guy telling him Woodling was dangerous and hit Murphy, he had the obvious signs of abuse on Murphy's face and arm, and he had Woodling hiding behind the door telling Murphy what to say. If Woodling decided to come at him with a complaint, Jake had the facts on his side.

"You had no right to do that! This is my house."

Jake pulled the hulk's wallet out of his pocket and confirmed his name.

"Don't you need a warrant for that?"

"Shut up."

Jake called Erin to have her run the name, but she'd left for the day. He called the dispatcher and got what he needed. Woodling had been arrested three times for domestic battery but was never convicted. Murphy was his most recent victim—but her case was dropped when she didn't show up for court.

Murphy appeared in the hall with a small suitcase on wheels and a plastic grocery bag stuffed full of clothes. But when she saw Woodling was conscious, she backed up and went into the kitchen.

Jake stepped over Woodling and joined her there. As she sat at the table, Jake positioned himself so he could see Woodling through the opening into the living area. The man's knees came up, and he rocked onto his side, then inch-wormed until he had his back against the wall. He eyed Jake through a veil of drying blood.

"Sheila," Jake said softly, "I'm here about the missing persons report on Nicholas Lange."

"I remember that."

Murphy had washed off her makeup, revealing purples and greens and yellows around her eye. It would make a nice picture for his defense if Woodling tried to stir something up. Jake reached for his phone, but didn't pull it out. She deserved better than for him to use her injury to protect himself.

"He went out one afternoon and never came back," Murphy said.

"Guy's a loser," Woodling shouted. "Can't believe you used to hang out with a punk like Lange." He struggled against the cuffs, muscles rippling across his shoulders. "Why you got me all tied up for? Let me go!"

"Settle down, Woodling. I'll let you up when she's gone."

"What do you mean, gone?"

Murphy jumped up from her chair and darted past Jake. She launched a kick that grazed Woodling's forehead before Jake wrapped her up and pulled her away.

"I'm leaving!" Murphy shouted.

"You going back to Lange? That little pussy?"

"He's a better man than you." She lunged forward again, but was too small and light to break Jake's hold.

"Then where's he been for the last, what, four years? Five? He squealed on the wrong guy and got what he deserved, that's what happened." Woodling laughed, then looked hard at Jake. He squinted, and his mouth drew into a thin smile. "That's why you're here, right? To tell her you finally found his skinny little skeleton."

Murphy spun in Jake's arms and looked up at him. Her face had gone slack and pale.

"I am sorry to bring you this news, Ms. Murphy. Nicholas is dead."

CHAPTER FOURTEEN

Jake took Murphy outside to get her away from Woodling's laughter. She cried, which made Jake three out of four for the day. Cassano hadn't cried, but he hadn't told her about the bodies. He knew it was the message, not the messenger, but it didn't make him feel any better.

They sat on the low brick wall that girded the front porch, waiting for the sister. Jake held his questions, hoping the sister's emotional support would help Murphy talk freely.

A late-model Nissan pulled up behind his Crown Vic, and a woman in surgical green scrub pants and a penguin-splattered shirt jumped out and hustled up the driveway.

"Angela!"

Sheila ran and met her sister on the driveway. Angela wrapped her in a hug, and together the women walked up to the porch.

Angela eyed Jake over her sister's shoulder. "Who are you?"

"I'm Detective Jake Houser." He pulled back his blazer to show the badge on his belt. "I came to talk with Sheila about Nicholas Lange."

"What about him?"

"He's dead," Sheila said, and began sobbing again.

Angela grimaced and held Sheila tighter.

Jake stepped onto the driveway and pretended to look at his phone. When Sheila's sobs wound down, he joined them on the little brick wall and eased into his questions.

Sheila took him through the preliminaries like someone who watched a lot of cop shows. "Nicky didn't have any enemies," she assured him. "No one would want to hurt Nicky."

"When Nicky went out that day, was he meeting Robert Graves and Donald Silva?"

"Why are you asking about Donny and Robert?"

He told them about the car, about Lange's and Graves's bodies, and that Silva had been missing ever since the car disappeared.

"Have all three of them been missing this whole time and you cops didn't even look for them?" Angela asked, anger in her voice.

"There's only so much we can do," Jake explained. "Adults pick up and move—run away, if you want to call it that—but they have the right to. Happens all the time."

"But *three* guys, all at the same time?"

"That would have raised more suspicion. Unfortunately, Sheila's report on Nicky was the only missing persons report filed. The officer who worked it never knew about the other two. In the report, you said he went out with friends—no names—and never came home."

"He was like that sometimes. Mysterious. 'Baby, I got to go out and do some business,' like that."

"Did 'business' mean a crime?"

Sheila looked at her sister, then shrugged. "I don't know. I always thought it was just macho talk."

"Did the three of them often hang out together?"

"Back in high school they did. Nicky called them the Three Amigos. But not so much after graduation."

"Was there a reason for that?"

"I don't know. I just know they hadn't hung out in a long time. Maybe that's why Nicky seemed so up that day, you know. Seeing his old friends."

They talked for a few more minutes, but Sheila didn't know about whatever had bubbled up between the three, and knew little about what Graves and Silva had done after high school. She displayed no deception indicators.

"How about you, Angela?"

Angela looked up. "Me? I never knew Robert. I knew Nicky—a screw-up, but nice. Nothing like ass-wipe." She jutted her chin at the house.

"Did you know Donald Silva?"

"I mean, sure, from the neighborhood. I graduated before Sheila started at East, but I remember he was a big deal in sports. Baseball and basketball." She rubbed Sheila's back and smoothed her sister's hair away from her face. She winced when she saw the eye. "Are you going to do something about this?"

"He already did." Sheila pointed toward the open front door.

Angela crossed the porch, stuck her head in the doorway, and barked out a laugh. Woodling called her a "stupid bitch," and she laughed again as she came back.

"Do either of you know Craig Morgan?" Jake asked. "He was a friend of Silva's. Rode motorcycles together. Goes by Lace."

They both shook their heads. Jake had gotten all he could.

After he gave Angela his card and wrote her address and phone number into his notebook, the two women left in the Nissan. Jake went back inside to handle Woodling. The air conditioning had lost the battle against the open front door, and the room was as warm as it was outside.

Jake crouched in front of Woodling and checked the wound. The bleeding had completely stopped, and the blood had dried and turned flaky.

"You gonna let me loose finally?"

"In a minute." Jake checked the big man for a concussion. His pupils were the same size and tracked Jake's finger without wavering. Jake covered each eye in turn and had Woodling look at things around the room at different distances. He was fine.

"I can see fine. I feel fine. Cut me the hell loose." Woodling turned his shoulders to bring his bound hands into view.

Jake stood and stepped back. "First tell me about the squealing." Rumors often grew from tiny seeds of truth, and squealing was a motive for murder.

Woodling licked his lips, then lifted a shoulder and rubbed it along his jaw. "You got no right to even ask me any questions when I'm tied up like this. How long are you going to keep me tied up? She's gone, ya know." Woodling banged his heels on the carpet. "I'd tell you if I knew, you can believe me on that. I'm an honest guy."

Woodling definitely knew something about the squealing. He'd displayed five distinct deception indicators: repeating the question to buy time, licking his lips, rubbing his face, attacking Jake's procedure, and trying to influence Jake's perception of him by claiming to be an honest guy.

"I saw Sheila's eye, and her arm, and it makes me think I need to get an investigation going into you," Jake said. "But maybe I'm wrong. Maybe you're the good guy here. Let me help you. I'd like to take the cuffs off and get out of here. This thing I'm asking about is a rumor, right? An old one. If a guy like Lange heard it, lots of other people did too, so no one's going to trace it back to you." Jake smiled.

Woodling looked at the floor for a long minute, working it through. "I don't know who it was he squealed on, but you should be able to find out."

"Lange was working with the Weston police?"

"Yeah, well, maybe. Might have been county."

"About who?"

"That's all I know. Honest, man. Like you said before, I'm the good guy here. Lange was the thief." Woodling licked his lips. "You can believe me, man."

Woodling was a bad liar.

"Let me know when you're ready to talk." Jake walked out the front door, leaving it open.

"Come on, man. Don't leave me all tied up. I'll tell ya!"

Jake stopped in the doorway and turned around.

Woodling met his gaze, then his eyes shifted away. Flakes of dried blood dropped to the carpet. "Don't you tell anyone it came from me. I'm no squealer." His eyes found Jake's again. "That's the deal."

"Agreed."

"Lange was squealing on his old pal Silva."

"About what?"

"Silva was supposed to be a big-time burglar—like a jewel thief or some shit. That was the word, anyway."

"In Weston?"

"Maybe it was Chicago. I don't know."

"Where did you hear this?" If Lange had offered up Silva to get a deal, it would have been through the arresting officer or later through the state's attorney. Neither one was likely to generate a rumor a guy like Woodling would hear.

"Man, I don't know. Around. Now cut me loose. That was our deal. That's all I know."

Jake peppered him with more questions, but Woodling didn't know anything else. He hadn't even known Graves was missing, though he remembered the name and shared a memory of Graves playing football for East Kirwin High. Jake extracted a promise from Woodling to stay away from Sheila Murphy, then cut the zip cuffs off and left.

He rolled down the windows as he left Woodling's neighborhood. The heat was fading as the sun dropped toward the horizon, and the air coursing through the car wicked away the sweat coating him.

He spotted movement in his rearview mirror.

Woodling.

Standing at the end of his driveway, waving a middle-finger salute.

Just another scumbag who got his courage back when he saw a cop's taillights.

CHAPTER FIFTEEN

Hogan called Bull as Houser drove away.

"I think we've got something here that could help us with Houser," Hogan said. "A thread we can pull on."

Bull's oxygen machine hissed into the phone. "What's the thread?"

"I followed Houser to a shitty duplex in east Kirwin. Past the mall off thirty-four. I was pretty tight up on him because the guy has no operational awareness. Mousy woman opened the door a crack, and Houser kicked it open and went in."

"You sure this is related to the Buick"—*hiss*—"and not some other case?"

"Ninety percent."

Hiss. "You said Kirwin. He call it in for a Kirwin patrol to back him up?"

"Nope. He was in there maybe fifteen, twenty minutes, then a woman came over and picked up the mousy woman. Houser stayed behind, but he's leaving now. Big guy with a bloody face followed him out of the house and is standing on the driveway flipping him off."

Hiss. "Sounds like a domestic."

"That's what I'm thinking, boss."

A long silence hissed.

"Houser didn't call it in," Hogan said. "That means—"

"Something happened he wants to keep quiet." Bull coughed. "Maybe something we can use."

"I think I should stay here and check this out," Hogan said.

"Do it. But remember, Bev's running this."

"I know, I know."

"I'll call her about this." Bull gasped, then sucked in a loud breath.

"Sounds good. What do you think about that jurisdiction angle she's chasing?"

"I got a call from Borgeson. He's working the mayor and a couple councilmen."

"Do you think it'll work?"

"Bev thinks it will."

"Okay, boss."

Hogan ended the call and went to talk to the muscle-bound freak standing in the driveway.

CHAPTER SIXTEEN

Jake mulled over what Woodling had told him as he drove through the development's narrow streets and out onto Ogden Avenue. If Lange had been squealing on Silva, that was a powerful motive. If it was true.

He pulled into the gourmet grocery store west of downtown Weston and parked away from the other cars. He called the dispatcher and had her look up the officer on Lange's last arrest—Nigel Brown—and patch him through. He was connected after a minute of clicks and static.

"What can I do for you, Detective Houser?"

"I'm calling about a shoplifting arrest you made a few years ago out at the Meijer store. Nicholas Lange."

"He's one of the guys you pulled out of the river." News spread fast in the Weston Police Department.

"Yes."

"I remembered him when I heard the name. Busted him for sticking one of the display laptops down the back of his pants and trying to walk out with it. Guy was an idiot."

"I heard he might have tried to trade his way out of it."

"A trade?" Brown was silent for a few seconds. "Yeah, that's right. Lange spouted about a big player he could deliver. I thought it was bullshit, but I had to tell the sergeant. You never know."

"What did the sergeant think?"

"He thought it was bullshit too, but kicked it up to that Paget County burglary task force. Just in case."

A county task force was an affiliation of separate branches of the law enforcement tree, and a rumor-generating machine.

"Do you know what happened then?"

"Nope. It was out of my hands."

"Thanks for your help."

Jake opened his notebook and wrote *Motive to kill Lange: Turning Silva in*. After a moment he scratched a question mark on the end of the sentence. It was possible, but he needed more than Woodling's story. Maybe someone from the task force would remember Lange and the information he had offered up to save himself.

Jake had a vague memory of the task force. The previous sheriff had pulled it together to look tough when the media was giving him hell for a rash of property crimes.

The media angle reminded Jake of Bev's interest in the case. The second body made the media possibilities so much juicier, and she probably regretted her weak attempt to take over the crime scene using that deputy. By now, she was probably looking for another way in. So be it. He'd work the case and ignore the politics. If she interfered, he'd handle it. Until then, he would move forward.

He made another call.

"Coogan."

Jake smiled. "Coogan? That's a hell of a way for a big shot attorney slash CPA to answer the phone. You sound like a bookie."

"Call in during office hours and Jessica will answer. She might even call you Mr. Houser. Would that suit your ego?"

"I need the name of someone on—"

"Did you hear the Cubs are calling up that kid from double-A to pitch tomorrow? Skipping triple-A completely. I have five of his rookie cards. All signed. If he does well, they'll be worth a fortune."

"Only if you sell them." Coogan hoarded baseball cards.

"Buzzkill. Who do you need to talk to?"

"Someone on that Paget County burglary task force."

"It's dead."

"When?"

"A few years ago, maybe more. Low conviction rates. The sheriff—this is before Bev—blamed the state's attorney and vice versa. Egos. The usual."

"I need to talk to someone who was on it."

"Remember Benny Larson?"

"From law school?"

"He was the Assistant SA prosecuting the task force cases. He's downtown with some blue-blood firm now. I ran into him at Dora's a few weeks back. I've got his work number here somewhere. Hold on."

Coogan dropped the phone on something hard, and the *clunk* in Jake's ear made him wince. While he waited, he flipped through his notebook. There weren't a lot of entries, but the case was coming together. If he nailed this down, it was solid motive for Donald Silva to kill Lange. But he still needed a motive for Silva to kill Graves.

Coogan came back on the line. "Jessica is putting all my paper online, so the napkin was out on her desk."

"The napkin?"

"Do you want the number or do you want to disparage my filing system?"

"I don't have a lot of time, so I'll just take the number."

Coogan read it off, and Jake wrote it in his notebook. "Thanks, Coog."

Jake dialed the number. Chicago attorneys worked long hours, so there was a good chance he'd find Benny still at the office.

A brisk voice answered, announcing a string of names Jake didn't recognize. He asked for Benny, but first he had to get past an assistant. He gave her his name and told her he was an old law school buddy, figuring that would carry more weight than telling her he was a cop.

Finally, he got through. "If it isn't old Marty Thomas." Benny laughed into the phone, a laugh so familiar Jake was hit with a swirl of memories.

"It's been years since anyone called me that," Jake said, grinning. In their first year of law school, an error in the class directory had put Jake's picture above the listing for Martin Thomas. People started calling him Marty, and the name stuck for a few months.

"Sorry, I guess you're *Detective* Marty now." Benny laughed again.

Jake gave Benny a few lubricating return laughs, then got to it. "I'm calling on police business, Benny. About the Paget County burglary task force from a few years back."

"Thank God they pulled the plug on that mess. It totally screwed up my conviction rate."

"How so?"

"The cases those deputies put together sucked."

"That bad?"

"This was before your cousin took over, though I don't know why you'd stick up for her. Not the way her dad... never mind. What do you need?"

Jake almost asked what Bull had done, but he didn't want to dive down that rabbit hole right now. "I'm calling about a specific case." He filled Benny in on the car and the bodies, and Lange's possible deal.

Unfortunately, Benny didn't remember Lange or any deal. "Why don't you call the sheriff or the SA's office?"

"I will if I need to get official. Right now I'm just getting a feel for what this guy was up to when he went into the river."

Benny was silent.

"Benny?"

"I think you're working something and don't want official attention."

Now Jake was silent.

A theatrical sigh, then: "I probably have something on it in my 2012 planner at home. I'll check it when I can and keep my mouth shut unless I'm subpoenaed."

"Thanks, Benny."

After the call, Jake considered his next steps. Silva was his focus: the man had taken the car, had gone missing when it did, knew both dead men, and had a reason to kill Lange. But did he have a motive to kill Graves? His mom hadn't helped with that question, but maybe Vicky Silva could. If she would talk to him about it; by now she would have realized her missing husband was a prime suspect. He needed something to wedge her open.

He flipped to a blank page in his notebook and wrote *Next Steps* at the top. He looked at it for a long time, but nothing specific came to mind. It happened in every case—the flat spot—but he wasn't worried. He had talked to a lot of people: Silva's wife, Graves's mom, Lange's ex, Mrs. Cassano, her neighbor, what was his name… Simari… and ex-SA Larson. Things were percolating, and something would break. If not, he would run them all through the wringer again.

That was his strength. He kept talking to people until he found his way to the truth.

CHAPTER SEVENTEEN

Jake left the car windows down, the night air deliciously cool after the hot day. As he turned east on Jefferson, streetlights popped on along his route as if he was the switch. Heading for home.

Home.

He'd been in the apartment for nearly a year, and still he didn't get that coming-home feeling when he walked through the door. Jake had enjoyed converting the dusty storage space on the second floor into a bachelor pad, but living there hadn't suited him. He wasn't sure if the problem was having to park in the alley, not having a green space to look over while he ate his breakfast, or the constant press of people. It was probably all of these and dozens of other things too small to register.

Whatever the cause, he'd rather be back in his commercial building on West Spring Street. There he'd had space to park a dozen cars inside, and his kitchen had had a row of big windows overlooking the Burlington Forest Preserve.

Traffic slowed as he neared downtown, and his building came into view a minute later. When he was a boy, the whole building had been off limits. The first floor had been a liquor store, and the second floor had held a private men's club. Those gray-haired grumps had raised a royal fit when he and Coogan snuck in on a secret meeting by scaling a downspout and prying open a window. Their first run-in with the police, at the tender age of eleven.

But Jake hadn't bought the building because of the memories—not directly. He'd bought it at Coogan's urging. Coogan had thought that living among places and people Jake had known his entire life would bring him out of the shell he'd built around himself after his wife's death.

So began this experiment in downtown living.

His reserved spot behind the building was empty. He slotted the Crown Vic into the narrow space and locked it up. The heavy, hot air in the stairwell bathed him with sweat as he ascended to his apartment. He'd painted the entry door a rich, glossy black, and it gleamed in the light from the skylight. He keyed open the door and stepped into the comfortable chill.

After hanging his blazer on a hook on the back of the door, he unloaded his equipment on the kitchen counter: gun in its holster, badge, cell phone, notebook, and sunglasses. He grabbed a Sam Adams from the fridge and settled into his leather recliner in the nook of the front bay window. He spun the chair to look at the room, a high open space with bookshelves covering the east wall and tall narrow windows the west. A small kitchen huddled at the back, and down a short hall were a bedroom and a large bathroom. A loft sat above the bed and bath.

Would he miss it?

It took him almost a minute to realize that asking the question meant he'd already decided to move back to West Spring Street. But the remodel wasn't wasted effort. He could rent the apartment out to some yuppie.

His phone clattered on the counter. He hustled to answer it, hoping for a break in the case.

It was Callie. He'd been so busy with his investigation he'd kept his mind off of her.

"Hey," he said. He returned to the recliner and sat down.

"How's the case? Now that it's a double, you want me to chase something down?"

"I've got it."

"I could work on the missing guy."

"I'm on it."

"Okay," she said, then went silent.

They'd had calls like this before, the silence dragging on until one or the other suggested they get together.

"How about I come—"

"No." Those nights were behind them.

"I'm sorry, Jake. If that's how you want it, that's how it'll be. Friends."

"Friends," he repeated.

"And sometimes partners."

"In crime… investigation," he said, his attempt at levity sounding flat even to him.

"Bye, Jake."

He ended the call and leaned back in the chair, the phone still in his hand. He thumbed the screen and pulled up his call log. For a moment, his thumb hovered over the callback button.

"No." He killed the screen and set the phone on the floor.

His reached for the laptop on the stool next to his chair. Work was his favorite distraction from the emptiness that sometimes flooded through him. He signed into the department's system and opened the investigative file Erin had started, but found he couldn't concentrate. He didn't have the focus right now to work on the murder book. He'd do it in the morning—when his mind was fresh and loaded with whatever connections and questions and answers his subconscious mind had bubbled up while he slept.

He set the laptop down and picked up the book he'd been reading: *1491: New Revelations of the Americas Before Columbus.* He'd been on a nonfiction kick lately. He found his place, but his eyes kept flicking to the street below, where couples, groups, and families wandered along. He cracked open a side pane of the bay window to hear the sounds of his community, then adjusted the blinds so those below couldn't see him—or he them.

Finally he settled back and lost himself in the pre-Columbian history of the Americas, something he'd thought he understood until he'd started reading this book. That was his favorite thing about reading non-fiction: the more he learned, the more he realized he didn't know.

* * *

Bull Warren watched the sun drop behind the trees and the sky bleed to orange and then slowly to black, turning the window into a mirror where the reflection of his once thick body made a pitiful lump under the covers. He turned away from the glass and clicked on the TV news. The Chicago TV stations were usually too caught up in their own filth to give the suburbs much coverage. Halfway through the broadcast a short video credited to the traffic chopper came on showing the Buick in the middle of Radar Grove in "idyllic west-suburban Weston," with a few people clustered around the trunk. But nothing about a second body. Good.

A jerking twist in his bowels clenched him into a knot. He needed to get to the bathroom.

Now.

If he failed to make it again they'd put him in diapers. *That* wasn't going to happen. He grabbed the call button but he'd had enough of the nurses for the day and let it drop. He held his gut against the building pressure and used the electric controls to raise the head of the bed and lower the side rail. He was gathering his energy to swing his legs over the side when a shape entered his peripheral vision.

"Boss, let me help you." Hogan held him upright with one hand, then lifted his skinny legs in the other and swung them over the edge of the bed. They dangled more than a foot off the floor. "Where're we going?"

"All the way to the goddamn bathroom." Bull gestured to the door a few feet away, then grabbed Hogan's arm. "Get me there and I can do the rest."

Hogan put one hand under Bull's arm and the other across his back, then boosted him off the bed and walked with him toward the bathroom door.

"I'm not a gazelle."

Hogan slowed and Bull clenched and they made it. Hogan helped Bull turn in front of the toilet and put his hand on the assist bar before letting go. Hogan adjusted the air hose so it wouldn't get pinched as he closed the door.

Success.

When Bull finished he called out and Hogan escorted him back to bed.

"Give me a minute." Bull's voice was harsh from air rasping in and out of his weak lungs. He inhaled hard through his nose. "Then tell me where we are." He leaned back on his pillow, nose-breathing to get the most from the cannula. He was lucky to have Hogan's help. The spitting image of his father, a man Bull considered closer than a brother after humping jungle with him in 'Nam. They'd been so stupid, but they'd survived it. Together. Each saving the other so many times they lost count of who owed who in a way that brought this closeness that left them each owing the other. A bond Ernie had somehow extended through his son.

"You look like him, you know." In the jaw and forehead. And he moved like him. Smooth and controlled.

"I know."

"Now tell me."

Hogan went through the day, fleshing out what he'd said on the phone about the domestic and then laying out who

Houser had been there to see and what happened inside the house. "Houser split the guy's face open. Check out the picture." Hogan pulled it up on his phone.

"Ugly bastard might look better with the scar."

"Problem is he's got a history of smacking women around."

"It's something." Bull shrugged. You worked with what you had. "Where's he now?"

"I dropped him off at the Edgar ER to get stitched up on my way here."

"Have him file a complaint." Bull wheezed. "Brutality. Then push it."

"He'll make a bad witness." Hogan pulled Bull's covers up to his chin and raised the side rail. "But as long as we don't take it all the way, it could do the job. Disrupt Houser enough to get ahead of this. What did Bev think about it?"

Bull couldn't remember. Had he called her? He'd meant to…he must have. He changed the subject. "Bev's working the phones. Got County Board Chairman Borgeson pushing the mayor and his council to let her take the case." Had he already told Hogan about that? Hogan smiled and patted his arm. Bull sniffed in a deep lungful. "They're stalling because they want the credit if Houser solves it quick. Another day goes by and things will change." A few more deep breaths. "Until then we just need a little luck to keep him from finding the document, or his way to me."

CHAPTER EIGHTEEN

Jake woke, gasping for air. He swung his head back and forth, lost, searching for a reference point. It was his bedroom, the gray of early dawn in the windows. The soft rush of his ceiling fan, then the distant clang of a Dumpster lid in the back alley. Normal sounds.

His breathing eased. He threw the sheet off and sat up, the fan chilling his sweat-drenched body. He knew from the sweat that what had woken him wasn't outside, or even in the room. It was in his head.

He swung his feet off the bed and onto the cool plank floor. He bent over with his elbows on his knees and rubbed his face with both hands. *Royce Fletcher*. The name burned him with shame.

He plodded into the bathroom, flicked on the light, and splashed cold water on his face. He toweled off, pulled on his robe, and padded out to the front window, bare feet sticking to the oak floor with each step. He opened the blinds and watched the dark lighten to gray as dawn approached. The dream had left a residual jitter in his legs. He sat in his recliner and rubbed it away.

Everyone had agreed it was a righteous shoot.

It was Jake's second case as lead detective back in Chicago, and he had become convinced the burglary of an electronics warehouse required inside information. So he and his partner, Lee Hilleman, started interviewing former employees.

Royce Fletcher bolted when Jake showed his badge in the doorway of the man's apartment. Fletcher pushed past Jake and knocked Hilleman down the stairs. Jake gave chase, Hilleman screaming that he was okay and to get the bastard.

Jake burst from the building's front door just in time to see Fletcher duck down the opposite alley. Jake followed, dodging garbage cans and pallets, and cornered Fletcher behind a string of retail stores off Halsted.

He pulled his gun—he had carried a 10mm Glock back then—and Fletcher turned to face him with a revolver in his hand. Jake's memory felt clear up to this point... but here it got fuzzy.

A surveillance camera had filmed the encounter—but from a lousy angle and with a lack of sound. Jake must have watched the recording a hundred times with his union rep before the mandatory Officer Involved Shooting hearing. The union rep pulled apart every frame to explore what could have been happening, so that by the time the hearing started, Jake wasn't sure what he actually remembered and what was merely one of the possibilities the rep had planted in his head.

Had Fletcher pointed the gun at Jake or held it out? Had Fletcher emitted an unintelligible scream when cornered, as Hilleman had testified, or had he yelled that he surrendered? Had Jake shot the man because he feared for his own life, or had the anger burning in him since his wife's death pushed him to shoot?

Light streaked across the sky as sunrise arrived. Jake rubbed his face and went to the kitchen to make coffee. He sat on a stool at the counter while he waited for it to brew, the dark roast's aroma cutting through the air-conditioned air.

Going to Fletcher's funeral had been a bad idea. Jake was less than a year removed from Mary's murder, and seeing the Fletcher family devastated by his violent death had been a spike in Jake's heart. He knew the pain they felt—that he had inflicted on them— because the pain of Mary's murder still filled him. Then, and to this day.

He glanced at his gun on the counter. It was small compared to the Glock he'd carried back then, but its purpose—its potential—was the same. He was glad the gun still had the power to remind him of the awesome responsibility it represented—and the devastating consequences of using it.

He poured himself a mug and sipped it as the room filled with light. When he finished his first mug he refilled it, grabbed his notebook, and settled into the recliner with his laptop. He started building the murder book, entering every conversation he'd had and every fact he'd collected. His memory was strong, but he referred to his notebook on every entry to make sure he had it all straight. When he'd gotten everything down, he poured himself the last coffee in the pot, then leaned back in the recliner and thought it all through.

Donald Silva had taken the Buick, it was found with the bodies of his two friends in it, and Silva had disappeared. It didn't take a great leap of logic to conclude he was either the killer or running from the killer. Finding him was key. Jake sent Erin an email to put out an APB and to start surfing databases for any trail Silva might have left behind.

As he left the apartment after a bowl of cereal and a quick shower, the buzz from his phone shot hope through him that one of his calls or interviews the day before had tripped something. He pulled it out as he went down the stairs, blazer over his arm.

"This is Houser."

He pushed through the door at the bottom of the stairs and out into the day. It was hot and bright, and the record-setting string of sunny days had baked away the humidity. He squinted up at the vivid blue, fished his new sunglasses out of his shirt pocket, and unfolded them over his eyes, blinking away sunspots.

"I got your email, and I'm on it." Erin's voice surged with triumph. "Plus, I've got two pieces of Buick-related news. First, I've narrowed down the date Cassano's car disappeared."

"How?" Jake rounded the corner into the alley where he parked his car.

"Cassano told you Silva took the car soon before she needed it to go to the Living Rosary, right? And we know it was 2012 because of the registration. The fourth Tuesday in October 2012 was the twenty-third—I called St. Theresa's and confirmed it—so the car disappeared no later than the twenty-second. That Monday. That's the same night Vicky Silva said her husband went out and never came home."

"Good work." Erin always came through.

Jake's car sat in the shade cast by the building to the east. He leaned against it, the fender cool through his thin gray pants. The stench from a restaurant Dumpster wafted over him but was pushed away by the morning breeze.

"Second, that same night—Monday the twenty-second—there was a strong-arm robbery outside a liquor store."

"And it involved the Buick?"

"Maybe. The perps were driving a Buick the same color as Cassano's. But the incident report's a little funky."

An incident report was filed for every 911 call. It was a simple form with boxes to fill in with relevant information like the time, victim's name, nature of the call, who responded, the response time, and more.

"How so?" Jake asked.

"Information is missing from the online report." Erin paused, as if to force him to coax it from her, but then went on, clearly too excited about her news to wait. "The officer's name, the victim's name, the location… they're all blank. I'll send you a PDF so you can see it."

"Maybe the victim took off and the responding officer was too busy with other calls to fill it out," Jake suggested. "No complainant means no investigation, which means no arrest." Weston police responded to an average of thirteen emergency calls on every night shift. There were only six cars out at a time, so things sometimes got busy and shortcuts were taken. "Was there anything else about the call that makes you think it's connected?"

"The description of the perps. I'm quoting: 'a big football player type and a skinny little guy dressed like a wigger.'"

A smile bloomed on Jake's face. Graves and Lange. This was the break he needed.

"The report quotes the victim saying, 'It was a misunderstanding.'"

"Anything about a third guy?"

Pearl Cassano was sure Silva had borrowed her car that night, so he must have been there Unless he'd known what was coming and left his friends to deal with it.

"No, nothing."

But the robbery was still a solid lead. The missing bits from the report—whether caused by officer neglect or data-entry error—might slow him down, but they should be in the responding officer's notebook. "Can you track down the responding officer?"

"I'll have dispatch check the duty log. We keep them here for seven years. I requested the original paper copy of the incident report. It's already in offsite storage."

"Who called it in?"

"Alex Mason." The clack of computer keys over the line. "No address in the system."

"Which liquor store?"

"The report doesn't say, but it *does* say the car exited the south end of the parking lot and headed east on Saller Road."

"That's out by the tollway and 59. Anything else?"

"Chief Arvind has been in to see Deputy Chief Braff. He wanted to know why we're not handing the case off to county."

Chief Arvind normally stuck to administration and left law enforcement to his deputies—who all loved him for it—but the man was sensitive to political winds.

"Is Braff holding fast?"

"Of course," Erin said. "One last thing. The *Tribune*'s stringer showed up at the six-thirty shift change this morning asking about Radar Grove. She left quickly, so probably got what she wanted, which would be your name."

"I'll keep my eyes open."

CHAPTER NINETEEN

Jake drove west and then north to Saller Road, a stub running between Route 59 and Bond Street that provided the strip mall facing 59 a back entrance. Businesses all along this stretch of 59 were still struggling to recover from the recently completed construction project that had cut them off from the highway for two years.

A soft morning breeze rustled stout weeds growing in the pinch where the building and the cracked asphalt parking lot met. Jake swung his car into the lot and drove slowly along the building. He found a ghost image of the word LIQUOR above the windows of the end unit. The store had failed.

He parked, locked the car, and walked up and peered through the window. There was nothing left inside but shelving and the front counter. He walked next door to Paget County Cleaners. As he stepped inside, a bell above the door announced him. A steam press hissed from the back, and the air, heavy and wet, held the pleasant scent of starch.

A scrawny man in a tie-dyed T-shirt with a patchy beard sat on a stool behind the counter. "A pickup, sir?" His smile was genuine and open.

"I'm looking for a guy who used to work at the liquor store." Jake pointed in that direction. "Alex Mason."

"The liquor store closed."

"I saw that."

"The economy, you know." Patchy Beard shrugged. "Then it took 'em two years to finish construction on the highway interchange. Can you believe it? We're lucky to still be here."

"Did you know Alex?"

"Everyone who worked there is gone."

"Obviously." This guy was working too hard to avoid Jake's simple question. "What's your name?"

"What do you need my name for?"

The bell over the door clanged, and a middle-aged woman backed through it with a load of dress shirts. Patchy Beard hopped off his stool and darted around the counter. His jeans were worn through at the knees, and his Chuck Connors gym shoes were covered with ink drawings of superheroes.

"I got ya, Mrs. H."

"Thank you, Levi." She gave up the bundle and sighed. "Twelve today."

Levi put the pile on the counter. His fingers scuttled across his keyboard. "Light starch. Hangers. Be ready Wednesday. Eighteen dollars." A small printer whirred. He tore off the pink slip it spit out and handed it to her.

"Thanks, Levi."

"See you then, Mrs. H." Levi sat back down. "Tell Mr. H good luck with the 5K this weekend."

The woman stopped at the door and turned back. "I *will* tell him. Have a good day."

She left, the bell ringing again.

"Let's start over, Levi," Jake said. He couldn't help liking the guy. "I'm Detective Jake Houser with the Weston Police Department. I need to talk with Alex Mason."

"What about?" Levi lifted a hip and settled back on his stool. "He's no criminal."

"So you do know him?"

"Thanks be to God." Levi squinted at Jake's chest.

"What?"

"Thanks be to God. You're Catholic, right? Guessing religions is like one of my hobbies." He pointed to Jake's neck. "The chain there, inside the neck of your shirt. Most Catholics wear a cross. Me too. See?" Levi reached inside the neck of his T-shirt and fished out a wooden cross strung on a piece of rough twine.

Jake's hand went to his chest, and his fingers splayed flat on the cross under his shirt. He hadn't reached for it in a long time. He lowered his hand. "About Mason."

"Can I see your badge? I can ask to see it, right?" Levi held out his hand.

Jake pulled his badge off his belt and handed it over. Levi examined it closely, first the photo ID, then the shield, his fingers running over the contours like he was reading Braille. "Houser. That's English, right? In England you'd be Church of England, but here you're Catholic." Levi handed it back.

"Yes." A relaxed Catholic. Jake glanced at his watch without seeing it. "Now, about Mason—"

"He's Catholic too."

"Levi—" Jake stopped, then started again in a calmer voice. "Where is Alex Mason?"

"He works at the Liquor Mart next to the Meijer. He's one of my squad. You want I should text him you're coming?"

"No, but thanks for your help."

"Bring some cleaning next time. Paget County Cleaners is number one!" Levi held up an index finger. "My uncle owns it."

* * *

On the way to the Liquor Mart, Jake caught himself running a finger over the arms of his cross. He wondered why he still wore it. But as he pulled into the massive store's parking lot, his thoughts returned to the case. If Alex Mason were to put a third man in the Buick during the robbery, that would confirm Jake's speculation that the three men had been together.

He stopped at the service desk to ask for Mason, approaching badge first to save time. The woman working behind the shoulder-high counter hitched herself up onto her elbows and reached for the badge. He held it higher, and she put her hand over his, squeezing it. He pulled his hand away. She took her glasses off and smiled.

"Well, well, well." She folded her arms and leaned on them, her breasts mounding from the top of her blouse. "An honest-to-god detective." Her voice was smoke-rasped and burbled with phlegm.

Jake recognized she was flirting, but even if he weren't working, he would have ignored it. Being "single" was an identity he couldn't quite accept. Erin kept telling him that Mary wouldn't want him to be alone, but it didn't change how he felt. He wasn't *single*—he was a *widower*. Even the thing with Callie was outside of that. It had just… snuck up on him. Through familiarity and proximity and a mutual… loneliness.

It hit him suddenly that Callie was right: what they had going wasn't a relationship. It never had been. It was a convenience. His text message had been a mistake.

"I'm here to talk with Alex Mason. Is he working this morning?" Jake swept his eyes around the store. The shelving stood only five feet high, but was topped with bottle displays that made it hard to see much from where he stood.

"That boy's never been a spot of trouble. I'll page him for you." She reached for a base-mounted microphone. "Mr. Mason to meet a visitor in the break room." She told Jake how to get there. "You be good to our boy, you hear me?"

Jake followed her directions toward the back. On the way, a skinny twenty-something with dark hair and round glasses merged into the aisle and quick-stepped ahead of him.

"Mr. Mason?" Jake said.

The man turned and smiled. "Yes?"

"I'm your visitor." Jake pulled back his blazer to show his badge. "I have a few questions for you about the incident outside the liquor store in 2012."

"Oh. Okay." Mason smoothed down the front of his orange apron with both hands. His name—*Alex*—was written in black marker in a white square on the chest panel.

"You called 911 the evening of October twenty-second about a robbery in the parking lot outside the store."

Mason clasped his hands at his waist. "That's the only time I've ever been involved in anything like that. I was happy to help."

"Even though you were wrong?" The victim hadn't pressed charges, so this was a reasonable skew of the facts. A skewed fact often generated more truth.

"Wrong?" Mason shook his head, looked around, then gestured toward the front of the store with an open hand. "Can we speak outside?"

He took off without waiting for Jake's response.

Jake put his sunglasses back on as Mason led the way outside and around the north corner of the building. He stopped in the shade amid a litter of cigarette butts. A tobacco pall hung in the air.

"I wasn't wrong," Mason said, clasping his hands again. "Those men did rob Mr. Siebert."

And just like that, Jake had the victim's name. "Mr. Siebert said it was a misunderstanding."

"I can't explain why he said that. He was a good customer before that. He never came back."

"Tell me about the two guys."

"Three guys."

Jake's pulse thrummed faster. Silva had been there.

Mason looked off for a moment. "The big one was dressed all in sports clothing. Shiny with team colors and numbers on it. I don't know what team—I'm not into sports. But it wasn't the Bears, I know those colors. He was the one who stopped

Mr. Siebert in the parking lot. The little skinny one wore baggy pants and a crooked baseball hat. He took the wine from Mr. Siebert."

"And the third one?"

"The driver stayed in the car. The other two kept looking at him. He leaned to look through the window one time, but I couldn't see what he wore."

"Were the men black, white, Latino?"

"White. All three. I shouldn't have called the little one a wigger like the officer quoted me in the report. I wasn't very PC back then." Mason smiled.

"What else can you tell me about Mr. Siebert?"

"He was a good customer. Mostly craft beer and Jack Daniel's. That night it was wine." He smiled again. "I helped him with the pairing. His wife was making a spicy lasagna."

Jake thanked Mason for his help, handed him a card, and returned to his car, happy to avoid the woman at the service desk. He was opening his car door when something Mason said hit him: he'd apologized for calling Lange a wigger, "like the officer quoted me in the report."

Jake caught up with Mason before he made it back inside. "Mr. Mason!" Jake stopped in front of him. "Did you see the police report?"

"I got a copy, just for kicks."

"Do you still have it?"

"Sure." He pulled out a smartphone, tapped away at the screen for a couple seconds, then held the phone out to Jake. "Here it is."

"You have it stored on your phone?"

Mason pointed up. "On the cloud."

Jake took the phone and shaded the screen with his hand. There it was. And it was complete—so the missing entries in the online report had resulted from data entry error, not officer negligence.

"Can you send me a copy of this if I give you my cell number?"

Mason took back the phone and stood poised with his thumbs over the screen. "Shoot."

Jake recited his number, and within seconds his phone buzzed in his pocket. "Thanks, Mr. Mason."

Mason smiled. "My friends call me Alex."

"Thanks, Alex."

CHAPTER TWENTY

Bull didn't like mornings in the hospice.

Every job changed shifts, and the fresh people assigned to him—the nurse and the patient services assistant and the dietician and the pharmacy assistant—came in to check him over. To poke and prod and wash. To measure his oxidation and pulse and blood pressure. To question his sleep and his appetite and even the consistency of his bowel movement: hard and pebbly like a rabbit's.

Today Doctor Death came in, too. Not Bull's own doctor, the guy he'd seen for forty years, but a hospice specialist. Bull tried not to think about the path a medical career took to land a guy in place like this, tending to people who were so certain to die within six months the government even got in on the action. As usual, the doctor spent nearly twenty minutes trying to talk Bull into going on morphine. Maybe they were running out of beds or the doctor had a friend who wanted this corner room.

Finally they all left, but before he could even relax, Bess Swanson in the room next door went. You would think the people who worked here would be so used to death—that's why the place existed, after all—they would close her door and wait for the funeral home to pick her up. Instead, every person on duty had to come and cluck over some little thing the dear departed had said or some little connection they had felt. It went on for at least an hour every time. Hell, Bull probably knew Bess better than any of them. She'd beat him at tetherball in fourth grade. Girl had been a damn giraffe.

He picked up a magazine and tried to read an article about the proposed health care bill, but he couldn't hang on to the thread of it. Either the bill was a muddled mess, or his mind was. He closed the magazine and tossed it on the table. The air concentrator thwumped away, pumping a hissing stream of air into the cannula under his nose. The air clouded around his face, drying out his eyeballs. He blinked and adjusted the hose.

His cell phone rang. Hogan.

"What do you got?"

"Houser's talking to the guy who reported the liquor store robbery that night."

Bull knew the defensive whine in Hogan's voice. The boy was sensitive to criticism and would look at Houser's progress as a personal failure. "Not your fault."

"I'm the one who cleaned that damn incident report."

Bull paused to pull in a few lungfuls. "You also came up with the idea to manipulate the construction schedule." A genius-level idea that had choked the liquor store off from customer traffic for twice as long as necessary, leading to its failure.

"But he still found the guy."

"Houser's good. But Bev is better."

"She just keeps telling me to—"

"Tell her about the robbery," Bull said. "And about Siebert." With Houser working that angle, the information had become need-to-know.

But nothing more.

* * *

Bev felt good about her morning. She'd planted stories with two reporters about how the budget cuts would force her to raise the fees her department charged to lawyers. Then she'd called the director of the Paget County Bar Association, another woman breaking the glass ceiling. They planned a series of leaks to the foreclosure and eviction practices that used sheriff services the most.

Her cell phone rang from the depths of her purse. She pulled it out. It was Hogan.

"This is Sheriff Warren."

"It's Hogan. I need to give you some more information about that document we're looking for. Silva and his pals stole it from a guy named Siebert the same night he was supposed to deliver it to Bull. A witness called in that theft as a strong arm-robbery."

Bev sighed. She had known there was more to the story. "Why are you only telling me this part now?"

"Houser just talked to the guy who reported the robbery that night. The clerk at the liquor store where it happened. Kid named Alex Mason."

She waited.

"I cleaned the incident report, but I guess I didn't do enough."

"What do you mean, you cleaned it?"

"I deleted parts of the online report and shredded the original."

"You tampered with—" Bev grimaced at the shrill tone her voice had taken. She put her hand over the phone and cleared her throat. "You altered the report, but Jake still found his way to the witness?"

"He won't suspect anything more than data entry error."

"Unless something else makes him rethink it."

"This guy, Mason. He knew Siebert's name—it was in the report even though Siebert had left the scene—and I doubt he's forgotten it. Witnessing a robbery was probably a big deal for him."

"So Jake'll be visiting Siebert next? The guy who had the document?"

"Siebert can't help Houser. He never understood what he had."

"How about telling me what's on this document?"

"Bull said not—"

Bev interrupted. She already knew what her dad had said. "Stay on Jake. Don't let him see you."

She didn't waste any time fretting about whether to call her dad. He answered right away.

"Hey, baby girl." He was strongest in the morning, and his voice was clear and energetic, but the background *hiss* from the air hose reminded her where he was. And why.

"Hogan says Jake has made his way to Siebert."

Her dad coughed, gravelly and wet. "Sorry, Bev."

"You okay, Dad?"

"Fine." He cleared his throat in a great rolling hack. "How's your jurisdiction grab working?"

"Borgeson likes it. He's pushing Mayor Dietz and his Weston council allies on it."

"Might work, but listen." He told her about Jake hurting the boyfriend of the woman who had reported Lange as missing.

"When did this happen? I just talked to Hogan, and he didn't mention it." *More secrets.*

"Last night. Hogan recognized what was going down"— *hiss*—"talked to the boyfriend."

"Last night," she repeated, an angry heat rising in her chest.

"Right before Hogan came here to visit." *Hiss.* "Told him I'd talk to you about it. I forgot."

"Hogan reports to *me*, Dad."

"My mistake, Bev."

"I need to know everything or I can't protect you."

"You do, now."

"No, I don't. Not even close. I don't know what this document is."

"Bev…" He coughed. "It's going to stay that way."

"I need—"

"End of discussion." The barked words ended in a cough that trailed on until dying into a wheeze.

End of discussion. Her dad never reversed himself once he'd laid that down. She chewed her lip. "This guy, the boyfriend, is he willing to file a complaint?"

"Hogan's already got it papered up."

"My department handles Professional Standards for Weston." Her dad knew that, but she was thinking out loud. "We can use this. I can even second Hogan to that group and have him take lead."

"Good! Sidetrack him with that"—*hiss*—"then take the case and we're clear."

"Then my detectives will follow the evidence and close this case."

"Well, not all cases clear," he said. "Fifty-fifty, give or take."

"We're doing better than that, Dad."

"That's great. Just so long as you keep your boys away from me and ours."

CHAPTER TWENTY-ONE

Jake got in his car and took a minute to examine the incident report Alex Mason had sent him. He spread his fingers on his phone's screen to zoom in on the bits of the incident report that had been missing from the online report. It was all there: the victim's name, the responding officer's name, and even the Buick's plate number. His new friend Alex was a good witness.

He called Erin and briefed her.

"I don't recognize the officer, Peter Thompson. Do you?" Jake knew most of the patrol division from the lectures he gave on interviewing techniques.

"Nope." Computer keys clacked in the background. "But Google gave me a Paul Siebert in the Cress Creek subdivision." She read off the address.

"I'm going straight over there."

"Hang on. I dug up something on Silva. He had a juvenile record, but it's sealed."

"Can we get into it?" Jake started the car and put it in drive, but kept his foot on the brake.

"Nope. And as an adult he's clean."

"That it?" He eased the pressure on the brake and started to roll forward.

"I talked to Ed Temple. He patrolled the Bends for thirty years until he retired in '09. Remember him?"

"No." Jake had returned to Weston two years before that, but the name wasn't familiar.

"Temple took a look at Silva when he hooked up with an old crook Temple had his eye on. Guess who?"

Jake remembered what Pearl Cassano had said—that her husband had taken Silva into his carpet business.

"Mr. Cassano." Jake stopped the car. That explained the wariness he'd sensed from both Pearl Cassano and her neighbor, Mr. Simari. "What was Cassano into?"

"He was a fence, but he never did time and was only arrested once, way back in the seventies. Temple never believed Cassano went straight, just that he got better at hiding what he did. Temple kept an eye on both Cassano and Silva but never caught them at anything."

"Anything on Silva's wife?"

"She's clean. Works as a bookkeeper at an office supply warehouse."

Jake released the brakes and got underway again. "That it?"

"I checked with the DMV. Silva's driver's license expired in March of 2013."

"That fits." Jake smiled. "Thanks."

The circumstantial evidence agreed with his gut: Silva had taken the car, killed the men, and had been running ever since. But why?

* * *

Bev's cell phone rattled across her desk, and she snatched it up. "This is Sheriff Warren."

"It's Coroner Jansen." His voice was a tight whisper. "I had them tear out the inside like you said."

She sat up straight. "And?"

"They found another body. Well, not a whole body, but extra bones. They're sending out divers to look for the rest of it back at the lagoon."

Bev slumped in her chair. Her dad's story didn't account for a second body, much less a third. "Any more paper?"

"You heard me about the body, right?"

"I heard you. Paper?"

"Some waxy cardboard like for Chinese takeout. That's it."

Bev ended the call, then paced along the window behind her desk, considering what she knew. Five years ago, Silva stole a dangerous document—then promptly disappeared. Now the car he was driving turns up with two bodies in it, neither of which is him.

This third body *had* to be him. But where was the document?

She didn't like continually being behind the story. She needed to get ahead of it. She grabbed her bag and headed for the door. She would paw through every last thing in her dad's house until she found answers.

CHAPTER TWENTY-TWO

Jake drove slowly through Paul Siebert's subdivision, an upscale neighborhood with tree-lined streets and high-end minivans and SUVs sitting in open garages. The entire subdivision had been built around a golf course, and twice Jake had to wait for a golf cart to cross in front of him, traveling from a green to the next tee box.

Siebert's house, a brick-fronted colonial with two minivans in the driveway, was on a cul-de-sac away from the golf course. A scrum of boys in nylon shorts and NBA jerseys were playing basketball on a portable hoop set up to hang over the street. Jake pulled around the circle, waving to the boys as they wandered out of his way, and parked down the curb from their game. He climbed out of the car and struggled into his blazer as he crossed the lawn toward Siebert's front door.

"Hey, five-o!" one of the boys shouted, and the others laughed.

Victoria Silva was right about the Crown Vic—it gave him away everywhere he went.

He rang the bell and waited, watching the boys, squinting against the sun, sweat running down the hollow along his spine.

The door opened, and suction rattled the glass storm door. He turned to find a teenage girl in yoga pants and a tank top.

"Yes?" She looked at him, then over his shoulder at the boys.

"Is Paul Siebert home?"

"Just a minute." She turned and disappeared.

The sun's glare against the glass prevented Jake from seeing deeper into the house, so he stepped to one side until the glare disappeared. The door opened onto an oak-floored foyer with a carpeted staircase running up to the second floor. Piles of folded clothes were stacked on the side of several of the steps. If each stair held the clothes for one child, then Siebert had six kids. A large pile of soft colors on the top step was probably the girl's, while the other steps looked to hold boys' clothes: shiny sports jerseys and cottons in tans and browns and reds. Jake turned back to the boys and wondered how many of them lived here.

The storm door creaked open, and cool air flowed out of the house and around him.

"I'm Paul Siebert." The man holding the door wore cargo shorts and an orange T-shirt from Rocky Mountain National Park.

"I'm Detective Jake Houser from the Weston Police Department."

The smile left Siebert's eyes but held on his face. "What… uh, do you want?"

"I'd like to talk with you about the incident outside the liquor store five years ago."

Siebert's mouth pulled into a hard line, and his eyes jiggered away. A long moment passed. "I suppose I should ask you in."

"Thank you."

Jake stepped inside. The house felt comfortable, the air fragrant with sugar and butter. He flapped open his blazer to get some cool air up under it as he followed Siebert through an arched opening into the living room. The house had been built before the infatuation with open floor plans, and the room was a simple space lined with mismatched desks, dim behind lowered blinds. A bookshelf against the near wall held a set of encyclopedias, several science dictionaries, and a dozen other reference works.

Siebert spun two desk chairs around to face each other and sat down in one of them, gesturing for Jake to take the other.

"During the school year the kids do homework in here," Siebert said. "During the summer they're mostly outside."

Jake was glad Siebert had started off with small talk; it helped build rapport and relax people. "Which of the boys out there are yours?"

Siebert smiled. "I didn't see who all's out there. Neighbor kids come over too. Five of them are with us."

With us?

Confusion must have showed on Jake's face, because Siebert explained, "Our boys are foster children. Two sets of brothers."

"Oh." Jake's experiences with the foster care system had all come while on the job. Many children in the system came from difficult situations that left emotional scars and behavioral problems. The Sieberts taking on five of them—all boys—was impressive. "And you have a daughter?"

"Annie. She's our oldest."

Jake wanted to ask if she was also a foster child, but he remembered that foster parents, and foster children, could be sensitive about being considered a "real" family, so he left it alone.

He smiled and pulled out his phone. "I need to confirm the incident report from that night. I have it here on my phone. Please tell me what happened. Then I might have a few questions."

Siebert's mouth pulled tight and his chair squeaked as he shifted his weight. He propped an ankle on the opposite knee. "It was…" He shook his head and put his foot back on the floor, then ran a hand over his face and grabbed the arms of the chair. He breathed out with a whoosh and then told the story, keeping it short: three men waylaid him in the parking lot and robbed him of his money and the wine he'd bought.

Robbed him. Not a misunderstanding like the report said.

Jake waited for Siebert to explain this, but when the silence lengthened he decided to move on. "Tell me about the men." He left his notebook in his pocket. He didn't want to interrupt the flow.

"The big guy…" Siebert's voice cracked. "He was… bad. Wore basketball shorts and a football jersey." He shook his head. "The little guy was, I don't know, almost comical. He had on baggy jeans and… I can't remember his shirt."

"Was the big one running the show?"

Siebert shook his head. "The other one. The driver."

Bingo. "Tell me about him."

"More polished. Dressed better, maybe. That was my impression, anyway." He rubbed his hands over his face. "White guy, all three of them were white."

"What made you think the driver was in charge?"

"Well, it's been a long time." He pulled his ankle onto his knee again and bounced his foot. "I'm sorry. I can't remember why I thought that."

Siebert had displayed a few indicators of deception—shifting his weight, touching his face—but not clustered, and his story matched Mason's. He wasn't lying; he was in emotional pain.

"How were the men together?"

"What do you mean?"

"How did they interact? Cooperative? Friendly? Did the driver yell instructions at the other two?"

"I don't think he said anything. The big guy was the one who… talked to me. The little one, he just, I don't know, heckled me, I guess is the best way to describe it."

Mason had observed the two looking to the driver for prompts or approval, but Siebert had been too focused on the men right in front of him to see that. At least not consciously.

"Why are you confirming the report now?" Siebert asked. He planted his feet and leaned forward. "It's been five years."

"The car they were driving that night was pulled out of the Paget River yesterday."

Siebert pushed back into his chair. "Oh."

"What's this?"

A tall, thin woman stood in the archway drying her hands on a patterned kitchen towel. She slung the towel onto her shoulder and wrung her hands, drawing Jake's eyes to her slender fingers, the skin red from some hot-water chore. There were probably a lot of those in raising six kids.

"Mrs. Siebert? I'm Detective Jake Houser. I was talking with your husband about the men who robbed him a few years back."

Jake stood and held out his hand. The baking smells came off her, now. And a new one: cinnamon.

"They were horrible men." She took Jake's hand and shook it once, squeezing hard, her flesh warm. "Call me Linda." She released her grip and stood next to her husband, a hand falling to his shoulder.

"That was their car," Siebert said to her. "The one they pulled out of the river with the bodies in it?" He turned back to Jake. "We heard about it on the radio."

Jake sat back down. "We've identified the dead men as Nicholas Lange and Robert Graves."

"And...?" Linda asked.

"And I came by to see if your husband could shed a little more light on that night. He may have been the last person to see the men alive."

The Sieberts exchanged a glance that probably communicated something in the private language a couple develops, but Jake couldn't decipher it.

"Are you saying the car went into the river that same night?" Linda asked. Tendons rippled in her forearm as she squeezed her husband's shoulder.

"We think so."

Siebert patted his wife's hand, then pulled it off his shoulder. "Why don't you get back to what you were doing?"

"Okay." With a tight hard smile she left, taking the delicious smells with her.

When she was gone, Siebert spread his hands wide. "I don't think I can help you further, Detective. I've told you everything I remember."

"Why did you refuse to file a complaint that night? You claimed it was a misunderstanding."

Siebert's chair squeaked as he fidgeted. "I didn't refuse. It was my choice, and I chose not to."

"Why?"

Siebert's face flushed, and he turned away. "I was ashamed, okay?" His fist pounded the arm of his chair. "Ever since then I've felt... I don't know. Like if I had stood up to them in that parking lot, things would have been different for us after. Instead..." His arms dropped to his lap, and his shoulders slumped.

Giving in to those men had damaged Siebert's perception of himself—and he still suffered from it. But he'd done the right thing. A few bucks and two bottles of wine were not worth taking on three younger men.

"Did they use a gun?" Jake asked.

Siebert shook his head. "I'm embarrassed to say, they didn't need a gun to rob me."

"They had a gun with them," Jake said. "If you had resisted you might have been killed. Giving them what they wanted was the right thing to do."

Siebert waved that away and scowled. "Maybe. I mean, sure. But back then?" His gaze wandered away, and memory played across his face in waves of anger and hate. "I was disgusted with myself." His voice dropped to a near whisper. "Absolutely disgusted."

Jake stood and pulled out one of his cards. "If you remember anything else about that night—about the third man, or anything else—please let me know."

He left Siebert stuck in the memory of the weakness he'd shown that October night. Jake regretted stirring it up, but at least now he knew why Siebert hadn't filed a complaint. He'd never wanted to think about what those men had done to him—what they'd taken from him—ever again.

CHAPTER TWENTY-THREE

Bev waited patiently for a chance to speak. The managing partner of the biggest foreclosure firm in Paget County was talking her through his many reasons why she shouldn't raise sheriff department fees. She'd already told him the increase came from the county board and not her, but lawyers liked to talk, and she was an elected official so she listened. When he finally wound down she pressed him to start calling the county board's officers and members, then got off the call as quick as she could.

She had more important things on her mind.

Hogan and her dad.

She pulled out her cell phone and called Hogan. She didn't even give him a chance to say hello.

"Where are you?"

"Houser is leaving Siebert's house. Wasn't in there very long."

"I called my dad this morning. He told me about Woodling."

"This morning? Said he was going to call you last night."

"Don't blame him."

"Not blaming, I'm just… never mind."

"You work for me. You report to me."

He was silent, but she waited him out.

Finally: "I know."

"Tell me the whole story."

He told her everything her dad had.

"Will Woodling cooperate?" she asked.

"Yes."

"We're going to use this. I talked to the lieutenant over Professional Standards. You're now seconded to that group, and you're taking Woodling's complaint directly to Jake's deputy chief. You have an appointment in forty-two minutes."

"Braff? Good. That'll be like yanking a dog's leash. I'll head right over there. Any specific instructions?"

Just the obvious, she thought. Then decided she'd better say it. "Avoid talking about how the complaint got to us so fast. And about Woodling's record."

"Got it."

Bev had barely put her cell phone down when her desk phone rang. It was County Board Chairman Borgeson, unhappy with how the jurisdictional argument was playing out.

"I've been pulling strings, but they're holding them too tight," he said. "Losing makes me look weak. I hate that."

She knew. "Even with the multiple bodies?"

"Those bastards don't want to give it up. Gonna call it a murder suicide."

"Who told you that?" Jake wouldn't do that without solid proof.

"The powers that be down there want to wrap it up quick even without a man to convict. Hell, easier that way, I expect. I've always said they manipulate their crime statistics to make those damn lists."

Borgeson was right: her effort to take the case over on jurisdictional grounds was taking longer than she'd thought it would. But the Woodling complaint should slow Jake down long enough for the jurisdictional argument to do the job.

CHAPTER TWENTY-FOUR

Jake's phone had buzzed while he was in with Siebert. Back in the car, he checked it: a missed call from Erin. He pulled off his blazer and called her back while watching the Siebert boys shooting hoops. The tallest Siebert boy lowered the hoop until even the smallest one could dunk on it.

"FIC Fanning found finger bones this morning."

"Okay." He folded the blazer on the passenger seat.

"These are *extra* bones. He'd already found all the finger bones for Lange and Graves."

Silva. It was the obvious conclusion, but he needed to convert that speculation to fact ASAP. "We need to get back out to the river and find the rest of him."

"Deputy Chief Braff sent the Water Rescue Team out there already."

"Good." WRT's members came from both the police and fire departments. The group spent more time training than doing, so they were always excited for real work. "See if you can track down Silva's dental records."

"I'm on it. What did Siebert have to say?"

Jake summarized their conversation.

"Sounds like macho nonsense."

She had it backwards. If Siebert had been macho that night instead of doing the mature, adult thing, he might have gotten killed. "Did you know he's got five foster kids living with him?" Jake had never met a foster family outside of the job. "Maybe six. I'm not sure about the daughter. The girl."

"One girl and five boys. That's a lot of sweaty kid flesh."

Jake laughed. "It is." The Siebert boys were all dunking on the lowered rim now. Rating each other like it was the NBA slam-dunk contest.

"I ran Craig Morgan through the databases," Erin said.

"What did you find?"

"Clean as a whistle. Not even a speeding ticket. Spent three years in the army. Now he's self-employed. Even bothered to get the city license for his business."

"Three years in the army? What were the dates?"

"December of 2012 to December 2015."

December of 2012. Just after Donald Silva disappeared.

* * *

Jake headed to Radar Grove to see what the WRT would find. He would need more than a few finger bones to even prove there had been a third death—a person can live without a few fingers, and the lab might not be able to extract a usable DNA sample from something so small after all that time in the water. What he really needed was the skull. That would prove the death *and* give him the best chance for an identification.

Traffic was light on Ogden, and he made it the few miles to Radar Grove in minutes. At the bridge over the river, a car full of teenagers with a canoe strapped on top were arguing with an officer Jake didn't know. Jake flashed his badge, and the officer waved him through.

A Chevy Sprint van, painted police blue with the Weston PD logo, stood at the riverbank, straddling the Buick's drag marks. Jake parked in the shade and crunched his way across the dried-out grass. The sun was straight overhead, strong and bright, and the air was still. Bugs chittered and twitted about, and the distant tollway droned in the background. Three divers were picking their way across the drying mudflats, fins in hand and air tanks strapped to their backs. The mud was a day drier now and had developed a crust that broke under each step the divers took. Swarms of flies buzzed into the wet holes they left behind. The smell hadn't gotten any better.

A short, thick man in a red jumpsuit and a Weston FD ball cap stood on the bank talking over a map with another man. Jake didn't recognize either of them. The civilian looked out of place in his corduroy pants and short-sleeved dress shirt.

"Gentlemen."

The two turned from the map.

"I'm Detective Houser. This is my case." The skin on Jake's neck tightened against the sun.

The men introduced themselves. The stocky fireman was Lieutenant Blaine of the Water Rescue Team. The taller one was Joe Knight, a geography teacher from Paget Community College. His buzz cut was so short Jake couldn't determine his hair color. He said Erin had called him in to help decide where to look.

"What's the plan?"

Knight pointed to the map. "We know how long the car was in the water and where it rested. This shows the hydrography of this section of the river and the lagoon."

Jake followed along, his gaze occasionally wandering to the three divers, who had reached the water's edge. The men formed a triangle to lean on each other as they put on their fins.

"The car was in this deep spot." Knight pointed at a swirl of lines indicating the topography of the hole where the car had settled. His map was a lot more detailed than the one in the park brochure. "It's unlikely the missing contents—the third skeleton—moved far. We expect to find the remains in this deep hollow, or close to it on the downstream side."

"If they don't find it there?"

"The current would carry it along here." Knight traced a finger south along the bank to where the water cut back to join the river. It was a lot of territory.

The divers pulled their masks down and eased into the water. Each lowered a probe in front of him as he disappeared under the surface, bubbles trailing behind.

"Now we wait," the lieutenant said.

Jake walked back under the shade and called FIC Fanning. "Duke? It's Houser. Tell me about the extra bones."

"Distal phalanges." Fanning talked in short bursts that juries loved. "Fingernail bones. Left thumb and forefinger."

"Did you find any more of him?"

"Fibula." Fanning paused. "Up under the driver's seat. Looked like the seat frame until we took it out."

"Leg bone, right?"

"The little one. The calf bone."

That brought him closer to proving there had been a death.

"Why did you take the seat out?" Jake asked.

"Jansen told us to strip the inside to bare metal. First thing out of his mouth when we came in this morning. That's why we found it." A shout in the background. "Hold on."

A voice came through Fanning's phone, growing louder as though approaching Fanning.

"… freaking metatarsus. Wedged inside the vent."

"Jake?" Fanning came back on the line. "You hear that?"

"A foot bone, right?"

"Yep. The extra bones are turning up in and around the front seat."

"Anything pointing to a cause of death?"

"Not my job, but no."

"Did you find the gun yet?"

"In the smaller guy's right hand." Fanning sucked on something. A straw, maybe. "Revolver. Thirty-eight. Fully loaded. All shots fired."

A smooth voice came over the line, its tone neither urgent nor excited.

"Is that Jansen?" Jake asked. "What's he doing?"

"Looks at every damn thing we pull out of the car. Calls it all in to someone on his cell phone." Fanning grunted a short laugh. "Doesn't like the bones, though."

This level of interest wasn't the Jansen norm. Whoever was on the other end of those phone calls was pulling Jansen's strings. Probably the same person who'd told him to have the car moved to the garage. "Any idea who he's talking to?"

"I'd be guessing."

Jake could do his own guessing: Bev or Borgeson. Or maybe even Bull from his hospice bed.

"Thanks, Duke."

CHAPTER TWENTY-FIVE

Jake walked the grove's perimeter, sticking to the shade, and found the section of thinner undergrowth where the park map showed the old road he remembered from his teenage years. He kicked through the soil and leaf clutter and found gravel. He called Knight over, who got excited at the opportunity to calculate the "world without us" scenario.

While Knight worked it out, Jake distracted himself thinking about Radar Grove's history. It was named after a top-secret radar training facility built there during the Second World War. Before that, during the depression, a Civilian Conservation Corps camp at the same location had housed hundreds of men who spent years improving the county's forest preserves and trail systems. Jake knew a lot of this thanks to Coogan—the local expert on the camp. Coogan had even helped their high school friend, Henry Fox, locate and excavate the old pit latrines. They'd found dozens of artifacts that enjoyed a short display at the Weston Settlement before going into its archives.

Knight estimated three to six years had passed since the road was last maintained, with four years as his best guess.

Jake ambled back over the river's edge. The lieutenant walked over from his van to join him. "Lagoon's so muddy they're working mostly by touch. Makes for slow going."

"What's the most interesting thing your guys have ever found?"

"Once we were looking for a gun that might have been tossed into a retention pond, and found a body instead. Turned out to be an old-timer who'd disappeared from his rest home a few years before."

As they stood in the baking sun, staring at the broiling surface where the air bubbled up, Jake's phone vibrated. In the sun's glare he couldn't read the screen to see who was calling, but he answered anyway. It was Erin.

"Deputy Chief Braff wants you to come in right away." A deep voice boomed behind her. "He says that's an order, not a request."

"What's up?"

"Yes, he's right here with me."

"What's it about?"

"I'll tell him you'll be in right away." The commanding voice faded, still talking.

"I can't leave now. The divers are still looking." He needed to be here, where the answer was.

"They can keep doing that. But you need to see Braff."

"What's this about, Erin?"

"A deputy from Professional Standards is making a scene."

The sheriff's Professional Standards Office handled disciplinary complaints for every police department in the county and had the authority to suspend officers and could even press criminal charges.

"Any hint who complained?" Jake asked.

"I heard the name Woodling."

Woodling? Complaining less than twenty-four hours after Jake encountered the guy? And why would Woodling want to start something when the beating he'd given his girlfriend was so clear on her face?

Erin seemed to be waiting for Jake to say something.

"It's nothing to worry about," he said.

She said nothing.

"Okay," he conceded. "I'll be there in twenty minutes."

* * *

Jake tried to prepare for talking with Deputy Chief Braff, but his focus kept turning back to the lagoon. Finding the third victim—it had to be Silva—changed everything. The politicians would now push him to make the quick and easy determination that Silva had killed his friends and then himself. But Jake's gut told him it wasn't a murder-suicide. He'd found no facts to support that Silva was suicidal, or that he had a reason to kill Graves. Even Silva's motive to kill Lange was weak. He just didn't see it; he'd never heard of a murder-suicide among three adult men outside of a workplace shooting.

Jake had a lot of work to do. Why the hell was Braff pulling him away from the lagoon now? Braff should know better.

That gave Jake pause. Braff *did* know better. Which meant he was taking Woodling's complaint very seriously.

Woodling's split eyebrow was probably what had gotten Professional Standards interested. But when Jake told them what had really happened, he'd be in the clear. Especially if Murphy backed his story. And even if she was too scared to tell the truth, her face and the bruise on her arm would speak for themselves. He should have taken a picture of her injuries. They would fade every day.

But the big question on Jake's mind was: How had a sheriff's investigator gotten on this so quickly? Even if Woodling had filed a complaint first thing this morning, this was too fast. And if Woodling had the juice to do this, the obnoxious ass would have spouted off about it last night with threats to get Jake fired. So Woodling had no juice. Maybe it was Sheila with the juice. Or Angela? But that didn't feel right.

Jake parked in the station's visitor lot and reached for his blazer, but then left it on the seat—Braff didn't stand on formalities. As he entered the building, Jake waved his way through security and past his co-workers to the double oak doors that led into Braff's office. They were closed. Jake reached for the knob, but a familiar voice stopped him.

"He told me to have you wait here, Jake. It'll only be a few minutes." Margie, Braff's admin, spoke from her desk across the corridor.

Jake had known Margie his entire life. They had sat together at many Warren family gatherings—back before his family was banished from them. Her dad's mother was a cousin of some kind.

"How's Thomas's thesis coming along?" Jake asked.

"Good!" Her eyes twinkled as they always did when talking about her children. "He defends it next month."

"And James? How's he doing in San Francisco?"

"He loves it out there. He has a new job as the controller at a bank."

"I'm glad to hear they're both doing well."

"James still asks about you from time to time." James had had a brief fling with being a cop, but got scared off the idea during a ride-along with Jake. It had been a busy night, with two domestics and an attempted rape.

"Tell him I said hello." Jake settled into a chair along the wall. "How's Bull?" he asked. Margie had always been tight with Bull and Bev. "I heard he's not doing well."

"Don't believe everything you hear."

"Well, if you happen to talk with him, please tell him I hope he beats it."

Margie smiled. "I'll do that."

Jake waited. Trying to focus. Braff wouldn't jam him up for nothing. He was a cop's cop. Not a bureaucrat. Whatever Woodling had said, and whomever he'd said it to, it had been serious enough to get Braff's attention.

A few minutes later the door opened, releasing a mumble of deep voices, and a big redheaded man in a lightweight suit emerged. The man glanced at Jake, then looked down at his cell phone as he strode by. He looked familiar, but Jake couldn't quite place him.

"Margie, who was—"

"Get in here, Houser!"

* * *

Hogan dialed the contact on his phone as he left Weston Police HQ. He stepped out into the heat, squinting against the harsh brightness, and moved into the shade by the memorial wall as the line rang.

"Is this Hogan?" A smoky, sensuous voice.

He smiled. "I have something you might be interested in."

She laughed. "Now I know it's you. Getting right to the point."

"Isn't that the way you like it?"

She laughed again. "Well, don't keep me in suspense."

"There's a brutality complaint against a detective in the Weston PD."

"I'm guessing this is off the record, then."

"Way off."

"Who?"

"The favored son."

"Not even a name, for crying out—wait, you're talking about Houser, aren't you?"

"That's all I can say. You'll have to use your amazing powers of investigatory journalism to get the rest."

"That *is* what I do. I'm already chasing Houser on the double murder at the river. Did this brutality complaint come out of that?"

"I can't say."

"Shit, it did, didn't it?"

"I can't say."

"Thanks, Hogan. I'll buy you a drink."

He smiled as the line went dead.

CHAPTER TWENTY-SIX

Jake followed Deputy Chief Braff into his office, the air icy and scented with coffee and leather. The DC was old school: buzz cut, short-sleeve shirt, clip-on tie. The badge on his belt gleamed as if freshly buffed. As he adjusted the blinds to block the sun cutting through, he motioned for Jake to take a seat in a grouping of leather club chairs and a couch by the window. Jake felt that sitting here instead of across the desk from one another was a good sign.

Braff sat on the edge of his chair and got right to it. "Tell me about Woodling."

Jake told the whole story, watching for a reaction, but Braff was completely still, eyes focused and intense. When Jake finished, Braff didn't speak for several beats, but Jake was used to that.

"Three things. One, when you identified yourself at the front door, was it loud enough for Woodling to hear you?"

"I—"

"I don't want your answers now." Braff held up a hand and popped up a thick stubby finger for each point he made. "Remember. Reflect. Answer."

Braff loved threes.

"Two, why didn't you call an ambulance for Woodling?" Braff let that sink in. "Three, why didn't you send the woman to a shelter?"

"Got it."

Braff stood and paced along the windows, hands behind his back. Finally, he stopped and faced Jake. "The Weston PD has a good relationship with the sheriff's department." He shifted his gaze around the room. "This…"

Jake sat up straighter. Braff was never at a loss for words.

"A complaint from a guy with Woodling's history should have been met with serious skepticism. Instead they're fast-tracking it." Braff shook his head, then met Jake's eye. "Something's going on that we aren't privy to. Political nonsense of some kind, no doubt. So we keep doing our jobs. Think through those questions, and we'll be ready."

"I will. Who was the big redhead I saw leaving your office?"

"The investigator from the sheriff's office." Braff pointed a finger at Jake. "But don't you worry about him. He's *my* worry. You keep working the case." He sat back down. "Now tell me about the bodies at the river."

Jake knew Braff read every update made to the online murder book, so he kept it brief, summarizing his interviews and the car's connection to the robbery at the liquor store. The only thing he didn't mention was the information missing from the incident report—no reason to get a civilian employee in trouble over a data entry error that hadn't slowed him down by much.

"With the third body up front, are you looking at murder-suicide?"

"The body's location is the only thing pointing that way."

"What's your gut telling you?"

"That it's not that. I'd need two more motives. I have nothing to explain why Silva would want to kill Graves, or why he would off himself. And I've never heard of a murder-suicide among three friends."

Braff waved toward the door. "Get back at it."

* * *

Jake checked his watch on the way to the car: 4:48 p.m. He wanted to head back out to Radar Grove, but decided to focus his energies where he could actually do something. He'd return to his apartment, update the murder book, and prepare answers to Braff's three questions.

He had his blinker on to turn down his alley when his phone buzzed. He turned off his blinker and continued north on Main Street while he answered. "This is Houser."

"This is Lieutenant Blaine."

Jake's pulse accelerated with expectation.

"We found the skull and the top of the spine."

"Perfect," Jake said. The skull confirmed they had a third victim and would make identification easier. It might even reveal cause of death. "I'll be right there."

As he headed for Radar Grove, he called Erin and gave her the news. She had already located Silva's dental records and had sent them to Doc Franklin.

"Can you call the coroner's office and make sure someone comes out to pick up the skull and deliver it to Doc Franklin ASAP?"

"I'm on it."

When Jake arrived at the park, the three divers were sitting at a picnic table that had edged into the shade as the sun dropped. Their wetsuits were peeled down to their waists, and their fins lay in pairs on the brown grass. They were drinking from plastic water bottles and laughing together.

Blaine waved Jake over to the back of his van, where a white plastic box with its lid off sat in the open door. "Here's what we've found."

Jake peered into the box, squinting against the sun and heat. The mud-stained skull looked complete and undamaged, its teeth white, a caterpillar of vertebrae snaking from it. He saw no obvious signs of trauma. A jumble of small bones and three ribs clustered around it.

"Good work, Lieutenant." He wiped his forehead. "The skull is exactly what we need."

"The boys can go back in, if you need them to."

The skull was enough to make an identification, but the cause of death might be in the bone record left in the river. "Can they work till dark?"

"Absolutely. Maybe they can find something else worth burying."

Jake looked over at the men. "What's that bottle on the table with them?"

"Wine. Still sealed."

Siebert's wine. "Bag it as evidence. The dead men stole two bottles of wine before they went into the river."

"Will do."

Jake stepped into the shade cast by Blaine's truck and watched the lieutenant herd his dive team back into the water then bag the wine as evidence and put it in the van. After the deputy coroner showed up and took the box of remains, Jake called Dr. Franklin to alert him that the skull was on its way. The doctor said he'd head right over to the autopsy suite. The identification was now in Dr. Franklin's hands. Even with autopsy protocol slowing him down, having the skull and dental records should make identification quick.

Jake's gut told him it was Silva—but his gut wasn't evidence.

* * *

Bev let herself into the house with the same key she used to wear on a string around her neck. It felt weird to be in the house by herself. Even though the two of them had lived there alone after her mom and brother died, her dad had always been home when she was. As an adult, looking back, she realized that must have been hard for a busy man to do.

Her dad kept everything important to him in his home office, so she swept through the rest of the house first to get it out of the way. She found nothing helpful.

She hadn't been allowed in the office alone as a kid, and the weight of that tradition descended on her as she crossed the threshold. She scanned the big room: hardwood floors, heavy wood furniture, dark wood paneling. Such a masculine space.

A few months before, she'd sat in the guest chair across the desk from her dad to discuss the manila folders still lined up along the left edge. They held his will and trust and medical directive and power of attorney and the details of his financial holdings. Neat and organized and labeled.

Now she sat in her dad's chair and swiveled to examine the family photos in silver frames arranged on the other end of the desk: solo shots of her and her mom and her brother. The largest frame held the last family shot ever taken. Bev had the same photo on her dresser at home, but it still pulled her in. She picked it up and rubbed a thumb on the glass above her mom's face, then her brother's and her dad's. Soon she'd be the only one left on this branch of the Warren family tree.

She set the photo down and started through the desk drawers, taking them one by one and giving everything she found a hard look. Utility bills and bank statements in one drawer, medical insurance and doctor bills in another, a jumble of pens and pencils and odds and ends in the lap drawer.

She turned to the credenza and began sifting through a lifetime of accumulated paper. Time passed, and the room darkened; she turned on the overhead light, then added the desk lamp and the lamp on the credenza. She had flipped through decades of tax records and dozens of files on Warren family history without finding a single word to help her, when her cell phone rang.

Bev looked at her phone. Jansen. She didn't like talking to the pompous fool, but she needed to know if the third body was Silva.

"Yes?"

"It's Coroner Jansen." He liked to refer to himself as *Coroner Jansen*, although tradition dictated he be called "the coroner" or simply by name. He'd once waylaid her at a Republican fundraiser and explained in excruciating detail that his research told him it was not prohibited.

"What is it, Jansen?"

"Dr. Franklin identified the third body from dental records the Weston PD sent over." He talked so fast his words bled together. "A man named Donald Silva."

Of course. Why had she spent even a moment hoping it wasn't Silva? By her dad's own admission, Silva had been blackmailing him, and now Silva was dead. Motive.

"What else in that car didn't make the list you sent me? Like those phalanges that sent them back out to the lagoon." The list had only covered the non-human items found in the car, so her complaint wasn't fair, but Jansen brought out the worst in her.

"I had FIC Fanning rip the guts out of the car. That's ho—"

She hung up on him; she didn't need to listen to Jansen congratulate himself for something she had told him to do.

She checked her watch. It was nearly eight. She called her dad. As she waited for him to pick up she chewed her lip, sweat breaking out across her forehead and down her back.

She jumped right to it when he answered. "Dad? The third body is Silva." She couldn't stop the quiver in her voice. "A triple murder."

"Or not." He sighed loudly over the hiss of his air machine.

"Or not?" Had he lost it? "What's the *not* scenario?"

"Silva kills the other two. Then himself. He was in front. The other two in the back. Classic murder-suicide." He spoke slowly, interrupting himself every few words for a breath.

"You're saying Silva had motives to kill both of them? Nobody will buy murder-suicide without solid motives. And not among three unrelated men, unless they'd been in a love triangle of some kind."

"You find what you look for."

"Dad, if you've got something, let me have it and I'll run with it when I get the case." Her detectives would follow the evidence, not look for evidence to fit a theory.

"When is that going to happen, baby girl?" Her dad pulled in a loud breath.

"I'm keeping the pressure on."

"Let's hope your strategy works." He hung up.

Hope? Her dad hated that word. He said hope was for people without a plan. She *had* a plan. It was just taking too long. She needed something else. Something more than the jurisdictional argument and the brutality complaint.

Board Chairman Borgeson's comment about crime statistics wormed into her tired brain. It was a major source of pride for Mayor Dietz and his council that Weston landed high on the "Best Places to Live" lists in several national magazines. They'd built a whole marketing plan around the lists, touting them on websites, banners strung across the shopping district, and advertisements in retirement and travel magazines. Their ridiculous obsession gave her an idea.

She pulled her iPad out of her bag and launched a Google search, then tapped her way through a few Best City rankings. Her memory was right: the ranking systems for all the lists used crime statistics as a factor, and none of them adjusted for clearance rates. Only the crime mattered, not whether it was solved. An unsolved triple murder and a cleared double murder-suicide would both count as three on Weston's murder total.

She dove into Weston's statistics. The city had had only one murder the previous year. A three hundred percent increase would drop the city's rankings faster than the Buick had sunk in the river. But because the bodies were on county land, Weston could legitimately exclude them from their stats—*if* the Weston PD didn't handle the investigation.

And the county board's methodology for counting crime and for evaluating her performance didn't rely on magazine ratings. She went to the county website and clicked through to the crime statistics and did some quick math. Three solved murders would put the department's murder clearance rate over sixty percent for the first time in decades. And if she included only the solutions without the murders, that would put her solve rate over seventy percent. Could she get away with that? Maybe. Statistics was a twisted business.

She leaned back in the chair, forcing her fingers through her hair. Maybe she could get the family out of this *and* give her career a boost at the same time.

But she still didn't know the whole story, and what she didn't know could hide a landmine. Somewhere in this room there would be a hint of the truth.

There was only one more credenza drawer to search. She pulled the handle. Instead of sliding out, it swung open. Behind the fake drawer front was a safe.

CHAPTER TWENTY-SEVEN

The sun had dropped near the horizon, but there was light across the sky as Jake jogged west on Jackson, then joined the Paget River Trail at Jefferson, enjoying the river burbling peacefully beside him. He'd had trouble focusing back at the apartment, too full of nervous energy in anticipation of the identification of the third body, and had decided a run would clear his head.

As he ran, he worked back through the Woodling encounter and prepared answers to Braff's three questions. One: he'd identified himself loud and clear so Woodling knew a cop was at the door. Two: he'd examined Woodling, and the man didn't have a concussion, so didn't need an ambulance. Three: Murphy had packed her belongings and left with her sister, a nurse, so Jake didn't need to direct her to a shelter. Check, check, and check. Besides, Woodling was a hothead with a history of domestic abuse. The complaint was just a distraction that would eventually go nowhere. He would give it no more attention than he had to.

He lengthened his stride as he passed under the Burlington Northern Railroad tracks, his footfalls echoing off the concrete. His gait felt smooth as he leaned into the low hill where the trail entered the south end of Radar Grove.

Then the Woodling complaint wormed back into his head.

It didn't make sense. The typical repeat domestic abuser whose live-in girlfriend carries the marks of abuse in plain sight wouldn't make a complaint—he'd keep his head down and hope it all went away. And Woodling's complaint had gotten traction too quickly. He would have called his local police department, the Kirwin PD, or if he was good at googling, maybe Jake's boss. But Woodling had done neither. Somehow he had found the exact right place to direct his complaint to get it acted upon immediately. And even then, the investigator's first step should have been to talk to Woodling and any witnesses before taking it any further. A short conversation with Murphy and her sister should have killed it. The bruise on Murphy's eye and the handprint on her arm should have been enough to put Woodling's credibility in question.

Jake continued through the park, the white crushed stone trail almost ghostly in the fading light. As he cut through the picnic area, he caught a glimpse through the trees of Lieutenant Blaine and his team packing up their diving gear in the light from floods mounted on the back of the truck. Jake kept moving, looping through the north end of the park and then turning toward home. He kept his pace, the trail flying by beneath him.

There was no way Professional Standards would open an investigation into him without talking to the sheriff. Everyone knew they were related. Unless... maybe she was driving this as part of her effort to take over the lagoon case? But how would distracting him with Woodling help her get the case? At most it would slow him down.

Maybe that was it. She didn't want him to solve it before she got her hands on it.

He crossed back under the tracks, the light fading fast now. At Jefferson, he cut back onto the Riverwalk. The brick path squeezed between the church and the river, then ran along the bluff that rose up along the bank where the old Bristol place had stood. The Bristol grounds—a giant house, a dozen outbuildings, and a pond full of enormous sunfish—had been a fenced-in no-trespassing zone when Jake was a boy. Old Lady Bristol had wandered the property shooting salt pellets at anyone stupid enough to climb her fence. She'd caught Jake fishing the pond once, but had let him scramble away unsalted.

From there the trail dropped off the bluff and onto the flats, where the city's yard-waste dump and a long string of riverside businesses— car repair, upholstery, piano tuning—had once stood. All that was gone now, replaced by the Riverwalk, a beautifully landscaped linear park running along the Paget River all the way through downtown. Fancy cast-iron streetlights dotted the brick sidewalk with pools of light.

As he passed the ballpark where his team had won the city championship when he was nine, he raised his fist in triumph, as he did every time he ran past. He sprinted the last half mile to the apartment. His hope that the identity of the third body would be waiting for him put extra thrust in his stride. He darted up the stairs and snatched his phone off the counter.

There it was—a text from Doc Franklin.

The body was Silva's.

Jake stretched and rolled a foam roller over his hamstrings and calves before taking a quick shower, finishing with the valve set to cold to reset his body's thermostat. As he stepped out, he considered whether he should go notify Vicky Silva right away. But she was a single mom with a full-time job, so disturbing her this late with this news didn't feel right. Besides, he had tough questions to ask her about her husband's mental state. Waiting until morning was the right thing to do.

He pulled on a pair of cotton shorts and a T-shirt and sat in the recliner with his laptop, notebook, and cell phone to document his efforts in the murder book. What a difference a day made. This morning he'd been almost at a standstill, his only avenue of investigation the missing Silva. Now they'd found Silva's remains and, thanks to Erin, had tracked the three dead men to a strong-arm robbery the same night the car most likely disappeared.

Jake entered the details from the incident report Alex Mason had given him. He started to describe how he'd found Mason, but that revealed that information had been missing from the incident report, which would only get the data entry clerk in trouble. He hit delete until the string of sentences was gone.

When he finished, he read back through it, corrected typos, and rewrote a couple sentences that didn't sound right. He still hadn't entered a theory. Some detectives jumped on a theory right away, but Jake had always thought that was a mistake. People liked to prove themselves right, so working from a theory too early could influence how a detective saw the evidence. He considered filling in the section with the double murder-suicide possibility, but he didn't want anyone to think he was selling it when he wasn't even buying it. He left it blank.

He went through everything one last time before hitting submit. Off it went to the database.

His phone rang, rattling against the oak floor. He didn't recognize the number. "This is Detective Houser."

"Detective? This is Angela Murphy. From last night?"

"Is Sheila okay?" Jake wanted to snatch the question back as soon as he'd asked it. He'd be calling both Sheila and Angela as witnesses if Woodling's brutality complaint went that far, and he didn't want to add a witness-tampering claim to that problem.

"She's fine. She's going to stay with me and look at her options."

"Good to hear. I appreciate the call."

"Well, I actually called for another, uh, reason."

"What can I do for you?"

"I'm wondering... Do you want to come out for a drink with me?" Her voice sped up. "It doesn't have to be tonight."

"No," Jake said. "I mean. That would be nice, but I can't socialize with people involved in a case."

"When it's over, then?"

Jake almost said sure, but that would only push the problem off into the future. "Angela, I'm a widower and—"

"I'm sorry. I—"

"I'm involved with someone. Was involved. Anyway, I—"

"Wait. You're turning me down because you're a widower? Or because you're involved with someone? I didn't follow that."

Jake didn't follow it either. But one thing was clear: he wasn't ready to date. The thing with Callie—which hadn't been dating—proved that.

"I'm sorry." He had nothing else to explain it.

"Well, thank you for helping Sheila last night. We both appreciate it."

"Sure." It came out as a sigh.

Angela hung up, and Jake put the phone back on the floor. Had he sent her some kind of signal that he was interested and available? Did he have it in him to do that? He started to turn that over, but then pushed it aside. Avenging the three dead men was more important than his private life. And a lot more interesting.

His thoughts kept circling back to two very different possibilities: a triple murder, or a double murder-suicide. The motive for a triple murder would be cinematic: a spree killing, or a psycho at work. Unlikely. And a murder-suicide involving three men was even more unlikely.

His gut said it was something else altogether.

* * *

Bev stared at the safe. Her dad wasn't sentimental about anything except his family, and she'd already found two drawers stuffed with family histories, so that wasn't what the safe held.

And the two of them had spent a long time in this room going over his estate plan without him once mentioning the safe, so it couldn't hold anything of financial value.

What then?

She knelt on the carpet and examined the safe. The numbers around the dial ran to one hundred. She wasn't a math whiz but figured there would be millions of possible combinations. Her dad's estate plan gave her all his financial assets and all his belongings, including the house and its contents, so he wanted her to have whatever was inside it. Was he waiting until the last second to tell her it existed and give her the combination?

She sat back down behind the desk, slid the file containing the will in front of her, and flipped it open. It was a simple document transferring all his property at death to his trust. The trust file was thicker, and the document longer, but it was mostly boilerplate. She was about to close the file when a penciled notation on the inside cover caught her eye. She lifted the file to the desk lamp. It was her dad's handwriting, block printing in pencil.

His birthday.

His.

It could only be her brother's.

She knelt in front of the safe and spun the dial. Its cold plastic turned smoothly. 4-27-73. She tried it left-right-left and right-left-right, but neither worked. She was sure about the numbers. Maybe safes used a different format for combinations than a bicycle lock?

She went back to her iPad and searched for videos on this model of safe. She found a demonstration by a safe company within twenty seconds. It was left-right-left, but with complete dial rotations in between the numbers.

She tried it. And this time when she grabbed the handle and pushed it down, the door swung open.

A page from a yellow legal pad hung down, taped to the top of the safe, blocking its contents. She pulled it out and read:

Bev: I leave you these files to do with as you will. I almost shredded them before going to hospice, but decided you should read them, then make that call. Use them or shred them. It's up to you now. You are the best of us and the best of me.

I love you!
Dad

Bev held the paper for a few minutes, his handwriting flooding her with memories of adventures they'd shared. A smile spread across her face, then faded. Her dad had hidden these files so she wouldn't find them until he was no longer around to explain them. That couldn't be good.

She set the note down and looked inside the safe.

The interior was like a dorm-room fridge with an adjustable wire shelf and a pocket in the door. But instead of beer and pop, these shelves held manila folders. She pulled them out in thick bunches and piled them on the floor, counting as she went. Twenty-two.

The files were labeled with names. She recognized most of them as Weston and Paget County politicians and administrators—councilmen, board members, trustees, commissioners, even a former police chief. And as she flipped quickly through a few files, she started to feel sick. The safe held secrets all right—but not her dad's. These files contained evidence of the private vices and mistakes of the people named on the labels.

Her stomach clenched and her hands shook. She grabbed a thick wad of files, intending to stuff them back in the safe, but stopped herself. Something in this stack might explain the mysterious document.

She went through the files, page by page, skimming for any reference to the Chicago Bears stadium deal.

She found nothing about it.

She put the files back in the safe and was closing the steel door when something rattled in the door pocket. She scooped out a small brown envelope that fit in her palm. It was oddly heavy. She found more of her dad's handwriting on the envelope: *Remember: Failure isn't Fatal.* The phrase rang with familiarity.

"Failure isn't fatal."

It was her dad's favorite phrase whenever he wanted to talk her into trying something again after she'd flubbed it the first time. She'd heard it at least a dozen times when learning to ride a two-wheeler, her dad running beside her holding the seat so she wouldn't wipe out.

She pulled open the flap and upended the envelope over her palm.

A gold coin slid out.

She'd never held anything so solid, so beautiful. The gold was shiny, and the woman in a flowing gown on the front and the flying eagle on the back were so finely displayed they struck her as art. Her dad had never shown her this coin; she would remember it. Where did he get it? Why was it in the safe? And why would it help him remember that failure wasn't fatal?

She took another minute to admire the coin, but as it had nothing to do with the stadium, she returned it to its envelope and the envelope to the safe. She closed the safe and shut the walnut door over her dad's secret files.

She plopped back into the desk chair and spun it to eye the drawers stuffed with Warren family records and tax returns. She understood her dad wanted to protect her, but she wasn't a little girl anymore. She needed to know what was in this mysterious document—what could be so damaging.

And then she realized: if there had ever been something that could damage him, he wouldn't have kept it at all.

She was wasting time.

CHAPTER TWENTY-EIGHT

The temperature was already climbing when Jake set out the next morning, so he cranked up the Crown Vic's air conditioner before calling Erin.

"I was just about to call you," she said.

"I'm driving up to notify Silva's widow." Erin read all the updates to the murder book, so Jake didn't need to tell her that Doc Franklin had identified the third victim. "Can you tell Braff I'm ready on Woodling?"

"He's right here. He wants—"

"Houser?" Braff's rough voice grated in Jake's ear after Erin's soft tone. "Now that it's confirmed it was Silva in the driver's seat, you leaning toward murder-suicide? In the seat, get it?"

"It's one of the things I'm looking at." The car's location added some weight to the theory—or at least argued against the theory of triple homicide. A triple-murderer trying to hide the bodies would not have left one body in the passenger compartment where a decomposition-loosened bone could detach and float out the window to be discovered—and a triple-murderer trying to make it look like a murder-suicide would have made the car easier to find instead of sinking it in the deepest spot in the lagoon.

"Right," Braff growled. "Keep on it."

Erin came back on the phone. "I called Mrs. Silva's office. She took the week off, so should be at home. You want me to do anything else on Woodling?"

"Can you find out about the investigator who visited Braff yesterday?"

"Will do."

"Oh, and cancel the APB on Silva."

"Already done."

He ended the call and dropped the car into gear. It was going to be a tough morning. He had to notify Vicky Silva her husband was dead, then ask her some probing questions.

He traveled west on Jefferson, then north on Mill. A pair of runners dashed across the street in front of him, and Jake had to hit the brakes, then pump them again, before he got the big beast under control. What the hell? He hadn't been going that fast.

As he approached Spring Street, another pair of runners paused at the right-hand curb. More wary this time, Jake pre-emptively pressed the brakes to slow down.

But nothing happened.

He pressed harder.

The car didn't slow.

Shit!

He passed the runners, and the car picked up speed as the road descended to pass under the railroad tracks. Just up ahead, a Jeep Wrangler was stopped in the street, its left blinker on as it waited for an approaching school bus to pass so it could turn into the Digital Realty parking lot.

Jake hit the brakes again, the pedal sinking all the way to the floor without resistance. Panic gripped his chest.

He jammed a fist into his horn. "Move!"

He couldn't swerve off the road to the right, because a Chevy Suburban was in the way, waiting to exit the driveway of Weston Auto Works.

He hit the horn again.

The Jeep suddenly lurched forward, swerving as the driver corrected the wheel. But it was still in the way, and Jake was coming too fast. He pumped the brakes over and over, hoping. The Crown Vic surged down the hill, the Jeep's bumper drawing closer even as it picked up speed.

Then Jake was past the Suburban. Immediately he jerked the wheel to the right, and the Crown Vic banged up over the curb, missing the Jeep's bumper by inches.

His right wheel dug into the landscaped berm in front of the Auto Works. He jerked the wheel back and fought the car straight, scraping past a light pole.

The car plowed into the scrub brush at the base of the railroad embankment, then nosed upward and jerked to a stop with a great rending of metal against concrete. A sudden explosion slapped Jake's face. His vision blurred and his head lolled loose on his neck.

But then he was back, ears ringing.

A car horn. Yelling. Both sounds were muted under the ringing in Jake's ears.

Jake unbuckled, then tried to open his door. It was jammed. He gave it a couple whacks with his shoulder, and it groaned open. He got out, and almost fell when the ground turned out to be farther away than he'd expected; the car's front end was levered up against the rising embankment. He opened and closed his mouth, stretching his jaw, then rubbed at both ears.

"You okay, Jake?"

Jake turned toward the voice. Bill from Auto Works.

"I think so." Jake swung the door shut, but it bounced back at him. "A little deaf."

"I bet. Air bags are louder than people think. Give it a minute."

Jake worked his jaw and rubbed some more. Improvement.

"Looks like the frame's torqued," Bill said. "What happened?"

"I couldn't stop. The brakes gave me nothing."

Bill pointed at the front of the car. "I don't think we can do anything about that."

The front end was mangled. A thin stream of radiator fluid was pooling on the ground, the smell rising up in a sugary fog.

"Think it's totaled?" Jake said.

"Probably. You want us to tow it somewhere?"

Jake stretched his back and rubbed at a sore spot on his chest where the seat belt had caught him. "Can you take it over to the city yard?"

"Will do. Need a loaner?"

"No, I'll drive my personal car. My place is only a couple blocks from here."

"Right. Okay. You going to call a patrol officer?"

That was the right thing to do, but it would bog Jake down in hours of bureaucratic nonsense. He needed to keep moving. Identifying the third body was a shot of momentum he needed to ride. "No."

"All right. Leave this to me."

Jake started walking.

* * *

Jake pulled his Mustang into Silva's driveway, the rumble from the tuned exhaust echoing off the house. As he headed for the front door, the scud of plastic wheels on concrete came from behind the house, followed by a peal of high-pitched laughter. Jake changed direction.

On the wide expanse of concrete between the house and barn, a boy—no doubt Donny Junior—was pedaling what looked like an over-sized Big Wheel, sliding it sideways in a continuous circle. Drifting, according to an X-Games television program Jake had caught while flipping TV channels. The boy had his mom's dark curls and pale skin. Jake paused to watch.

Movement in the barn's open door. Lace, standing guard. His eyes on the Mustang.

"Lace," Jake called out, then walked over. His back and chest were sore from the crash but loosened as he moved.

"What are you doing here?"

"More questions for Mrs. Silva."

Lace's shoulders flexed, corded muscle and veins rippling. "You trying to make some extra money off the mileage or something?"

"What do you mean?"

"Yesterday you had a cop car."

"Oh—I had some trouble with the Crown Vic this morning."

"So that's your personal car? I've always liked how they tune the exhaust on those Mustangs."

"Thanks." Jake gazed into the shop's shadowy interior. The BMW was gone, with nothing in its place. "What are you working on today?"

Lace gestured toward the house. "Thought I'd stay handy in case she needs me."

"She'll probably appreciate that. Were you a mechanic in the Army?"

Lace cocked his head, then shook it. "Just a grunt."

"What made you join up?"

"I was a dumbass kid and college wasn't going to make me a man."

Lace's eyes drifted toward the house, and Jake followed his gaze. Vicky Silva pushed open the screen door and stepped onto the back stoop. She wore yellow cotton pajamas and was barefoot. She let the door slap shut, then sat down on the steps, holding a big coffee mug in two hands. She sipped from it, eyes locked on her son.

"How's she been?" Jake asked quietly.

"She's tough."

"She needs to be."

Jake left Lace and walked across the concrete. Vicky frowned as he approached.

"Bad or worse?"

"Good morning." He sat down beside her, the concrete rough and cool through his thin pants.

"I doubt it."

She kept her gaze on her boy, and Jake took the opportunity to look at her. Thin red lines spidered across the whites of her eyes. The crumpled end of a handkerchief stuck out of her shirtsleeve. Her right hand went to a delicate gold cross hanging from a thin chain around her neck. She hadn't been wearing it on his first visit. She slid the cross back and forth on the chain: *zzzip, zzzip, zzzip.*

"Don't try to ease into it." She glanced at him but then her eyes went back to little Donny.

Years of experience hadn't made notifications any easier for Jake—or made him any better at them. But he knew loss—had lived it himself—and knew it was best to deliver the news quickly. "We found your husband's body last night. He was in the car with the other two."

Vicky let out a small gasp, then pulled her lips tight. "Did you wait until today to tell me so I'd get a good night's sleep? If that was your plan, it failed."

"I'm sorry."

He turned away to give her a moment before he started with his questions. The boy spun his wheeled contraption around the concrete, looking up at his mother and flashing her a goofy smile every time he passed them. They sat in silence, watching the boy, until Vicky let out a single sharp sob. Jake turned back to her. Her pale cheeks ran with silent tears.

She pulled the handkerchief from her sleeve and wiped her eyes and cheeks. "Ask your questions."

Jake started with her husband's relationships with Graves and Lange.

"You're asking whether Donny had a reason to kill his friends."

"Mrs. Silva," he started. He was planning to deny it, then realized she was tough enough to handle the truth. "Vicky. It's a scenario I have to explore. With Donald in the driver's seat, it looks like he controlled the situation, which means it's possible that he—"

"Killed his friends and then killed himself." She dashed her coffee into the grass and stood. Her face had gone red. "That did *not* happen!" Her voice shook. "Come up with another theory." She yanked open the screen door and went inside, a string of sobs bursting from her before the door slammed back against the jamb.

Jake stayed where he was, watching the boy spin his trike in a continuous drift. Lace still stood in the barn doorway. He shook his head, then turned and disappeared into the shadows.

Victoria Silva's pain reminded Jake of his own when his wife was killed. That night was seared into his memory, in vivid detail. Mary had left him at a restaurant table to run back to the gallery for something she'd forgotten—he didn't ask her what it was. He wanted to go with her, but she insisted he enjoy his beer and promised to be back before he finished it. She wasn't. Then a squad car sped by the restaurant windows, lights flashing and siren wailing. The wailing stopped, but the lights kept pulsing from down the street. Where the gallery was. As soon as he completed the thought, Jake was out of his chair and running. He made it to the scene before the ambulance arrived, but he was too late to do anything for Mary.

She had surprised a for-hire thief in the act of robbing the art gallery. The thief slit her throat and left her to bleed out, then bolted out the front door, only to be crushed under a city bus less than two blocks away. The department poured a massive amount of overtime into the investigation, but the man who'd hired the thief, the man who'd set the whole thing in motion, was never identified. Jake's revenge had been incomplete, so his pain continued undiminished.

Donny stopped his big trike with the front wheel against the bottom step between Jake's feet. "My mom's sad and my dad is dead."

Jake pulled his mind out of the past and smiled at the kid. He looked like he was about eight or nine. Could a kid that young understand death? "I'm sorry."

The boy gave a sad little smile. He pedaled the trike backwards, flicked the handlebar, and did a reverse spin that he converted into forward motion with smooth grace.

* * *

After a while, Donny left the big trike and went and sat on the swing set, feet scuffing in the dirt, his eyes on the back door. The yard was deeply shaded, and the thin grass was holding green against the drought. The sobbing inside had ended, and the sounds of a running faucet and clattering dishes sounded through the screen door.

Jake waited.

Finally, Vicky came back outside.

"I made a fresh pot," she said, handing him a mug. "Cops all drink it black, right?"

"Thank you." He sipped the strong brew.

"Donald didn't kill anyone. Not his friends, and not himself." She sat down and waved at her son.

"We're still investigating and haven't reached any conclusions."

"But I know how cops work. You decide what happened and then set out to prove it." She sipped her coffee and looked at him through red-rimmed eyes. "Are you going to tell me that's not right?"

"Cops develop theories, but we work the evidence. Help me here. Tell me about Donald's relationships with the other two men."

Vicky opened up about her husband and his old friends, and Jake didn't detect any deception. The men had been close in high school. Vicky had gone to the same high school, graduating two years behind them, but had been aware of all three. Back then, Graves was the BMOC, Lange was a near-dropout who only went to school to hang out, and Silva was the quiet bad boy, riding a motorcycle to school in any weather but a blizzard. Jake asked Vicky about the falling out Mrs. Graves had hinted at, but she saw it as nothing more than the growing apart she had described during their first conversation. No animosity involved on any side.

She pointed to the barn. "Lace has kept Don's old bike running all this time, just in case. I moved the carpet van to the shop to give Lace more room here."

"Shop?" The itch of a revelation crawled up Jake's spine, but he held in his excitement.

She looked away, watching her son on the swing. "It's in the building Pearl owns."

"I need to see the shop."

She looked him in the eye. "You know, I didn't mean it yesterday when I said I'd rather he was dead."

"I know."

"I'll get you the key."

CHAPTER TWENTY-NINE

Jake found Silva's carpet shop in a cluster of prefab concrete buildings between Fifth Avenue and the Burlington Northern Railroad tracks. Silva's building held five other small businesses offering services like convertible top repair and furniture refinishing. All the units were the same: a roll-up door high enough for a truck, a steel service door, and a window in between. Faded paint spelled out CARPET INSTALLATION on a warped square of plywood above the window of Silva's unit.

Jake squinted against the glare off the concrete, the reflected heat blasting. He pulled off his blazer and folded it on the passenger seat before getting out of the car.

"If you're looking for a carpet installer I can recommend ya one." The voice came from the neighboring shop, an upholstery business. A slight man with a round paunch stepped from the shadow of its roll-up door, a hand lifting to shade his eyes. "Oh, you're a cop."

"Yes." Jake's gun and badge were in plain view on his belt.

"If you're here about the carpet guy, nobody been working out of there since I've been here."

"Nobody?"

"Not that I seen, anyway." The man eyed Jake, apparently waiting for an explanation.

Jake held up the keys. "The landlord set me up, so I'm good."

"Vicky? She's a nice lady." The man scratched his gut. "Okay then." He went back inside.

Jake found the right key on the second try. The door swung open on squeaky hinges, revealing a darkened interior; the window was painted out. He took off his sunglasses and slipped them in his shirt pocket, then reached in and ran his hand along the jamb until he found the switch. The overhead fluorescents came on unevenly, one starting with a flicker before popping on and buzzing.

Jake stepped inside and closed the door. The air was cooler in here, but musty and stale. He wandered through the space taking in the tools, carpet remnants, and tall racks holding rolls of padding. To one side stood a small forklift, and in the area behind the garage door was a van with an extra long body. Probably needed for hauling twelve-foot carpet rolls.

Jake circled around the van and noticed that in the corner, behind a carpet rack, was a walled-off space, with an open loft above it cluttered with cardboard boxes. The door into this space had two deadbolts—even though there'd been no deadbolts into the shop itself. Jake gave the double-bolted door a hard rap. His knuckles met the strength of solid-core steel under a thin wood overlay.

His pulse kicked up, and he smiled. This door protected something worth looking at.

He pulled the keys out, found the right ones, and opened the door. When he flipped the light switch, a grid of can lights in the ceiling came on, lighting the place as bright as a photo studio.

Glass-fronted wood cabinets lined the three near walls, and on the far wall, above a leather couch, framed drawings of motorcycles sat on shallow shelves. A recliner that matched the couch rested under a lamp in the corner, a steel door in the wall behind it, and a tall table sat in the middle of the room, a single high-backed stool pulled up to it. Dark wood cabinets, leather, the wall covered in art... Jake recognized a man cave when he saw one. But it hadn't been used in some time; everything was now covered in a thin layer of dust.

A pair of three-drawer filing cabinets were tucked in one corner. Jake pulled on a drawer, but it was locked. He tried the others, and a random selection of cabinets—all locked. He pulled out the key ring, but every key was too big for these little locks.

The glass-fronted cabinets held hardback books stacked flat, with clear covers like at the library. Jake recognized many titles, from Hemingway and Fitzgerald to Paretsky and Grafton. Valuable, if they were the right editions and in excellent condition. Silva was apparently a collector.

Jake dragged the recliner away from the steel door, thumbed open its three deadbolts, and pulled it open. It led to the alley behind the shop. He stepped through into the shade cast by the ivy growing in the fence along the railroad tracks. He looked back and forth behind the long building—there was nothing there but discarded furniture and trash blown into the fence. But at the far end of the building, he spotted the rear end of a car with a whip antenna arching up from the rear bumper. A cop car.

Curious, he walked that way, the entire vehicle slowly coming into view. The big redheaded investigator sat in the driver's seat, talking on a cell phone.

Jake's pulse thrummed faster.

He's following me!

Jake advanced in the shadow along the fence until he could overhear this end of the phone conversation.

Big Red wasn't talking about Jake, or even about Woodling. He was talking about Silva.

CHAPTER THIRTY

"Now Houser's in Silva's old carpet shop."

Hogan was parked in the alley at the end of Silva's building with his windows down. Out of sight, but close enough to hear the Mustang's rumble when Houser left. The hot air wafting through the car smelled faintly of industrial solvent. "Been in there for about ten minutes."

"Can you see what he's doing?" the sheriff asked.

"No windows. But I've been in there. Searched every nook and cranny. There's nothing for us to worry about."

"You're sure it isn't in there?"

"It's not in there!" Hogan took a breath and lowered his voice. "And it wasn't in his house or his barn."

"How sure are you it's not in the car?"

"I've seen Jansen's list and talked to him. It's not in the car."

"You haven't looked at the car yourself?"

Hogan pulled the phone away from his mouth, then re-gripped it. "Your call. Do you want me to keep watching Houser or go look over Jansen's shoulder?"

"How do you think my dad's doing?"

"Well… I, uh… Your dad's as tough as God ever made a man."

Silence. Then: "How much would this document hurt him?"

"Bull thinks it's a smoking gun."

She sighed. "Stay on Jake. When he quits for the day, go look at the car."

"I'll stick with Houser," Hogan said. "For as long as he keeps moving."

* * *

Bev turned to the window and gazed out into the sun-scorched day. She sipped her coffee, holding the bitterness on her tongue for a moment before swallowing. The files in her dad's safe had kept her up most of the night. She'd only scanned them for references to the stadium deal, but she'd seen enough to understand what they were.

The so-called "tools" he'd left her to handle problems that bubbled up when he was gone.

By blackmailing people.

She chewed her lower lip, her vision clouding with tears. Her dad wasn't the good guy she'd always thought he was. She let that settle, the truth curdling her gut. How had she never seen it? He was her dad, so she was biased, but still. Her mind went back to the hours she'd spent with him going through his medical bills and financials. He'd held nothing back. There was no extra money there.

So if he hadn't made money from the files, why did he have them? What good were they?

Her mind got stuck on the word. *Good.* Her dad had been all about doing good. Always working on some charitable event or cause. Sunday nights while she'd done homework, there was almost always a meeting going on in their dining room for one cause or another. She'd even started calling her dad "The Do-Gooder" because of them. Hell, she'd forgotten that. It went back to junior high school. She'd wanted them to join a father-daughter bowling league on Sunday nights, and he'd said nõ. And he *never* said no to a father-daughter activity, so she'd lashed out with the nickname. He'd told her Sunday nights were reserved for those meetings. She remembered a few of the projects: food drives and after-school programs and women's shelters. But there had been many more.

The Do-Gooder.

So maybe he'd used the files to do good. To encourage people in power to do the right thing. Because the ends justified the means. He'd said that to her many, many times.

She wiped her eyes. That was it. Of course, not everyone would agree with how her dad weighed the means and the end. Certainly not the people in the files. And it wasn't her way of doing things. But she could accept it.

Unless he'd killed these three men.

Her stomach roiled. Was that why her dad wanted her to take over the case? Not just to find the document, but also to protect him from a triple-murder charge? That would explain why he'd mentioned that not all cases were solved.

Her stomach heaved, and her throat burned with bile. She gulped a slug of coffee to wash it back where it belonged.

No. She couldn't believe that. She didn't believe that. This mysterious document would point her to the real killer. She needed to find it—or at least figure out what it was.

Before Jake did.

Jake was good, too. Growing up, he had always done the right thing. She remembered one time when the two of them walked to Casey's Foods during a family party to buy more ice. The cashier gave them an extra dollar in change, and Jake immediately returned it. Bev had nearly pulled his arm off trying to stop him. She'd wanted to use the dollar to sneak over to DQ for a soft-serve cone. But Jake always took the high road. Hell, the highest road.

Of course, that was all before he spent a decade on the job in Chicago. That cesspool might have changed him. And he was bound to harbor some ill will toward her dad. The Houser family hadn't attended family gatherings since the early eighties, and Bev spent years angry with the Housers for the snub—until she learned it was her dad who had done the snubbing. Could that create enough animosity for Jake to railroad her dad if he found the document? She hoped not, but she didn't want to find out. She needed to take this case and find the real killer.

She picked up the phone and made a call.

"Chairman Borgeson, please."

When the chairman came on, she explained her idea to use crime statistics, and Weston's obsession over its rankings, to convince Mayor Dietz to turn the case over to her.

"I love it, Bev." The chairman only called her sheriff in front of the media, and then only after his assistant told him to. "Dietz is super sensitive to that rankings bullshit. They have an eye on rankings for every decision they make in that damn town. It's ridiculous."

"And this case hurts them whether they solve it or not."

"Oh, I get it." Borgeson laughed. "And I get how it will impact *your* stats. *And* your budget."

"My budget, sir?"

"Don't play me, Bev Warren. I was planning to cut your budget. The press you'll get for solving this case would force me to leave it. Nicely done."

Bev smiled. With Borgeson sure of her motives, he wouldn't look for a different one.

"I'll work this bug into Dietz's ear ASAP." He chuckled again. "He's at his noon Rotary right now. I'll catch him as he leaves. This is great."

After hanging up, Bev placed another call.

"Rieser here." Doug Rieser sat on the Weston Board of Police Commissioners and had been Bev's homecoming date her junior year at Weston Central.

"Doug, it's Bev."

"What's up, Sheriff?"

"I want to talk to you about a case."

She explained how the Radar Grove murders would impact Weston PD's statistics.

"But Houser's on that," Doug said. "I know you don't like him, but he's practically automatic."

"I don't have anything against Jake. He's my cousin! Anyway, it's not about him solving it. The case hurts Weston's rankings either way."

Doug was silent for a minute, and she waited him out.

"I mean, I see your point. But why do you care?"

"Chairman Borgeson wants me to take it. County forest preserve and all that."

"Yeah, the word came down he's pushing for it. Frankly, that was enough to make the mayor want to keep it, but…"

"But?"

"You know how the mayor feels about crime."

"If you don't count it, it doesn't count?"

"Ha!" Rieser chuckled. "I haven't heard it put quite that neatly, but yeah."

She waited again, and he came through for her.

"Okay. Thanks for the heads-up. The mayor's entire re-election campaign is based on those ratings, so… I'll see what I can do."

"Thanks, Doug."

CHAPTER THIRTY-ONE

Jake listened through the end of Big Red's call, then returned to the shop through the back door. He threw the deadbolts, jogged through the shop to the front door, and locked it, too.

Back in the man cave, he returned the recliner to its place against the back door and sat down, his mind spinning with what he'd heard. Big Red was definitely the sheriff's investigator Jake had seen leaving Braff's office. But Red's phone call had been about Silva, not Woodling.

Jake pulled out his notebook and wrote down everything he'd overheard, then read through it. Big Red had clearly been talking to Bev—he'd referred to Bull as "your dad"—he'd spoken to her like she was his boss, and he'd promised to keep following Jake. Was Bev running a parallel investigation until she got her hands on the lagoon case? Jake had seen no hint of that, and people didn't hesitate to complain when they'd already told their story to another cop. Besides, following Jake around wasn't investigating—it was keeping tabs on him. Spying.

He shook his head. *Don't be paranoid! It's not about you!*

So it had to be about this thing Big Red was looking for. Big Red had searched this shop, and both Silva's house and barn, and Jansen was searching the car. Which meant Silva had it—whatever *it* was—with him that night. And whatever this thing was, Bull thought it was a smoking gun: conclusive evidence of a crime.

He called Erin to see what she'd learned about Big Red.

"Where are you?" Answering a phone call with a question was practically her trademark.

Jake told her, but not about being watched or the conversation he'd overheard. Until he understood what Big Red was up to, he would keep that to himself. "What did you learn about Woodling's complaint?"

"Woodling lives in unincorporated Kirwin just within the Paget County line, so it makes sense for him to contact our sheriff. But I know a clerk over there who confirmed no call came in, and he never signed the visitor log at the sheriff's department, so he didn't walk his complaint in either."

If Woodling didn't call or visit the sheriff's department, then someone there must have gone to see Woodling. "Did you find out who the investigator is?"

"A deputy named Warren Hogan. He's been with the sheriff's office for twelve years. Moved here from somewhere back east. He's been Bev's assistant since she was elected."

"Big redhead?"

"That's the guy."

"If he's Bev's assistant, what's he doing on a Professional Standards investigation?"

"My friend checked, and no official paperwork was put in to move him to that department. But he works for Bev, so…"

"Thanks, Erin."

Jake put his cell phone away. He didn't like where this was going. Hogan worked directly for Bev and was searching for some *thing* Bull thought was a smoking gun. Silva had this thing the night he died, so the deaths and the mysterious thing could be connected. Was Bull connected to the deaths? If he was, then Bev's interest in taking the case wasn't professional—she was in it to protect her dad.

Jake's stomach fluttered, and heat rushed to his face.

Could that be true? Could his own relatives be involved in these deaths?

If it was true, and Braff found out, he would yank Jake off the case. If this case was mixed up with Bull, then the associated politics would be a powerful force that could influence another detective. Jake, despite the *technical* conflict of interest, would chase the truth wherever it led him. That's all he wanted: the truth.

The flutter turned into a swirl of nausea. He leaned back in the recliner to let it pass. It faded, but lingered. *Bev and Bull? Christ!*

CHAPTER THIRTY-TWO

Jake decided to take a closer look at Silva's collections before leaving. He had no trouble picking the locks on the cabinets and drawers in the man cave. During a summer working at Weston Lumber he'd learned to pick locks, and he carried the tools in a hidden pocket on the back of his belt. He knew if Bull had been worried about anything in here it would be long gone, but the contents might still help him understand Silva, and that was worth a few minutes.

He started with the glass-fronted cabinets. Every book he checked was a first edition, and many were signed. Jake knew just enough about book collecting to know Silva's collection was worth real money.

He then turned to the filing cabinets. These were about half full and contained other collectables: binders filled with stamps, carefully wrapped porcelain figurines, old metal toys in their original cardboard boxes.

One drawer contained three black binders labeled INVEN-TORY. Jake flipped through them. They were listings of Silva's collections, backed up with receipts in his name—proof of ownership. Which meant none of these items could be loot from the crimes Lange had offered to disclose about Silva, or stuff Cassano had acquired as a fence before his death.

He locked everything up, then sat on the high stool, thinking back to the conversation he'd overheard. Hogan had told Bev he'd searched the shop and that nothing in it was worth worrying about. Which meant Bev hadn't already known that. When that thought settled, Jake followed it to a logical conclusion. Bev didn't know because she hadn't been involved in whatever had gone down five years before. She was just playing cleanup.

Jake looked over the transcript he'd made of Hogan's end of the call. He'd told Bev he would "stick with Houser." They either thought Jake would lead them to this thing they were looking for, or they wanted to stop him from finding it.

But how could Hogan stop him?

Shit!

He pulled out his phone and searched through his contacts. Bill answered after the first ring.

"Bill? It's Jake."

"I was going to call you."

"Tell me."

"When I got your cruiser pulled off the embankment I took a look at your brakes. I know the city works on its own cars, but I was curious, you know." His voice dropped into a deeper tone. "Jake... someone cut your brake lines."

"Did you take the car in?"

"Yeah. They weren't expecting it, so they told me to drop it in the back of the yard and they'd look at it when the paperwork catches up."

"Did you mention the brakes?"

"I did. I thought it was important."

"Thanks, Bill."

Jake ended the call. News about his cut brake lines would run up the command structure fast. When Braff heard it, he'd want answers. Answers Jake didn't have.

For as long as he keeps moving.

Hogan's odd wording hadn't struck Jake before, but it did now.

Hogan had already tried to stop Jake from moving.

Did Bev know what Hogan had done? She couldn't. Jake had known her his entire life. He could fault her for being too interested in media attention and politics, but he'd trust her to do what was right. Not like her dad. And this was all about her dad. Jake was sure of it. Bev was just trying to protect her dad.

Just.

Writing always helped him think, so he flipped his notebook open to a clean page and listed what he knew as fact.

1. *Bev tried to take over the crime scene.*

2. *Bev pushing to take the investigation.*

3. *Bev pushing the Woodling complaint.*

4. *Hogan following.*

5. *Hogan's conversation connects Silva to Hogan and to Bull and also to Bev.*

6. *Lange gave the burglary task force Silva's name—the task force was soon disbanded.*

7. *Hogan works for Bev.*

8. *Hogan is searching for something Bull thinks is a smoking gun. Something they think Silva had with him that night.*

Jake stared at the list, then circled three and four. If Hogan had followed Jake to Woodling's house, he had seen enough to take a closer look. That explained the speed of Woodling's complaint and confirmed Bev was pushing it to slow him down. That was her doing.

But that couldn't be true about the brake lines. That had to have been Hogan. And Bull.

He pocketed his notebook, locked up the room, and left the shop. He got in the car without looking in Hogan's direction, but spotted the cruiser rolling after him in his rearview mirror as he pulled away.

CHAPTER THIRTY-THREE

As Jake turned right on Mill and drove under the viaduct and up into downtown, Hogan followed. Jake wondered if Hogan had been following him since the beginning, laying the whole investigation at Bull's feet. If that were true, then something Jake had done—some person he'd visited?—had triggered the cut brake lines. Siebert? Vicky Silva? Cassano? Graves?

He needed to shake Hogan off his tail, and he knew exactly how to do it.

Jake wound through the edge of downtown and north on Jackson to Riverfront Park. It had a giant parking lot that served Centennial Beach, the little league field, the skate park, and the playground. It also had a back exit through the VFW parking lot that a non-native like Hogan probably knew nothing about. Jake turned into the lot, keeping one eye on Hogan. The deputy sheriff pulled to the curb on Jackson, which wouldn't do. Jake drove deeper into the lot, until Hogan's car was out of sight, then parked by the left field fence. Hogan's car nosed into the image in his mirror, then backed into a spot two rows over from the lot's entrance. In the sun. *Perfect.*

While Jake waited for the big man to get comfortable and less attentive from sitting in the bright sun, he would make a few calls, then use the VFW's back exit to slip away.

He checked the call log for the Chicago number he'd called the day before. All his opposition—Hogan and Bev and Jansen and Bull—had come from the county, and the task force was a county operation. He needed whatever Benny could tell him.

Larson's daytime secretary wasn't as much of a ball-buster as the night help, and Jake got right through.

"Larson here."

"It's Houser." He waited for a Larsonesque crack but got nothing. "Wondering if you'd found your 2012 notebook yet."

"I can't talk today, Houser. The shit hit the fan on my toxic tort case. I gotta—shit, never mind. Just not today. I'll find it tonight."

"All I need is—"

The line went dead.

Jake checked the mirror. Hogan was still waiting, his face angled Jake's way.

Jake flipped through his notebook for Vicky Silva's number. Their conversation had been nagging at him. She'd brought up the carpet shop abruptly, without a question to lead her there. She'd wanted him to know about it. To see it.

He found her number and dialed.

She sounded better, her voice looser. "What did you think of the shop? See anything that might change your mind about the murder-suicide idea?"

"The back room is full of locked cabinets. Do you have keys for them?"

"I do, but I can tell you what's in them." She paused, then went on when he didn't ask. "Donny's collections. He was into books and all kinds of old things. Coins and stamps and toys. I've sold off the coins."

"Just before your husband went missing, there was a Paget County investigation into him as a burglar. Are those collections things he stole?"

"Nonsense," she said. No hesitation.

"I've confirmed the investigation," Jake said.

"Oh, I believe you." A laugh that was more of a sigh. "Every couple years a cop or a deputy sheriff would harass Don. Mr. Cassano had been a fence thirty or forty years ago, and the police wouldn't forget it. Don even let them in to check his collections against their stolen property reports."

Jake skipped to the question he'd called to ask. "Why did you want me to see the shop?"

"*You* wanted to see it." She paused. "But you're right. I wanted you to see it too."

Another long pause. He waited. A faint *zzzip, zzzip* of her sliding cross came over the line.

"A person who commits suicide has given up," Vicky said finally. "He's filled with despair. He has nothing to live for." Her voice grew stronger as she talked, convincing herself as she worked to convince Jake. "That wasn't Don. He was busy with work, and he had more interests—in his motorcycles and in buying and selling to build those collections—than anyone you'll ever meet. And he was devoted to us, little Donny and me. I have no doubt he loved us. There's no way he killed himself."

"I see," Jake said, though he didn't agree with her argument. A large percentage of people who committed suicide had no reason for doing so that an outsider could recognize. Less than half left notes, and most of those contained instructions or apologies, not explanations. Police had to prove a death was a suicide from the hard evidence at the scene.

"Your husband's been gone five years. Why haven't you rented out his unit?"

"I'm not cheating Pearl, if that's what you're asking. She and I talked it over, and the other units more than cover the building's expenses. So we agreed to wait. Until we knew. For sure."

There had probably been a lot more emotion in the decision than that. Judging from the way Pearl Cassano had talked about Silva, she held on to as much hope as Vicky.

Jake had gotten all he needed for now, so he thanked Vicky and ended the call.

If Silva was clean, and used to proving himself clean, he had no motive for killing Lange. And Jake still had no motive for Silva to kill Graves. Vicky Silva had known nothing about the so-called falling out Mrs. Graves mentioned, but maybe her husband had kept the details from her. Or maybe there was something to it Vicky didn't want to share.

Jake needed to push Mrs. Graves until she coughed up the whole story.

He could apologize later.

CHAPTER THIRTY-FOUR

Jake checked the distant form of Hogan sitting in the sun, then dropped his car into gear and started forward. If Hogan didn't know about the back exit through the VFW parking lot—as Jake suspected—he'd wait in place, expecting Jake to turn around and drive back out.

Jake followed the long curve out of Hogan's sight, then threaded his way through the VFW parking lot and onto Jackson. He checked his mirror.

He was free.

* * *

The Graves home looked as it had on Jake's first visit. Real life wasn't a horror novel, so Mrs. Graves's grief had had no effect on her foursquare; its front was as neat and welcoming as the first time he visited. The thought reminded him of his duty to Mrs. Graves. Although Jake's primary duty was justice for the dead, he also had a duty to the survivors—like Mrs. Graves and Sheila Murphy and Victoria Silva. It was his job to treat them with dignity and tenderness and understanding.

He put on his blazer, then climbed the steps. Mrs. Graves's heavy tread again crossed the floor to meet him at the door. She opened it before he knocked, this time dressed for the day and wearing makeup that softened the dark circles under her eyes. It didn't help the redness in them.

"Detective?" She ran her large hands down the wrinkled pleats of her skirt.

"I'm hoping we could have another conversation." Jake took off his sunglasses, smiled, and tilted his head. "Still trying to understand the relationships."

"Well…"

He stepped toward her, and she politely moved aside to let him through the doorway.

An open magazine on the wingback chair in the front window revealed she'd been sitting there and had spotted him through the lace curtain. He smelled coffee brewing. He smiled again, being careful not to overdo it. "Can you spare a cup coffee?"

"Of course!" She brightened and ushered him into the kitchen.

Cups of coffee in hand, they sat down at the kitchen table. Jake looked over at the casserole dishes and cake plates crowding the counter.

"Your friends pulled out all the stops with the food."

"It's the ladies from church." An awkward smile. She gestured toward the fridge. "The fridge is full too. Would you like a piece of coffee cake?"

"The coffee's fine." He waited for her eyes to come back to him. "We found Donald's body in the car with Robert and Nicholas."

"I figured you would," she said, through a strained smile.

He sipped the coffee. It was strong and almost too hot to drink. He set it down to cool and let the silence build, watching Mrs. Graves admire the food she'd received, probably enjoying the attention from her friends and neighbors. His gaze swung to the counter and then to the drawings taped to the cabinets. The drawings looked familiar, somehow.

His wife had tried to teach him to appreciate art. Mary had earned a bachelor's in art history while he was getting his law degree, and she landed a job with an art gallery in River North when he started with the Chicago PD. She used to say that every artist signed her work even if she didn't write her name on it. It was about the subjects chosen, the colors used, how a line was laid down, how shading was done. And in these child's drawings, Jake finally understood her point. These drawings used the same subjects and were done in the same styles and with the same colors as the drawings in Vicky Silva's kitchen.

"Please tell me about the drawings."

Mrs. Graves's mouth tightened, and her bony hands clutched together. "My grandson drew them." Her eyes went from picture to picture, brightening as she went, a smile growing on her face. "I watch him two evenings a week—when his mother has class—and we draw pictures together."

"The Silva boy."

"There's not a drop of Silva blood in that sweet boy. But Robert never took responsibility. He wasn't good at responsibility."

"Please tell me how it was back then."

She was quiet for a moment, her gaze moving from the drawings to Jake and back to the drawings again. "Robert was still young with a future and possibilities. People hired him because they knew him from football. He always had money in his pocket. Victoria was a few years younger than the boys, and she wasn't like she is now, all confident and professional. She was interested in Donald, but he was always too busy. So she settled for Robert. I don't like saying that about Robert, but that's the right word. Settled. He never loved her either. Not to be with forever. Then Victoria and Donald got together, and they were together ever since."

"But she was pregnant and—"

"The boy was Robert's." A tear squeezed from her left eye. "He never claimed his son. My grandson. Never even gave him a second thought."

"How do you know the boy was Robert's?"

"I know how to use a calendar." Mrs. Graves sniffed and grabbed a paper napkin from the holder on the table. She wiped her eyes and then her nose before crunching it in her big hand.

"Did they all know? Don, Victoria, Robert?"

She shrugged. "Counting to nine isn't hard."

No, it wasn't. Then Jake remembered what little Donny had said that morning: *My mom is sad because my daddy is dead.* The boy had said it before his mother had a chance to tell him about Donald.

"Does little Donny know?"

Mrs. Graves squeezed her eyes shut, and twin tears tracked down her cheeks. "I told him myself just a few months ago. It's our little secret. I wanted him to know I'm his grandmother, not just some babysitter."

They talked for a few more minutes. Jake got nothing more out of her, but now he had a lead on a plausible motive for Silva to kill Graves. A biological father could insert a lot of tension into a family dynamic.

As Jake stepped out onto her front stoop, he saw no sign of Hogan. But as he walked to his car, a motorcycle came roaring down the street. The rider backed off the throttle, and the engine's rumble broke into loud pops and a long crackle. The bike braked and swerved into Graves's driveway.

The big man riding it wore a full-face helmet, but the black jeans and sleeveless T-shirt gave him away, as did the bike—the Yamaha XS650.

Jake followed the driveway around the side of the house. "Lace? What are you doing here?"

Lace set his helmet on the bike's seat. "I'm here to put in a new toilet valve. How about you?"

"Follow-up questions."

"Like your follow-up with Vicky this morning?" Lace frowned. "She deserves better than to have you—"

"I had to tell her," Jake said.

"So you told her. Are you done?"

"How well did you know Robert?"

"I didn't know him at all. When Mrs. Graves needs help, Vicky sends me over and I earn some easy cash."

"How about Lange?"

"Never met him."

Jake peppered Lace with more questions but detected no deception from the man: he'd only known Silva.

CHAPTER THIRTY-FIVE

Hogan looked up to see the tail end of Houser's car as it pulled away. He lowered his visor and scrunched down in his seat.

A minute went by, then another.

He sat back up.

"What the hell?"

He drove down the long stretch of pavement where Houser had parked and found a back exit through the VFW's parking lot.

"Goddamn Houser. Made me look like a fool again."

He grabbed his phone and found the sheriff's number. He bit his lip and dialed. When she answered, he jumped right to it. "I lost him after he left the carpet shop."

He waited for a response but heard only silence.

He licked his lips, then squeezed the phone. Finally he said, "He drove down into that park behind the baseball field by that big outdoor pool—Centennial Beach—and parked. I didn't know there was a back exit through the VFW parking lot."

"Did he ditch you on purpose? Did he make you?"

"No. He didn't look at me or speed or make any suspicious turns."

"Why did he go there?"

"Looks like he parked to make a few calls." Silence. "Lots of shade here."

She was quiet for a long minute, but this time Hogan waited her out.

"Maybe the Woodling complaint distracted him as we planned."

"Maybe."

"Jansen talked me through everything they found in the car, but I'd still like you to look it over."

"I can head up there now."

"When you're done with that, go find Jake." She ended the call.

Hogan scrolled through his contacts and held his thumb over Bull's number, but then put his phone in his pocket and headed north to look at the Buick.

* * *

Bev squinted against the glare as she made her way up the wide concrete walk leading to Edgar Hospice. Trees lined the sidewalk, but they were still a decade from being big enough to cast any useful shade. Bev didn't mind; her duties kept her at her desk or in meetings, so she didn't get out much during the day anymore, and she missed the sun, the warmth, the air moving across her skin. Today the air was hot and dry and carried the faint dusty smell of the prairie grasses to the west.

She paused outside the hospice door to prepare herself. Her dad was strong, but his fighting days were behind him. The stomach cancer and COPD had won. Eventually he'd go on morphine. The doctor said that would signal the end, because taking enough morphine to soften the pain would suppress his breathing, and the fluid build-up in his lungs would kill him.

As she spun through the revolving door into the frigid air conditioning, she hunched her shoulders and clasped her bag to her stomach. Her nose twitched against the faint tang of cleaning products and the musky human scent. She signed in at the desk, sharing a smile with the receptionist, then walked the familiar long gauntlet of open doors. Her dad was at the end, in a corner room. He had wide windows looking south and west, providing a nice view of the trees separating the health complex from a 1960s-era subdivision of split-level homes.

Bev paused in the doorway of his room. Her dad's once massive body looked small beneath the covers bunched under his arms. He had a glossy news magazine propped in front of him and reading glasses perched on the end of his nose, but the tilt of his head told her he was asleep.

She entered the room, not worried he would hear her over the constant *chukka-chukka* from the oxygen machine. The machine was cranked up to maximum to compensate for his failing lungs. When the cannula wasn't enough, they'd put a facemask on him. And when that didn't do the job, it was over.

Bev set her bag on the chair in the corner and stood next to the bed, looking at her dad. She couldn't shake off the files she'd found in his hidden safe. But he was more than that safe and those files. He'd done a lot of good. And if he'd used those files to do good, then—

"Hey, baby girl." He closed the magazine on his stomach and pushed himself up higher in the bed. His face split with a big smile.

He'd called her that as long as she could remember. There had been a decade or so when that had bothered her—she was a grown woman, damn it!—but that was long ago.

"I wanted to see how you're doing."

"Could have called." He pulled the glasses off and tossed them on the cluttered table that spanned the bed.

"Well…" She wanted to ask him about the safe and the files, but she couldn't.

He tilted his head, and his mouth made that little pursing it did when he analyzed her. *Damn it.* The machine pumped away, and up close the oxygen hissed under his nose. He adjusted the air hose, then leaned back on his pillow.

"You came to ask me something."

"It's fine, Dad." She waved a hand. "It can wait."

"Can't say that to me anymore."

He adjusted the hose again, sniffing in a long breath. His eyes were soft pools of blue above his gentle smile, the same understanding look he'd given her so many times over their lives together.

"You want to ask me about Silva."

She wiped her eye where a tear threatened to slip out. "You've always read me like an open book."

"It's been just the two of us for over thirty years." He sniffed in some more air.

She gulped back a sob, nodding. Her dad had been right there for her from the day her mom died. He'd done it all. No nannies. No housekeepers.

"Ask your questions." He put the magazine on the table.

She set aside the hard questions she couldn't bring herself to ask. "You told me Silva got the original document and was holding it over you. That you had to pay him off."

"I did say that."

"You *said* it, but it wasn't true."

"I hired Silva to get it." He coughed and wheezed. "Silva and his guys took it from Siebert outside the liquor store."

The relief was a weight lifting from her shoulders and an unclenching in her chest. Silva hadn't been blackmailing him, so her dad had had no motive to kill the man.

"Then Silva disappeared?"

"Yes." He told her the rest of it: about the document coming to light, and his efforts to get it back and destroy any record that it had ever existed. The story made her stomach roil. She thought of the old maxim: the cover-up is worse than the crime. But he still wouldn't tell her what the document was.

"If it comes out," he sniffed in a few breaths, "my enemies will use it against me. Against you, too. Just to get at me. You take over, and we're good. How's that coming?"

"I'm trying a new angle."

"Tell me."

She explained her idea.

He laughed. "Perfect."

"Chairman Borgeson is pushing Mayor Dietz," she said. "I also called Doug Rieser—he's on the Board of Police Commissioners—to work the chief."

"Calling your homecoming date!" Bull coughed and sucked air through his teeth. "Ballsy."

"The things you remember!"

They talked about the past for a while, but Bev was too worried about her father's newest version of events to focus. Was this the real truth?

Maybe.

But it was too… timely. Too convenient. Eliminating a motive for killing Silva just as his body was identified.

Why was she second-guessing him?

Because of the files in the safe.

CHAPTER THIRTY-SIX

Jake left Lace to his handyman work and walked back toward his car. His phone vibrated in his pocket as he grabbed the Mustang's door handle. He didn't recognize the caller, but he gave his cell number to a lot of people during the course of an investigation, so that wasn't unusual. "This is Detective Houser."

"Detective! I'm glad I got ahold of you. I have a deadline looming and want to give you an opportunity to comment."

Jake didn't recognize the voice. "Who is this?"

"Bess Simpson with the *Tribune*."

Jake was familiar with Simpson's work. She was good. She must have been the stringer Erin mentioned showing up at shift change the previous morning, asking about the lagoon case. He wondered what she'd been doing since then.

"Go ahead and ask your question so I can give you my 'no comment' and get back to work."

"I'm calling about the excessive force complaint filed against you."

Jake's "no comment" got stuck in his throat. How had she found out about the complaint? As he pondered that question, his silence stretched.

"It has to do with the Radar Grove case, doesn't it?"

"I can't talk about a disciplinary proceeding while it's ongoing, Ms. Simpson."

"Ongoing, huh?" Simpson chuckled. "I was starting to think it was a rumor. The clerk who handles the complaint log at the sheriff's department said there is no such complaint."

Jake gritted his teeth. He should have stuck to a bald "no comment." Now he'd confirmed what her original source had told her. But why was the clerk in the sheriff's department giving her the runaround? Maybe there really was no complaint and it was all just Hogan and Bev.

"Maybe it resolved itself," he said.

"Did you use excessive force while investigating the Radar Grove case, Detective?"

"Of course not." If no one else at the sheriff's department knew about the complaint, Simpson's source was probably Hogan himself. Or maybe even Bev. "I suggest you talk to your source again, Ms. Simpson."

Jake hung up and got in his car.

The motive for Silva to kill Graves lost its luster as Jake drove back to Weston. Silva was smart enough to count to nine, so he must have known he wasn't Donny's biological father from the beginning. And Vicky's relationship with Graves hadn't been a secret, so Silva would have known who the real father was. Which meant there was no motive unless something new had set Silva off.

Maybe Graves had decided to assert his parental rights and take Donny away from Silva? But even if he established himself as the boy's biological father, all Graves would get was visitation and a bill for child support. And after ignoring the boy from birth, he might only get the bill. Still, it was possible. Graves's lawyer might have kept the possibility of that outcome to himself so he could cash a fat retainer check.

His phone shuddered in his pocket, and he answered it. "This is Houser."

"I searched our archives for the paper copy of the incident report—the original—and it isn't there," Erin said. "But I noticed something on the copy you sent me from your phone."

"What?" Jake switched lanes to avoid the turn lanes by the mall.

"The report says the victim declined to press charges."

"I remember." He'd already covered this ground with her, and with Siebert.

"The victim left the scene before the responding officer arrived, so later that night—"

"Someone talked to Siebert and got that quote," Jake finished. He should have thought of that himself.

"Which means there should be a victim report."

"Can you find it for me?" Jake stopped for the light at Eola Road, the rumble of the Mustang's exhaust reverberating off the trucks stopped on either side of him.

"Where are you?"

"Heading up to look at the Buick."

"I mean right now. I'm hearing a rumbling."

"I'm driving my Mustang today," Jake said. "Can you find the victim report?"

"I tried, but there isn't one. It should be referenced on the e-report with a link, but there's only another blank."

"The responding officer at the liquor store would have made the victim visit while the rover covered."

"That means Officer Thompson talked to him," Erin said, more keys clacking. "He quit the department within a month after this. Why are you driving your own car?"

"Had some trouble with the Crown Vic." The big car would have handled this road better than the low-to-the-ground Mustang. He swerved around a hole big enough to swallow a dog.

"What kind—"

"See if you can track down Thompson. And can you get into the county's family court database and see if Graves filed anything about custody or visitation on the Silva kid?"

"It's his?"

"Looks that way."

"Well, well. Hang on." She click-clacked away for another minute. "Robert Graves, Robert Graves. Hmmm. No, nothing like that." More clacking. "Nothing under Silva, either."

"Thanks." Maybe Graves hadn't gotten past the talking stage.

Jake turned north on Route 59, where the freshly paved surface was as smooth as glass.

"One more thing, Jake. Deputy Chief Braff wants to see you today at five sharp. To hear your progress on the lagoon case and to talk about Woodling."

Progress. "We're calling it the lagoon case?"

"Why not?"

"Tell Braff I'll be there."

Jake shouldn't have been surprised by the summons. If Bev had manufactured the Woodling complaint to distract him while Hogan looked for whatever it was they were after, then it made sense that she'd want keep the pressure on by pressing Braff. But Jake couldn't tell Braff any of that.

He checked his watch. He had an hour. Enough time to go up and look at the car.

* * *

When Bev came back from seeing her dad, she closed her door and told her secretary to keep everyone away. Her new perception of her dad was a knife twisting in her gut. He'd lied from the beginning. First, he'd basically said Silva was blackmailing him, and then he'd said Silva was working for him. Was this latest version of events the truth, or was he *still* lying to her?

She ignored the office noises outside her closed door and the spikes of pain in her temples. She needed to know the truth: about her dad, about the mysterious document, and about the dead men. She wasn't going to get it from her dad or from Hogan. That much was obvious. So she'd get it for herself.

She needed to find a place to start. A loose thread to unravel.

She paced along the window. Within a few minutes, she had a plan—or the start of one. Her dad's story started with a land deal. And the recorder of deeds kept records on all the real estate transactions in the county.

She sat down at her computer and got to work.

Within a half hour she'd found a map of the proposed Bears stadium project in the *Tribune*'s archive. She figured out how to convert the location to a series of property identification numbers, one for each lot that made up the bigger parcel. Armed with the PINs, she examined the listing of every legal paper ever associated with the lots, hoping the name of a bank or investor or landowner would jump out at her. There were dozens, and the system was not only slow, it repeatedly kicked her out and asked her to re-prove she was a human being and not a data spider.

She had no luck until she got to an option to purchase the largest parcel. It had been held by GADBW, LLC. Something about that name tickled her brain. She googled the company and got only a single hit: a barebones listing at the Secretary of State's Business Records Division archive, its details lost to time.

Damn it.

She spun in her chair and looked out at the forest, but the dense greenery didn't calm her. The company name felt so familiar…

And then it clicked. Grant, Abby, Daniel, and Beverly Warren. GADBW.

Her *dad* had owned the company holding the option. He hadn't just worked to bring the stadium here for the county's benefit—he'd also tried to benefit from it personally.

She squeezed her eyes shut and covered her face with her hands.

CHAPTER THIRTY-SEVEN

"We're done with the car." FIC Fanning's voice came from deeper in the building, echoing faintly off the metal walls.

Jake had entered the coroner's garage through the steel service door. The big open space smelled of oil and hot metal. He spotted Fanning's wave and joined him at a garage bay where the Buick sat in the harsh glare of a circle of halogen work lights on three-legged stands. The mud had been hosed off it, and Fanning's team had stripped the interior down to the corroded metal.

"The car bits are over there." Fanning pointed to a pair of brown tarps stretched out in the next bay, covered in a jumble of parts and pieces. "The rest is on the table. We sent the bones to the coroner."

After putting on a pair of gloves from a dispenser on the wall, Jake bent over the table. It held three sets of keys, mud-stained synthetic clothing on hangers hooked over the table's edge, a wad of paper that might have been an owner's manual, five shoes, two wallets, a few items of women's jewelry, a rosary, pieces of plastic and paper fast-food containers, a cup with a straw sticking out of its lid, and a wine bottle.

"Where's the gun?"

"Off to ballistics."

"Were you able to trace it?"

Fanning shook his head. "Not registered."

"Could you identify the cartridge maker?"

"Guntech."

That matched the box under Graves's couch. But it was the little guy—Lange—who'd held the gun.

Jake continued examining the items on the table.

"Funny thing," Fanning said.

FIC Fanning was famous for understatement. Jake stopped and looked up.

"Jansen was very interested in what we got out of the car."

"He *is* the coroner," Jake said.

"In this stuff." Fanning pointed at the table. "Not the bodies."

The coroner's role didn't extend beyond cause of death, so Jansen had no reason to be interested in any of this stuff, except the gun. But Jansen was doing what he was told, and Bull was interested in some thing Silva had that night.

"Did he focus on anything in particular?" Jake asked.

Fanning shrugged. "Looked at all of it. Tried to pick apart the owner's manual. He was on his cell while he pawed through it. Sounded serious."

"Did he find anything that interested him?"

"Neither of them did."

Jake smiled. *Here we go.* "Who else?"

"The sheriff's man came in a half hour ago and did the same thing, except no phone calls. Hogan's his name. *Warren Hogan.*"

Jake had known the redhead's name was Warren but somehow hadn't connected it to Bull Warren. Now it didn't feel like a coincidence.

"Did he take anything?" Jake pointed at the clipboard. "Can I see the inventory to compare it against what's here?"

"Jansen said no inventory." Fanning held up his clipboard. "I made him put it in writing."

Fanning folded back a couple of pages to display an inventory sheet with a long sentence written across it: *Coroner Jansen instructed FIC Fanning not to perform an inventory of the nonhuman contents of the subject vehicle.* Jansen's signature was scrawled underneath it.

"Damn." A screw-up like this could torpedo the case in court. Jake pulled out his phone and took a picture of the page.

"Yeah." Fanning flipped to a document at the back. "I did one anyway. Jansen isn't my boss. Hogan didn't take anything."

Jake smiled.

Fanning stuck the clipboard under his arm. "You'll have to wait for the official word from Doc Franklin, but I looked at the third skull when it came in. Professional curiosity. The guy had a broken neck."

"From the car hitting the water?"

"Probably not. In a car crash you typically see a flexion-distraction fracture. The abrupt forward movement when the impact whips the head forward breaks the vertebrae, fracturing them in the posterior and middle columns." Fanning pantomimed the action with his right hand being the neck and snapping forward. "This guy suffered a fracture-dislocation." Fanning used his hands again. "Multiple vertebrae broken across all three columns and significantly dislocated. Typical of a violent downward twisting motion." He grabbed his right hand with his left and twisted it down and to the side.

That was a lot of words for the FIC. "What causes that?" Jake asked.

"Someone cranking the head down and to the side."

A man couldn't do that to himself. "How definite?"

"Definite about the type of fracture." Fanning shrugged. "Not about the cause."

"Murder, not suicide."

"Not my call."

It was the coroner's call. Although the law still allowed the coroner to have an inquest—a hearing with witnesses and a jury to determine cause of death—in modern practice the coroner made the decision on his own after reviewing the autopsy reports. Dr. Franklin's autopsy reports typically contained bare facts without speculation—so the report on Silva would only list the type of fracture. Jansen would be free to conclude it was caused by the car's impact with the bridge or with the water. With the coroner's determination in hand, the politicians would have a solid handle to declare the case a double murder-suicide. And because the state's attorney was basically a politician, it would also influence him.

To counter the weight of all those institutional voices, Jake needed concrete proof. All he had so far was his gut—and the statistical improbability of a murder-suicide occurring among three unrelated men outside of a workplace shooting. But statistics were for economists and administrators and would get him nowhere. Police work was mostly about the exceptions to the statistical norm.

He now knew that Bull and Bev were interested in something Silva had with him in the car. He needed to know what this thing was that they were after; then he could unravel their part in it.

Jake looked through the rest of the items on the table. The ring with the little brass keys was probably Silva's. The wallets confirmed the identities of Lange and Graves and held wet bits of paper, some green. The wine bottle confirmed Siebert's story. The only items that looked out of place were the pieces of women's jewelry: three bracelets with silver and gold balls, and a gold claddagh ring. The claddagh—two hands holding a heart—was an Irish symbol for love.

"Where was the jewelry?"

"It was all in the little guy's pocket. Except the rosary. It was wrapped around the steering wheel with two metacarpals snagged in it. Hand bones."

"Silva was tied to the wheel?"

"Maybe. Or maybe I'm wrong about the spinal fracture and he held it when he killed himself." Fanning shrugged again. "Repentance."

Jake examined the rosary—black beads on a silver chain with a silver centerpiece and crucifix. The centerpiece was a claddagh, just like the ring. "It's Irish."

"Yep."

Jake stepped away from the table and walked over to the car. The heat off the lights was intense as he bent into the passenger compartment. The car was in drive, and the key in the ignition had a plastic fob printed with the name of a local realtor. Jake re-examined the bullet holes in the trunk lid. Six of them, as he'd remembered, so there had been no shots fired before the men went into the trunk.

He stepped back out of the heat. Either the killer hadn't known Graves had the gun, or he'd believed both men were dead when he put them in the trunk.

Last, Jake examined the car parts spread over the tarps. Fabric still clung to the door panels and hung in wet shreds from the seats. The metal parts were rusty, but the plastic and vinyl bits were mostly intact.

"What have I missed?" he said.

Fanning pointed to a flat rock laid out with the car parts. It was about the size of an automotive shop manual. "Found that on the floor under the driver's seat."

Jake could think of only one reason for a rock to be there: to hold down the gas pedal. And that didn't jibe with suicide.

The evidence was circumstantial, but it was beginning to add up to a triple murder. Silva was dead by the broken neck. He was then propped in the driver's seat with his hands tied to the wheel with the rosary. The rock held down the gas pedal.

He checked his watch. He had twenty minutes to get back to Weston and meet with Deputy Chief Braff.

CHAPTER THIRTY-EIGHT

Jake spent the drive back to Weston thinking about what to tell Deputy Chief Braff. Most of his progress had to do with Bev and Bull and the item they were after—and he wasn't going to tell Braff any of that until he understood it completely. He would also say nothing about Hogan tailing him, or about the cut brake lines, or Jansen's bonehead maneuver with the inventory.

Braff would definitely ask about the murder-suicide theory. It fit some facts, would clear the case, and would end the political conflict with the county. Jake would counter with the solid facts that were inconsistent with that theory: the spiral fracture, the rosary around the steering wheel, the rock found in the car. He would also tell Braff that all three victims were criminals—even though Silva had been too smart to get caught—and that he was looking into whether their deaths were connected to a criminal enterprise gone wrong. If Braff bought that, he'd give Jake more time to work the case.

With enough time he could figure out what Bev and Bull were looking for.

He would have to stay away from the incident report, too. With Bull so tied into this case, the missing information now looked more likely to have been due to intentional deletions rather than data entry error. Bull certainly had the connections to get that done. He wouldn't have been able to remove the report altogether, because all reports were logged to track emergency calls and responses. But he could have deleted the pieces of information that might lead to—

That was it.

The deleted information was specifically chosen to protect someone or something. Looking at exactly what had been deleted might reveal who or what Bull was protecting.

Jake pulled into the next parking lot, a bowling alley, and parked beneath the patchy shade of an elm tree struggling to survive being planted in a concrete-bordered island. He pulled up both versions of the report on his phone: Mason's original and Erin's PDF. Then he took out his notebook and created a list of the information missing from the online report: the Buick's license plate number, the victim's name, the liquor store's name, the store clerk's name, and the responding officer's name.

Why these?

Jake stared at the list, mentally arranging and rearranging the items as he looked for connections. What did each item tell him?

Time passed as he worked the problem—and then the answer hit him in a sudden burst of clarity. Each piece of information would have led him to either Silva or Siebert.

The plate number led to Mrs. Cassano, which led to Silva. Mason's name led to Siebert's identity. The liquor store's name led to Mason—and thus to Siebert. The responding officer's name led to the officer's notebook, which would have contained the notes from which the report was written—in other words, the whole story.

Jake thought it through. If the goal had been only to hide Silva, Mason's name could have been left on the report, as it was unlikely he would remember the license plate number. And if the goal had been only to hide Siebert, there was no reason to delete the license plate number, because it only led to

Silva. So whoever had tampered with the report had wanted to hide Siebert *and* Silva.

They wanted to keep the two men from being connected on that night.

Why? Their meeting in the liquor store parking lot was a chance event. Siebert in the wrong place at the wrong time. But what if that assumption was wrong? What if—

Jake's phone buzzed.

"Deputy Chief Braff is waiting patiently," Erin said.

"Patiently?" Jake closed his notebook and slid it into his pocket. "That doesn't sound like him."

"That is correct."

Jake dropped the car into gear. "I'll be there in less than five minutes."

CHAPTER THIRTY-NINE

Jake checked his watch as he hustled down the hall. He was less than ten minutes late.

Deputy Chief Braff met him at his office door. "Damn it, Houser. I'm getting squeezed to let the sheriff have this damn case."

As he waved Jake inside, his arm bumped Erin.

"If I could catch Jake for a minute before you two get started?" Erin gave him one of her Braff-melting smiles.

"No can do, Erin." Braff checked his watch. "I got a date with the wife tonight."

"I'll stop by your desk when we're done," Jake said to her.

Erin nodded as the door closed.

Jake headed for the club chairs, but Braff's voice pulled him up short.

"Over here." He pointed at his desk, then sat behind it.

Shit.

Jake took a chair in front of Braff's desk.

Braff clasped his hands in front of him, his elbows and forearms on the desk. "Why didn't you report the cut brake lines?"

Jake relaxed. It was just about the car. "Reporting it would slow me down. I know the pressure you—"

Braff held up his hand. "You think this mechanic who works in the Silva woman's barn did it? Maybe he killed Silva to go after the wife. I hear she's a looker."

Jake hadn't thought of the scenario, but didn't see it. "I've put away a lot of people, Chief. Probably just one of them getting some revenge."

"Maybe. But I'm putting Diggs on it."

"That's not necessary, Chief. I've—"

"It's already done." Braff slapped his desk. "Now about the lagoon case. The mayor, three councilmen, and a police board commissioner have called—"

"I can solve—"

Braff held up his hand. "They'd rather you give it up than solve it." He clenched his big fists. "Statistics."

"What about statistics?" Jake asked, but he thought he knew the answer. Weston had been obsessed with its rankings in "best city" lists going back to the sixties. His dad had once explained how important the rankings were back in the days when the western suburbs were population bubbles along the commuter train lines into the city. As the suburban population grew, there'd been a constant fight to annex land and attract developers. Weston won most of its battles to become the largest Chicago suburb, making many Weston businessmen rich in the process.

"If we hand this case over to the sheriff, the deaths won't count on our stats because the bodies were found on Paget County land."

"We're handing it over?" Jake's stomach twisted. He needed to know the truth about Bull and Bev. And if Bev took the case, he'd always suspect her result was tainted.

The right thing to do was come clean about Bull and Bev—right here and now. But if he did that, Braff would turn the case over to the Illinois Attorney General. The AG was a democrat and would love going after Bull and the standing sheriff—but would he go after the truth? Or would he just make hay with the political opportunity?

No. Jake had to finish this himself. He needed the truth. The dead men deserved it.

Braff gave Jake his hard, fiery stare. "Don't ever accuse me of being a politician, Houser."

"Sorry, boss."

"I'm telling you all this so you know what I'm fighting against here. That's fine. That's my job. But I want to be sure I'm being a hard-ass for a reason. You going to solve this case?"

"I don't think it's a murder-suicide."

Braff clenched his hands again, then stood and started pacing behind his desk. "If it's not, it's not. Talk me through it. Did Silva have motives against the other two?"

Jake laid them out. "Both are weak, and Silva didn't break his own neck."

Braff stopped pacing. "You have something solid there? You've seen the autopsy report?"

"FIC Fanning says Silva suffered a spiral fracture to his neck that was more likely from a manual twisting than a crash impact." Jake used Fanning's hand gestures to demonstrate both.

Braff winced. "Silva was murdered too?"

"It's more likely, according to Fanning."

"*More likely* isn't exactly solid." Braff grunted and sat down. "What else you got?"

Jake explained about the rock and the rosary, two solid facts that were not consistent with suicide.

Braff shook his head. "I got the sheriff practically begging me for this case, Jake. Kirwin residents found in a county park, no Weston moral imperative here—and that's all you got? Why not let Bev take the hit? Tell me you got something else. Anything."

"All three dead men were criminals." Jake laid out the criminal records for Lange and Graves, then explained his suspicion

Silva was a thief, and told Braff about the contents of his man cave. Even if all the collectibles were clean, the money to buy them sure didn't come from laying carpet. "They might have been involved in some criminal enterprise that went wrong."

"Okay." Braff checked his watch. "How about Woodling?"

Jake stood and started moving toward the door. "It won't be a problem." Now that he knew why Bev was pushing the complaint, he was sure it would disappear when the case ended.

"You work through the three questions I gave you?"

"I did, and I'm ready."

"I got a reporter hounding me. Says she got an anonymous tip about a brutality complaint against you. She wants a sit-down with you on that and the lagoon case, too."

"I—"

"I told her to contact the media liaison, but keep your eyes open. She's liable to come looking for you."

"She called me already."

"Well don't talk to her!"

"I didn't."

Braff put up a hand. Jake stopped at the door.

"You've done great work for us, for this city, so I'll give you more time, and I'll take the heat for it." Braff sounded almost apologetic. Then his voice hardened. "But with so little going, I gotta shorten your leash. You've got twenty-four hours to wrap this up. Then it goes to the sheriff."

Braff gave Jake a long hard look. He didn't release it until Jake nodded.

CHAPTER FORTY

Bull clutched his stomach. Pain rolled through him in undulating waves, peaking in spasms that made his whole body clench and left his arms and legs trembling.

Christ!

Something had broken through in his gut. A new finger of tumor worming through him.

Another burning stab.

He wiped a slick of sweat from his face.

"Mr. Warren?"

A nurse, but he couldn't tell which through his tear-blurred vision.

"Your oxygen saturation has dropped too low. It's your gasping. You're not getting enough air through the cannula. I'm going to put the mask on you, okay?"

He nodded because he couldn't speak.

She pulled the cannula off and wrestled the clear plastic mask over his face, stretching the elastic bands over the back of his head. She plugged the air tube into it, and he began gulping down air with his mouth wide open.

After a few minutes his vision cleared, and the worm inside him retreated. He released his tensed muscles and sank into the bed.

"Thank you," he said. Now he could see it was Becca. The Packers fan.

She smiled and left the room.

He flapped the sheet to pull cool air under the sweat-soaked cotton.

His cell phone rattled against the table, the noise faint under the hiss of air flowing through the mask and around his face. He fumbled for it and finally got a lock on the cold metal. It was Margie. He sucked in a lungful as deep as he could, pulled the mask partly aside, and answered. "Bull." He hoped his voice sounded stronger to her than it did to him.

"I called to let you know the deputy chief is pushing Jake to let Bev take the case. He's getting it from the mayor, the commissioner, and a couple councilmen. They're worried about the crime statistics. That was genius, by the way."

"Good." The word came out like it was wrapped in duct tape. "That was all... Bev."

"Are you doing okay, Bull?"

"Peachy." He pushed the word out in a bark. "Thanks for... calling."

"You want me to come sit with you?"

"No—*shit*." A tendril of fire dug through his stomach.

"I'll be right there."

His vision faded, pulsing in and out, and his fingers began to tingle. He scrabbled them against the sheet, searching for feeling. He struggled to push the mask back in place and...

...

...

Light built slowly, colors growing.

Bull told himself to blink, and his eyes obeyed.

The air machine's pump and hiss invaded his consciousness, and he almost smiled at hearing the sounds he'd come to hate. He wasn't dead.

He closed his eyes. He could still get this done and protect Bev from the taint of his past. Pain stabbed through his gut, fire probing through his entire nervous system to convulse his toes and fingers.

There was something in his hand.

"Bull?"

He opened his eyes. Margie sat next to him, his hand in both of hers.

Another wave of pain clenched him. "Morphine!"

She dropped his hand and ran from the room.

Bull accepted his failure. If he was going to help Bev, it had to be now.

CHAPTER FORTY-ONE

With Braff putting him on the clock, Jake itched to get moving, but he still stopped by Erin's desk on the way out. She already had her tennis shoes on and her purse on her lap, and she was shutting down her computer.

"Before you sign off, I—"

The screen blipped off.

"Did you find the officer who wrote the incident report? Thompson."

"That's what I wanted to talk to you about." Erin pulled a spiral-topped notebook out of her bag and flipped through it. "He quit less than a month after the thing at the liquor store. Now he works at Weston Running Company."

Jake wrote down Thompson's name, address, and phone number as Erin recited it. "Anything on why he left the force?"

"In his exit interview he said he wasn't cut out for it."

Not everybody was.

* * *

Weston Running Company was only a couple doors down and around the corner from Jake's apartment, and he knew it well. He'd taken up running in the spring and had bought his first pair of running shoes there after an analysis of his stride and foot strike. While driving toward the store, Jake called ahead and confirmed Thompson was working.

Jake turned down the alley to park behind his building, and found Callie Diggs crouched in his parking space. An evidence tech was squatted beside her, swabbing something off the pavement with a long Q-tip.

Jake rolled down his window, his gaze settling on Callie's curves. She looked good. As always.

"What did you find?"

Callie stood up and came to the window. "Brake fluid. Your brakes were cut here. I have a tech checking your car for trace and prints, a uniform checking the city's camera network, and another talking with the two restaurants that have cameras in the alley."

"Going all out," he said. He was worried that she might find her way to Hogan and interrupt his investigation. Or worse. But Hogan was a seasoned cop; he should know how to avoid leaving trace and prints behind.

"You okay?" Callie asked. "I saw the car."

"Fine."

"Done," the tech said, stepping away.

Jake rolled up his window and pulled into the spot.

"What does your gut say?" Callie asked as Jake got out of the car. "Think it was this mechanic? Craig Morgan?"

"My gut says it wasn't him."

"Then who?"

Jake shrugged. "Could be anyone from the last twenty years."

Her eyes bored into his. "Okay. I'll let you know what we get from trace and video."

"Sounds good."

The tech stood to the side, waiting. They must have come together.

"He's waiting," Jake said, nodding toward the man.

"You sure you're okay, Jake? Want me to come over later and—"

"No," Jake said. Then tried to soften the rejection. "I'm fine."

Callie nodded and walked away.

Jake waited a minute to be sure she'd cleared the area before he walked around to the front of the building and over to the Running Company. It was just a few shops down, past Dora's Café and the Subway sandwich shop. It buzzed with activity—both treadmills were spinning in the back, and a half dozen people were trying on running shoes at the benches scattered around the miniature running track painted on the floor. A trio of women near the front corner examined racks of brightly colored running clothes.

A stocky and well-muscled thirtyish guy with a receding hairline squatted in front of a businesswoman trying on a pair of lime-green shoes. His eyes pierced Jake's with an intensity that gave him away. Jake motioned with his head for Thompson to meet him outside, then pushed back through the door and leaned against the bicycle rack in front of the store.

Thompson came out a minute later.

"Thompson?" Jake asked.

"Yes."

They shook hands.

"I'm Detective Houser with—"

"I know who you are." Thompson shot a look back inside. "Let's talk over here." He led Jake along the sidewalk and into the alley between the shoe store and the sandwich shop. The reek of rotting food and the buzz of flies came from a pair of Dumpsters behind the chain-link fence closing off the back half of the alley.

Thompson folded his arms. "I've been off the force for almost five years. What do you need?"

"Right before you quit, you responded to a strong-arm robbery at a liquor store on 59."

"I remember."

When Thompson pulled his gaze away, Jake knew the man had something to tell him. "You followed up the report by talking with the victim."

Thompson's shoulders slumped. He fell back against the wall and slid down to a squatting position, hands rubbing his face. Jake stayed silent, not wanting to interrupt whatever seethed through Thompson. The story would come out without any more prodding.

After a long minute, Thompson turned his face up to Jake. "Is she dead?" His voice was hoarse and squeaky.

"Tell me what happened that night."

"I didn't get up there for nearly two hours." Thompson tried to hold Jake's gaze like a good cop would, but kept breaking off. "A semi had flipped over on the eastbound toll ramp and I had to handle traffic control for the EMTs. I didn't think there was any urgency in getting to Siebert's—the robbery happened at the liquor store, so Siebert wasn't in any danger at his house. My sergeant agreed."

Up there. Thompson's story skipped the liquor store completely. Jake let the silence stretch, then gently entered it. "And?"

"When I got there, something was off." Thompson bunched his hands into fists and pressed them on his knees. "The wife answered the door and she... she wasn't hurt—not that I could see, anyway. But something was wrong. I told her why I was there, and she looked nervous, and then her husband—the robbery victim, Paul Siebert—came to the door. He pulled her away and stood there blocking my view of her. He seemed surprised to see me. I explained about the 911 call and that I had to take a victim report. He cut me off and said there was no need. It was just a misunderstanding. Said he gave the wine to those guys of his own free will and the liquor store clerk misunderstood. Then he tried to close the door."

Thompson's face was red and ran with sweat. He looked up at Jake. "But their demeanor was so off, I stuck my foot in the opening. It spooked him. I told him I needed to talk with his wife again to make sure she was okay." He shook his head. "The wife came back to the door and said she was fine."

"She's still fine," Jake said. "This isn't about her at all."

Thompson sighed and wiped his brow, then transferred the sweat in a smear down the leg of his khakis. He stood up, one hand still on the wall. "Then what is it about?"

"The car driven by the guys who robbed Siebert that night was found in the Paget River two days ago." Jake considered what he should tell the man. He decided Thompson was okay. "There were three bodies in it."

"You sure it was the same car?"

"Yes."

"She's okay? Mrs. Siebert?" He wiped his face again, fresh sweat popping out on his forehead as soon as his hand passed.

"She's fine," Jake said.

"That's why I quit the force. Domestics. Too hard to figure out who's lying."

Jake had taken hundreds of domestic calls as a patrol officer, and he knew exactly what Thompson was talking about. "Mr. Siebert told you the incident in the parking lot was a misunderstanding? Was that a lie?" Siebert had admitted the crime to Jake, so it obviously was.

Thompson's gaze faded into his memory. "I… guess that's possible. But why would he lie about it?"

"To get rid of you."

Jake could see the whole story now. Siebert had been robbed, then went home and took out the emasculation on his wife. Thompson picked up on that when he arrived—so Siebert wanted Thompson gone. A run-of-the-mill domestic. Even in Weston there were dozens every day.

"Well, it worked," Thompson said.

"Why didn't you file a victim report?"

"I had to file the incident report, but he said it wasn't a crime, so no victim report. I didn't log it for detective follow-up either." Thompson wiped his face again. It had lost its red tint but was still slick with sweat. "You think the bodies are the same guys from the liquor store?"

"I can't tell you anything more, and please don't share what we've discussed with anyone." Jake folded his sunglasses back over his face. "But I *can* tell you I've seen nothing to indicate Mrs. Siebert is being abused." The Sieberts had looked happy, and close. They must have worked through their problems. Maybe taking on the foster kids had brought them together again.

"Good," Thompson said. "I've been thinking about her for five years."

Jake left him there, still sweating.

* * *

Bev spent the next couple of hours at her desk examining everything she'd ever believed about her dad. Her new understanding was like a lens that showed everything in a different focus; all the little whispers she'd heard over the years now painted a picture she didn't like and couldn't reconcile with the man who had been such a great dad.

She tried to apply this new focus to the mysterious document and the real estate option contract her dad had bought. If the stadium project had made it through the state legislature, her dad would have sold the option—his right to buy the land at a stated price—to the Bears. And he would have made a gigantic profit. Because her dad wasn't a member of the Paget County Stadium Administration, it wasn't against the law for him to try to profit from the stadium deal. But if the option was legal, then how did he "stray from the straight and narrow," as he'd said in that first phone call?

The missing document was about that straying.

She mulled that over for a minute. The answer came to her with a thump to her stomach.

It had to be about how he'd managed to pay for the option. The plot of land was over a hundred acres, zoned for commercial use—which made it worth millions. Would the option have cost a half million? More? She'd been through his finances and his tax returns. Her dad had never made a lot of money, and his biggest assets were a mortgage-free house and a modest retirement account. And none of his friends or relatives had that kind of money available to loan him for a real estate deal.

So where did he get it?

She spun her chair to face the window.

He'd had some kind of county job at the time. Something to do with disabled adults. No, it had been more than that, but she couldn't drag it out of her memory. She'd been all wrapped up in her own childhood dramas and problems.

She spun back to face her desk and pulled up the county website. She clicked through the various elected positions and county departments, but nothing fit her vague memory of the job he'd had. He'd been proud of that job, she remembered that, because of the work he'd done and because—that was it! The governor had appointed him. It was a state job.

A little more typing and clicking, and she had it. Public administrator for Paget County. In addition to helping disabled adults, the PA also handled the estates of people who died without someone to administer their property. The PA searched for heirs, collected the deceased's assets, and filed a probate case in county court. Now she remembered her dad complaining about how long it took for the lawyers and the court to get through the myriad of formalities even when there was no one around to dispute anything he was doing.

Shit. Her hands trembled on the keyboard and sweat popped on her forehead.

Assets, and no one to complain. *That* was how he'd funded the purchase.

He probably planned to return the money after he'd made his killing. He didn't steal the money—he borrowed it. It only became theft when he couldn't pay it back.

She closed her eyes against the lies she was telling herself. If he did this, it was theft from the beginning.

But she shouldn't condemn her dad without hard facts, no matter how obvious the conclusion seemed. She went into the Paget County court system and started sifting through the online probate records. When she managed to remember the name of the lawyer her dad had used in court, things started coming together quickly. She soon had a list of thirty-seven probate cases the attorney had handled in the two years before her dad bought the option.

It would take hours to comb through all thirty-seven files, and what did she hope to find? If her dad had stolen from one of these estates, he would certainly have been smart enough to keep the court file clean. Or at least, clean enough to withstand a passing inspection. She needed to narrow things down.

She scanned the list, hoping a name would jump out at her.

Two did.

Jedidiah Sublett and Seamus Doherty.

Both names were familiar from a lifetime in Weston and school field trips to the historic settlement. The Sublett name was on several parks in Weston, and the Performing Arts Pavilion at North Western College was named after Seamus Doherty.

Bev clicked her way to the Weston Heritage Society web page and read the extensive biographies compiled on both men.

There it was. Jedidiah Sublett had collected gold coins.

Like the one in the safe.

A picture was forming in her mind. A sequence of events. Purely speculation… but it made sense. It had the ring of truth.

As public administrator, her dad had handled Jedidiah Sublett's estate. The man had owned a collection of gold coins. Her dad stole the coins to buy the real estate option. He intended to... what? Re-purchase the coins later, after the deal? Return them to the estate somehow? She had to admit that seemed unlikely. And she'd never know, because the stadium deal fell through, and he lost the money.

The missing document must somehow reveal all of this.

He'd kept one coin. A souvenir of some sort. And when the plan fell apart, it came to symbolize his failure.

She opened a new search page and googled the phrase written on the little brown envelope in her dad's safe: *Failure is not fatal.* Variations on it were attributed to lots of people, but with a little more clicking she found "Success isn't permanent and failure isn't fatal" by Mike Ditka, the Chicago Bears' Super Bowl coach.

Bull loved Da Coach.

She sat back in her chair. She was guessing, she knew. The evidence for her conclusions was far from courtroom-worthy—thank God. But it was enough for her.

Enough for this.

Damn it!

CHAPTER FORTY-TWO

Jake thought about Thompson as he walked back toward his apartment building. It must have been tough for Thompson to admit he didn't have what it took to be a cop. Plenty of cops had that same self-realization, but lied to themselves and stayed on anyway. That was a situation that was bad for everyone.

Jake's next stop was just around the corner: Jansen's clothing store. It was time to find out what he knew and who had been giving him his marching orders. Jansen's bonehead order to Fanning about the inventory had given Jake the leverage he needed to pry that information loose.

He strode down the street and stepped inside.

Jansen's store was in a dinnertime calm. The coroner was in a back corner arranging a display of patterned socks that were on sale for fourteen dollars a pair.

"Coroner Jansen?"

Jansen turned with a broad smile that disappeared when he saw Jake. "Detective Houser." He turned back to the socks. "What do you want?"

"Because you're an elected official I'll give you the option. We can talk here or down at the station."

Jansen spun, his face reddening. "How dare you!"

"How dare *I*? *You* ordered FIC Fanning not to perform the legally required inventory of the Buick's contents, and *that* could let a triple murderer go free."

Jansen spluttered. "That's not what happened." His gaze darted around the store. "Let's g-go to my office." Jansen spun on a tasseled loafer and quick-stepped away.

So far, so good.

Jake followed him up a stairway, across a loft displaying casual wear, and through a door into an area walled off across the back. Jake shut the door behind them. Past a scarred table scattered with empty fast food bags, and a crowd of racks jammed with wool coats, sat a tight grouping of mismatched metal office furniture.

The coroner sat in a chair behind a cluttered desk. Jake stayed on his feet.

"So what *did* happen?" Jake said.

Jansen rocked back in his chair and met Jake's gaze briefly before looking away. "I just told him to wait until he was completely done," he squeaked. "That's all."

Jake pulled out his phone, found the picture he'd taken, and read from it. "Coroner Jansen instructed FIC Fanning not to perform an inventory of the nonhuman contents of the subject vehicle." He turned the screen toward Jansen. "Sound familiar?"

"I didn't write that."

"You signed it." Jake put his phone away, then settled into a chair as if he had all the time in the world. "Why?"

Jansen's old chair screeched as he tilted back, his hands rubbing his face. "I just wanted him to wait on the inventory until he was completely done."

Anchor point movement and face touching: a cluster of deception indicators.

"He was *already* done when you signed this."

Jake waited a beat while Jansen pulled out his cell phone and searched the screen. Then he asked:

"Did you kill those men?"

"Of course not!" Jansen's face went pale, and his cheeks puffed out like he was about to puke.

"But you're covering it up—and that makes you an accessory after the fact. A heavyweight felony. Serious prison time."

"It wasn't like that!" Jansen looked at his phone. "Just let me make a call and I can clear this up."

"If you want to call a lawyer, tell him to meet us at the station." Jake stood and motioned for Jansen to come with him.

"No, no, no." Jansen shook his head and pushed his phone away. "No lawyer and no phone."

Jake sat back down.

Jansen gaze went everywhere but to Jake. "I was supposed to report on everything in the car *before* it made it to the paperwork. Every single thing. Even garbage."

"Did Bev tell you what she was looking for?"

"No, she just—" Jansen's mouth clapped shut, then he gulped.

"Tell me what she asked you to look for."

Jansen bit his lip and looked at his phone. "I'm sure it's nothing like what you're saying." Finally he met Jake's eye. "She's your cousin!"

"What did she tell you to look for?"

Jansen shook his head, then wilted under Jake's hard gaze. "She didn't say, exactly. She just told me to tell her about everything we found in the car before we wrote it up. After I went through all of it with her, then Fanning could have done the report."

"Did you find what she was looking for?"

"No."

"What would have happened if you had found it?"

If Jansen had thought that far ahead, he was smart enough not to admit it. He remained silent.

"As you went through the stuff with her, what was she most interested in?"

"Not the gun, and that was the only interesting thing in there."

Jansen looked away, his chair squeaking as he shifted his weight and licked his lips. Jansen was lying, or holding back something weighty.

"Tell me."

Jansen took a deep breath and let it out. "She had me spend a lot of time on the few bits of paper I found. She even made me paw apart the owner's manual."

They're looking for a piece of paper.

Jake peppered Jansen with a few more questions, but got nothing more out of him. He told Jansen to keep the conversation to himself, though he wasn't really worried about him talking. The coroner would be too embarrassed to admit to the sheriff that he'd given her up.

* * *

"Jake! Did you listen to the game yesterday?"

Coogan leapt off the opposite sidewalk and loped across the street, his long arms swinging. An SUV slammed on its brakes and its horn blared. Coogan gave the driver a wave and an apologetic smile.

Coogan had been Jake's best friend since second grade, his roommate through college and law school, his best man, the head pallbearer at his wife's funeral, and was his go-to guy on Weston history.

"I'm afraid I missed it," Jake said. "What happened?"

"That kid they brought up from double-A pitched his first start."

"How did he do?" A new kid making his big league start for the Cubs always meant possibilities to Coogan. After the Cubs won it all in 2016—finally defeating the dreaded Billy Goat curse—everyone hoped it was the start of a dynasty.

"He's got the stuff," Coogan said. "You want to get dinner? Judy's at her sister's place this week."

"I can't. Chief's got me on a short leash. But I wouldn't mind your thoughts on this case if you have a few minutes." Sometimes putting his thoughts into words as he explained a case to Coogan was all it took for Jake to see everything clearly. Other times, Coogan's sharp mind caught something Jake missed. It was always worth the effort.

"Sure," Coogan said. "Shoot."

Jake led his friend a few steps down to the Mustang and walked him through the case. "I haven't told the deputy chief anything about Bev or Bull, or even Jansen," he finished. "But he found out about the brake lines."

"Did Hogan do that? You have to do something."

"Not if I want to hang on to the case."

Coogan's lips pursed, then he nodded. "Right." He started pacing the cracked asphalt. "Give me a minute."

Jake kept quiet during the long silence as Coogan worked through it.

"This paper is probably a legal document, because nothing else has such significance," Coogan said at last. "It's the key. If they thought it was in the car, then Silva must have had it. If he was a thief, maybe he stole it. Figuring out who he stole it *from* might help."

Jake liked the theory. Silva *was* a thief—he'd robbed Siebert that same night, after all—so the document could easily have been stolen. Hell, maybe Silva had stolen it from Bull.

"I think you're right that Hogan is Bull's tool," Coogan continued. "He personally selected Hogan as his daughter's assistant. Now he's only got days to live, and he's got Hogan doing what he can't do himself."

"What do you know about Hogan?"

"His first name is Warren, which tells you something." Coogan tapped his temple. "I remember an article in the VFW magazine a couple years ago. Hogan's dad and Bull both volunteered right when we got serious in Vietnam. Marines. Did two tours together. Went through some serious stuff."

That explained why Big Red was named Warren.

"I think you're right about Woodling's complaint," Coogan went on. "It came too fast, and because it isn't on the sheriff department's complaint log and Hogan wasn't transferred to Professional Standards, we can conclude it's not real. Not official, anyway. If that's the way they want it—to keep it from being public and attracting attention they want to avoid—maybe you should flip it on them. Treat it like it's official and give it to your union rep. That should get them to shut it down fast."

It was a good idea, but Callie was Jake's union rep, and he wasn't sure he wanted to pull her any further into this. She knew him too well for him to get away with not telling her the whole story.

Although if he *did* pull her in, he had no doubt she'd eat Hogan for lunch.

He walked Coogan out of the alley. "It's an interesting idea. You've given me some things to think about. Thanks for your help, Coog, as always."

"Be careful, Jake. Cutting your brake lines is serious."

CHAPTER FORTY-THREE

Jake headed north to confront Mrs. Cassano about Donald Silva taking over her husband's business fencing stolen property—to see if that would shake something out of her. It wasn't subtle, or pleasant, but with Braff putting him on such a short leash, he needed to push. Once he had her riled up about that, he'd ask her about any connection her husband had to the Warren family. He had nothing to lose, and she was tough enough to take it.

As he was crossing the tollway, his phone rang. Erin.

"Jake? I had some time on my hands, so I took a look at Paul Siebert." One of Erin's jobs was to wrangle witnesses, which included evaluating their credibility.

"Find anything interesting?" Jake asked.

"Two things. First, seven years ago, before the Sieberts moved to Weston, their son was taken and murdered."

"What?" Jake swallowed, his stomach suddenly loose. "Where did that happen?"

"Downstate. Mount Logan."

"Jesus." The Sieberts must have been destroyed.

"Yeah. Not exactly relevant, but I thought you'd want to know."

"I'm glad you told me." Jake's mind spun through his conversations with Siebert. He didn't find anything to indicate they'd experienced that devastation.

"But I did find something that *is* relevant. Or could be."

"Go ahead."

"Mr. Siebert was on our local cable station."

Jake cleared a lump from his throat. "For what?"

"You know that TV show, *Flea Market Finds*? They came to town, and Weston Community Television filmed the auditions. Mr. Siebert took an old desk in to get looked over. The expert found a secret drawer."

"Was there anything in the drawer?"

"A paper of some kind. The article I found on the Patch website didn't say anything more about that part of it, but the date is what struck me."

She paused. She sometimes went for the dramatic effect.

Jake waited.

"It was a week before the liquor store robbery."

* * *

Bev flicked at the pages of her planner, thinking about Margie's news. The doctor had explained how the morphine would accelerate her dad's condition—meaning his death. She wasn't ready. She didn't want to be alone, and she didn't want to be left with this new perception of her dad. She wanted him to explain it away—for everything to go back to how it had been a few days ago. If she could just talk to him. But Margie had said her dad didn't want anyone visiting tonight while he got used to the painkiller and the oxygen mask.

Should she go see him even though he didn't want her there? What if he died before she could ask him about the option and the estate?

She dithered—indecision her dad would hate. *You can't freeze when faced with bad options*, as he'd said many times over the years. You had to gather the facts, identify options, pick one, and then go all in. Full commitment to the chosen path was the most important factor in success.

Facts? Options? Pick?

Go or not go. She balled her hands into hard knotty fists. She'd let her dad have his way. She'd stay away tonight.

She turned her mind to the Radar Grove case. Her jurisdictional play and the worm in the mayor's ear about crime statistics were both bubbling away out there, but they were taking too long. She needed to push the Woodling complaint. Maybe have Hogan pull Jake in for a sit-down. That would eat up his time and screw with his head.

But finding the damn document was her first priority. If she was right about what it would disclose, it would destroy the memory of everything her dad had done for this county. His legacy.

She had to find it.

But Jansen had pulled the Buick completely apart, and both he and Hogan had examined every last item in it. It wasn't there. Maybe it had once been in the car, and time and water had destroyed it? That would be for the best. But she couldn't take that for granted. If it was out there somewhere, Jake could find it.

The phone rang. Caller ID said it was the Weston PD. She pulled her chair to the desk, squared her shoulders, and picked up. "This is Sheriff Warren." She was proud her voice sounded strong.

"Good evening, Sheriff. This is Deputy Chief Braff." The sound of violins came through the phone.

"I hear music," she said, buying time. She should have expected a call; Braff was an up-front kind of guy. "Where are you?"

"Doherty Hall. My wife likes music."

"What can I do for you, Deputy Chief?"

"I gave Houser twenty-four hours, then it's yours."

Damn it. Putting Jake on a deadline would kick his efforts into high gear. The opposite of progress. "Why wait?" She took a long breath to slow herself down. "Is Detective Houser chasing down a last lead? We can chase it down as effectively."

"Sheriff, I think you know I don't play politics. I gave Houser the time because he's as good as we got and he's done more with less. But if he hasn't made an arrest by this time tomorrow, I'll hand over what we have and the case is yours."

That was the longest speech in her acquaintance with the man, and she believed every word of it.

"Understood, Deputy Chief. I just hope this delay doesn't end up being an issue."

Braff hung up without another word.

CHAPTER FORTY-FOUR

All Jake could think about was the document in the secret drawer in Siebert's antique desk. If he was right, it pulled together everyone involved in the case. Siebert found a document hidden in an antique; Silva robbed Siebert; Silva's car ended up in the lagoon; and Bull was now looking for an important paper he thought was in that car.

What had Siebert stumbled upon in that desk?

And the document's discovery was on video. Everything Jake needed to know about the document might have been recorded on that TV show. Hell, maybe the guy who found it even read the whole thing out loud.

He passed the turn to the Bends and continued on toward the industrial park where the cable company had its office and studios. Playing hardball with Cassano about her husband's criminal past and any connection to Bull Warren would have to wait.

He pushed through the door into the cable station offices. The lobby was no bigger than the one at his dentist's office, and not as nice. Matching chairs, upholstered in stained brown fabric, lined two walls, forming an 'L' around a square table layered in magazines. The far wall held a sliding pass-through window and a wooden door with a red neon sign above it throbbing ON AIR. An air freshener filled the room with a floral scent thick enough to taste.

Jake looked through the window into a cubicle holding an empty chair and a desk cluttered with paper and binders. He checked the door and found it unlocked. It opened to a narrow hallway running straight back through an expanse of cubicles, with a suspended ceiling giving way to exposed ductwork. Bright lights shone across the space from the back of the building, and he smelled hot electronics and burnt dust.

He was about to yell "Anyone here?" when he remembered the ON AIR light.

He headed toward the activity. A stocky guy with brown hair going gray, his arms loaded with spreadsheets, cut into the hall from the cubicle farm and bumped Jake into the wall.

"Oh! Sorry." The man stopped and examined Jake over his glasses. "We're live back there. Can't have visitors."

Jake introduced himself and showed his badge. The man introduced himself as Mark Strimel, the station's CFO, bookkeeper, and scriptwriter. When Jake explained he needed to see old footage, Strimel led him to a tiny cubicle crowded with two chairs and a desk. Three large monitors were turned on, two jammed with window upon window of spreadsheets and PowerPoint files, the third showing a muted picture of a studio where a kid who couldn't be more than twenty was talking so excitedly it could only be about sports.

Strimel pulled a stack of printouts off the guest chair, then sat himself in the fancy ergonomic chair. He swiveled to the far monitor and clicked a few times to bring up what looked like a digital library catalogue.

"This is our video inventory. It's indexed so we can reuse video for generic background." He gestured to the monitor. "Staging shots when we have a story about a park, or a school, that kind of thing."

"The video I need was made about five years ago. It was taken when the program *Flea Market Finds* came here to audition people."

"I remember that." Strimel clicked and typed for a minute. "Yeah, here it is. Indexed as 'Flea Market Finds Auditions.' October thirteenth, 2012." He paused. "Hmm. This is strange."

"What?"

"Well it's indexed, but the field for the file size says zero." Strimel pointed at the screen. "See here?"

Jake leaned forward. "So you had a video, indexed it, and what? It was deleted?"

"Let me check the log. It tracks any changes to the file." Strimel typed and clicked. "Shit."

"What?"

"One second." Windows popped open and closed on the screen, and Strimel started shaking his head. "Gone. Completely."

Jake gritted his teeth. "What happened to it?"

"It was deleted a few weeks after it was created. November eleventh."

Filmed a week before the car disappeared, deleted within a month after it. "What about backup?"

"It would have been backed up before it was deleted, but that backup is long gone." Strimel pointed at the screen that held the catalogue listing for the empty index entry.

"Does the system show who deleted it?"

Strimel shook his head as he clicked through to another window. "It just says an administrator did it. Back then our security was kind of weak and we were all administrators."

Bull had gotten to it.

CHAPTER FORTY-FIVE

Jake's phone buzzed with a call as he left the TV station complex. Paget County Sheriff. *This should be interesting.*

He pulled to the curb. "This is Detective Houser."

"Detective Houser." A deep voice. "This is Deputy Hogan from the Sheriff's Professional Standards Division. As your deputy chief has probably told you, we are investigating an excessive force claim from a Mr. Woodling."

Jake considered throwing what he knew in Hogan's face, but that wouldn't get him anywhere. "He did tell me."

"We'd like to hear what you have to say about the incident."

"I'm tied up with a couple cases right now. I could meet with you next week."

"His accusations are serious, and we thought you'd appreciate a chance to tell your side of the story." Hogan paused. "We're offering you this informal opportunity to explain because of the good relationship between our two departments."

"Well thank you, Deputy. I can come in next Monday."

"Tomorrow would be better, if you want to get in front of this. Woodling's also talking about a civil claim. He had to get stitches."

"Text me with a time and place. Goodbye, Deputy."

A real complaint was supposed to go through several levels of review before the involved officer had to say a word on the record. This offer to "get in front" of Woodling's complaint meant Coogan was right: the complaint wasn't official. It was just a distraction to waste his time while his clock ran out.

Jake pulled out of the industrial park and onto Ogden. With the videotape gone, his only source for information on the document was Siebert. Jake would pick the man's brain until there was nothing left in it.

CHAPTER FORTY-SIX

Bev stared out her office window without seeing anything. Her dad had been on morphine for almost two hours. He knew what that meant even better than she did. His end was coming. Was he scared? She sure as hell would be. She—

Her cell phone buzzed against her desk. She spun her chair and grabbed it. Hogan. She doubted it would be good news.

"I found him. Picked him up near his apartment," Hogan said. "He was just at the Weston Cable Access Station."

Christ! "Dad said you handled the video back then, right?"

"Yes. Nothing to worry about there."

"But he clearly knows about the Sublett document." She said the name as if she'd always known it.

"Well… I, uh, he must know there was a document in the desk, but that might be all he knows. Might not know that name, or what the document says."

She'd been right about Jedidiah Sublett. "We get the case tomorrow at five."

"Weston PD agreed to turn it over? Good work."

"Finally." She smiled at Hogan's approval, but only briefly. Jake was too good. "A lot can happen between now and then. We need to slow Jake down." She said it before realizing what that might mean to Hogan. "By pushing the Woodling complaint harder."

"I did like you said and asked him in for a sit-down. Tomorrow. I'll schedule it for mid-morning to break up his day and keep him busy as long as I can."

"Let's hope that does the job." She winced at her own wording. A leader acted, she didn't hope.

"I'll have him come into the station. If he admits to hitting Woodling I'll slap the cuffs on him. That'll hold him for the day."

"Absolutely not," Bev said. That would only bring the attention they had so far avoided.

"You sure?" Hogan asked. "Bull would say—"

"I know what he would say." *When you commit, you have to go all in.* But arresting Jake was too far. "By the way… he went on morphine two hours ago."

Hogan sighed. "That's it, right? Morphine means he's near the end."

"Yes." She was glad she had Hogan to talk to, and the admission surprised her. "I'm going over to see him." She had to see him, right now, even if he didn't want to see her. "If you want to—"

"No, I'll keep on Houser. Fixing this so you don't suffer for it is important to Bull."

CHAPTER FORTY-SEVEN

As Jake exited the industrial park he spotted Hogan in his rear-view mirror. The only thing that would bring Jake to the cable station was the document found in Siebert's desk, which meant Hogan—and therefore Bull and Bev—now knew he was on to it. He considered confronting Hogan directly, but decided against it. The man wouldn't scare like Jansen had.

Jake went straight to Siebert's house. During the first interview, Siebert hadn't said a word about the document. Had he been lying? Jake mentally replayed that portion of their conversation and didn't spot any indicators of deception. But Siebert still had to know something about the document. Even one tiny fact could unwrap the whole case.

As Jake drove through Cress Creek, the sun dropped and the shadows lengthened. He powered down the front windows to let the cool evening air sweep over him. On both sides of the road, walkers and runners and children were out enjoying the cool evening air after the hot day.

Siebert's cul-de-sac was empty of hoopsters, but a basketball lay in the gutter across from the hoop. Jake stopped his car short of it.

He walked across the well-worn lawn and up onto the stoop. As he raised his hand to rap on the glass, he peered through his reflection to a circle of heads bowed in prayer around the kitchen table. He waited until the heads lifted—an excited babble breaking out as arms reached for the platters of food—then knocked.

The girl at the near end of the table bounced up and came to the door.

"Yes?"

"I'm here to see your dad."

Mrs. Siebert appeared behind her daughter.

"I've got this, Annie." She waited until her daughter returned to the table. Then, "It's a little late for a visit." She didn't open the glass door, and the slight muffling made her voice sound deeper than he remembered it.

"I'm sorry, Mrs. Siebert." Jake put on his most gentle smile. "I have a few follow-up questions for your husband."

"He's not here." She crossed her arms, then looked past Jake and up the street.

"Will he be back soon? Could I wait in the homework room?"

She crossed and re-crossed her arms, still looking up the street. "Here he comes now."

A minivan came down the court. Beyond it, Jake spotted the front of Hogan's car parked around the corner.

"Come in." She opened the door and ushered Jake into the study room. "You can wait for him here." Then she headed back to the kitchen.

Jake double-checked the desks to make sure none of them could qualify as antique—which they clearly didn't. A clamor sounded from the kitchen as the kids welcomed their dad home. Jake wondered what that felt like.

Then Paul Siebert entered the room.

"We've started dinner, so I hope this won't take long, Detective…?"

"Houser," Jake reminded him.

Siebert gestured at the chair Jake had sat in on his earlier visit. "You have some questions for me?"

Jake sat down and waited for Siebert to take his chair before answering. "Someone told me about you being on TV to have a desk evaluated. It sounded interesting. I wanted to see it."

"That desk." Siebert's lips tightened and he shook his head. "It's in the basement. Come on."

Siebert sprang up, and Jake followed. As they skirted the dinner table, the aroma of roast beef made Jake's mouth water and his stomach rumble.

"You okay, Dad?" The tallest boy stood up, his chair emitting a long squeak against the oak floor. The other boys rose in his wake.

"You guys eat." Siebert patted the air with his hands. "This'll only take a minute."

The basement was carpeted, with a pair of sofas angled around a video game system plugged into a giant TV. It smelled of sweaty teenagers. A jumble of video game disks spread across the TV stand and clustered on the floor around it. Around a corner a door opened into an unfinished space holding a cluttered workbench, the house mechanicals, and the desk.

Siebert pulled the cord hanging from a bare bulb, and the room flooded with harsh light. "The desk."

The tension again.

"Tell me about being on the show," Jake said.

"What's this got to do with those bodies?"

"Just covering all the bases. It's how we do it."

Siebert shrugged. "The desk didn't make the show because it was only worth like a thousand bucks according to the guy who looked it over."

"But there was a video on local cable?"

"I guess so." Siebert eyed him. "The Weston cable channel filmed us. I never saw it."

"I heard about a secret drawer."

The question didn't faze Siebert. He pulled out the desk's lap drawer and pointed at the shallow tray in the bottom of it.

"There was a thin wood covering over that space, but it was pretty obvious once the guy pointed it out. More forgotten than secret."

Siebert said nothing about the document.

Jake examined the desk. It was a narrow writing desk with curved legs and nice proportions. The top had an inlaid border of intricately cut geometric shapes. The drawer's front was splintered, and there was a deep dent and a crack where the drawer met the desktop. Someone had pried the drawer open.

"Was the desk like that when the appraiser looked at it?"

"No." Siebert's voice was gravelly with anger. "We got robbed."

"When was this?"

Siebert pursed his lips, and then his gaze found Jake's. "A week or two after the liquor store."

The news sent a shot of adrenaline through Jake. This was not a coincidence. Someone had come looking for the document.

He kept his voice steady as he asked Siebert about the robbery. Siebert told him it had happened one night while they were out of town visiting family. Not much was taken—some cash in a sock drawer, some jewelry, a couple watches. Jake detected no deception, but Siebert still said nothing about the document.

"Where did you get the desk?"

"My wife bought it at an auction out at the county fairgrounds. That was a couple months before I took it to be looked at. Old office equipment and furniture and junk like that."

The original owner's identity might shine some light on this. Erin could track down the auction details.

"It's a shame they damaged it," Jake said.

"I only locked that drawer because it had a lock on it. So of course the robbers broke it open." Siebert gazed at the desk with a wistful smile. "They ruined it."

"What did they get out of the drawer?"

"There was nothing in it."

"I heard the appraiser found a document in it."

Siebert looked at Jake, then back at the desk. "Well, that's right. He found it in that tray in the bottom of the drawer."

"Do you still have it?"

"If I did, it would still be in the desk." He shrugged. "Maybe I tossed it."

No deception. If Silva had taken the document from Siebert that night at the liquor store, or even mentioned it, Siebert would remember. Shame had burned every detail of that night into his memory.

"Do you remember what the document said?"

Siebert's mouth twisted, and his gaze drifted as he searched for a memory. He shook his head. "I don't."

"Did you report the burglary?"

Siebert leaned against the desk and shook his head.

"Back to the liquor store," Jake said, watching Siebert carefully. "Did they search your car? Go through your pockets?"

"They just took the wine and my money." Siebert's gaze held firm, his hands still. Then he pulled the cord, plunging them into darkness softened by light spilling in from the other room. "Do you think those three guys were after the document?"

"I don't," Jake said. "But because these things all happened around the same time—you being on TV, the liquor store, and the robbery here—procedure requires me to consider them together."

"Nobody in that parking lot said a word about the desk or that paper."

Jake detected no deception.

"Well," Jake said, "thank you for your time. Sorry about interrupting your dinner."

"It's not a problem. I'll walk you out."

Siebert led Jake back they way they'd come. The platters of food were mostly empty now, the boys shoveling in the last bites on their plates. Linda and Annie were done and waiting. The plate at the head of the table was covered in foil.

"Dad?" Annie stood from the table. "We heard through the vents what you guys were talking about." She gestured toward the floor. "I know something about the paper in the drawer."

Bingo.

Siebert motioned for Annie to come with them, and they went back into the study room. Jake took his old chair and Siebert his. Annie sat beside her father and gave him a smile, and he put a hand on her shoulder. The obvious affection between them struck a hollow spot of longing in Jake's heart.

He cleared his throat and got to work. "When did you see it, Annie?"

"Right after the guy from the TV show found it. The next day, I think." Annie pressed her hands together, then sandwiched them between her thighs. "When I scanned it into the computer."

Jake scooted forward on his chair. Annie pulled her hands from between her thighs and brushed her hair behind her ears. Her smile spread—she was happy to be helpful.

"You scanned it?"

"We'd just gotten our first scanner, and I was trying to figure out how it worked. The pages were there on the desk—it was here in the study room, except back then it was Dad's office. So I tried it out."

"Did you save the scan?" A buzz shot up Jake's spine at the possibility.

Annie shook her head. "That computer died a couple years ago. We lost everything." She looked at her dad. "Remember?"

"Hell, we don't even have that scanner anymore. Technology ages faster than I do."

"What do you remember about it, Annie?" Jake asked.

"It said 'inventory' on the top and had a long list of things on it with quantities. Fifty of this, a hundred of that."

"What kinds of things?"

"Coins," Siebert blurted. "I just remembered the appraiser said it was coins."

"Why would he have to tell you it was coins?"

"Well, it didn't list 'one hundred quarters' or anything like that. It used the name of the coin and the date."

"Like Buffalo nickels and Mercury dimes?"

Siebert frowned. "I've heard of those. But these had names like…" He squeezed his eyes shut, then snapped his fingers. "Double Eagle. That was one. And Saint something."

Jake had watched enough westerns to know a Double Eagle was a gold coin. "Does that sound familiar, Annie?"

"I'm sorry, but I don't remember that."

"But it said—"

Siebert interrupted. "You're more interested in this piece of paper than the guys who robbed me."

"Just covering all the bases, Mr. Siebert." Jake realized his questions, and his posture, were getting pointed and aggressive. He leaned back in his chair. "So the inventory was for a store or a museum?"

"No, it had a man's name on top of it. I remember the last name because it's the same as the park next to school. Sublett. The first name was Bible-sounding."

Every kid in Weston knew the Sublett name from elementary school trips to the Weston Settlement Living History Museum. They were a founding family, and the name was on that park, as well as on a middle school on the south side. But the family had one more recent member. "Was it Jedidiah Sublett?"

Annie smiled. "That sounds right."

"Did you recognize the name, Paul?" Jake eyed Siebert carefully, watching for deceptive behaviors.

"I didn't. We'd only just moved here. Now I know it, of course."

No deception.

Jake thanked both Annie and her father, and Siebert walked him to the door. Jake felt good about this interview—he'd gotten far more than he could have hoped. He now knew Bull was after a list of gold coins owned by Jedidiah Sublett. A list he'd been after for at least five years. A list Bull thought Silva had with him when the car went into the river—but which was so potentially damaging that Bull had ordered Hogan to search Siebert's house and Silva's shop just in case. But he'd never found it. If he had, he wouldn't still have Jansen searching through the car.

And he wouldn't have Hogan following Jake.

What would Hogan do if he thought I found it?

When he figured out the connections between the players—Bull and Silva, and now Sublett—he would know why the list was important.

And then the whole case would unfold like a flower opening.

CHAPTER FORTY-EIGHT

As Bev walked down the hospice's hall, her desire to see her dad grew into a need to confront him so strong her heart started racing. Even the chilly air conditioning failed to cool the heat burning off her.

She would ask him about the coins flat out. And insist he answer.

Her steps were a fast *thft-thft-thft* down the carpeted hallway. She slowed as she approached his door, preparing herself, then paused in the opening.

The mask covered the lower half of his face; air hissed out around it, and the machine chunked away in the corner. He was so completely still, she feared he was already gone. She squeezed her grief into a tight ball and swallowed it down.

Then his chest rose with a wet stuttering breath. After a pause, it fell and rose again and settled into a steady rhythm.

Bev's body unclenched, her anger dissolving so fast she felt like a balloon deflating.

"It's like that."

Bev flinched. The voice came from the chair in the corner by the air machine. A nurse in pink scrubs with a magazine on her lap.

"What's like that?"

"He doesn't breathe for a bit. Ten or twenty seconds sometimes. Then he's back to normal." The nurse stood up, slipped the magazine under her arm, and edged toward the door.

"Thank you for sitting with him."

"I'll leave you alone." The nurse lowered her head and ducked out, leaving the door wide open.

Bev swung it closed and pushed until it latched. She circled the bed, frowning at the reflection in the window: a middle-aged woman with hunched shoulders and a purse so large it could hold a cat, her dad's shriveled form huddled under blankets on the bed behind her.

He lifted his head, and his eyes tracked her. She turned from the window and came to his side, bending to get her face close to his.

"Hi, Dad." She dropped her bag on the floor, grabbed his hand, and reached out to stroke his head. His scalp was cool and rough with stubble. A tear started to pool in her eye, and she blinked it away. "I'm sorry I couldn't stay away like you wanted. But... well... you're my dad."

"And you're my baby girl." The mask and hissing air muffled his voice, and she had to strain to hear it. "Sorry about the morphine. I just—"

"It's okay." She stroked his head, love flooding through her, refilling the spaces the departing anger had left open within her.

He was quiet, his breath burbling slow but steady, his eyes open and on hers. She dragged the chair over from the corner and sat holding his hand and watching him.

His eyes closed. After a few minutes, his breathing stopped. She reached for the nurse button, dangling below the bed on its thick cord, and held it—but she didn't push it. If this was it, she was with him, and he was comfortable.

She released the device, and it swung away from her.

Then he was breathing again. He opened his eyes. They crinkled, but the rest of his smile was hidden behind the oxygen mask.

"Case?"

She forced a smile. "Weston's turning it over tomorrow at five."

"Good." His eyes drooped closed. "… deserved what he got."

She missed the beginning of that. "Who did, Dad?"

"Silva." He barked it out. "Shouldn't have held out on me."

Her head reeled, and she grabbed the bed's side rail with her free hand. *Held out on me.* Her dad had admitted to hiring Silva to get the document—but maybe when Silva saw what was written on it, he recognized the power of it and used it to blackmail him. Motive. Why hadn't she seen it?

Because you didn't wanted to see it.

As simple as that.

"I've got this, Dad. We'll get this Sublett issue behind us." Had the morphine opened him enough to tell her about the document? "What document should I be looking for?"

"I was going to give it all back." He coughed and went still. Only the weak rise of his chest told her he was still there.

"It's okay, Dad." She stroked his lumpy head. "I'm sure you would have."

She would finish this. For him. Whatever it took.

CHAPTER FORTY-NINE

Jake ignored Hogan tailing him as he drove back to the apartment. It was full dark now, the night air cool as it rushed through his open windows and over his skin. He parked in the alley and checked his phone as he plodded up the hot stairwell. He had one text, from Hogan—setting their meeting for ten the next morning at the sheriff's department.

Jake unloaded his equipment onto the kitchen counter, heated up a can of chili, and dumped it over some brown rice he'd cooked a few days before. He ate while he flipped through the sports page. Then he sat in the recliner by the front window and called Callie.

She answered on a half-ring. "I'm glad you called," she said. "I've got some info on Morgan. His neighbors love him, but I heard stories about him shutting down a loud party and catching some guy who'd been stealing neighborhood Amazon packages."

"So he's protective," Jake said.

"Exactly. Maybe he's feeling protective of Vicky Silva."

And maybe he had been in 2012, too. Jake rolled that around, but it didn't catch.

"Any prints or usable trace on my car?"

"I'll get to that. I stopped by Silva's and talked to the wife."

"You're only working on Morgan."

"Vicky Silva knows him and lives in the neighborhood, and he works in her back yard. Anyway. She said he used to be like her husband's shop mascot, always following Donald around in the barn. A scarecrow of a guy always lurking. Then he joined the army and came back a man. She is *very* impressed with his transformation."

"You sound like you think there's something between them."

"Not yet, but there will be. I think she rented him the barn to keep him close. For when she was ready."

"You're stretching things," Jake said. But maybe not by much. Morgan's interest in Vicky Silva was more than neighborly.

"Just interpreting what I heard and observed. Now about your car. No prints or trace. We do have video showing a man wearing black crawling under the car. Big enough to be Morgan, but that's all I can say. But I'm not done. I'm heading over to interview him right now."

"Let me know how it goes. But I called about something else."

"Help with the case?"

"No."

A muffled shout sounded from outside. Jake looked through the blinds to see a pack of teenagers on the sidewalk in front of Dora's. Pushing and laughing.

"Friends again?" Callie asked.

He wanted that, sure. But not "friends" like they'd been until a few days ago. And not like they'd been before that, either: two co-workers who went their separate ways at the end of the day. He wanted real friendship. But that wasn't why he'd called.

"I'm calling you as my union rep."

"Really? I haven't received notice of a beef."

"It's complicated." He told her about his encounter with Woodling.

"That's just two days ago!"

"And Professional Standards called me in for a sit-down tomorrow."

The teens screamed again. Jake adjusted the blinds so he could watch them. Cop instincts.

"Without any investigation? What about our written notices and—"

"A reporter said there's no paper record of the complaint at the sheriff's department."

"There's something you're not telling me."

"Nothing you need to know for tomorrow," he said. "At ten. In the sheriff's office."

"Okay. You are *not* required to be there, so I'll take the meeting alone. Straighten them out. But I'll want the whole story eventually."

Jake remained silent.

She sighed. "Okay, Jake. And I'm sorry about... us."

As Jake hung up, the word "us" was a fuzzy echo in his head. That was as close as she'd ever come to describing what had gone on between them as a relationship. Could that morph into friendship? He couldn't envision it. Not yet. He'd have to let it go, and see what developed.

He scanned the street below. The teens had moved on, and everything was quiet.

He decided to wait on the murder book and first see what the Weston Historical Society could tell him about Jedidiah Sublett. He found a slew of entries when he searched the name, including a detailed biography that ran on and on. The family came to town within a year of Weston's founding and immediately became a big player in land speculation. They also developed the gravel pit that became Centennial Beach, and they owned a brewery. The family grew and then, within a single generation, petered out. Jedidiah was the last surviving member. He was extremely generous with his family's wealth during his lifetime before dying alone and without heirs in 1983.

The entry Jake was looking for was smack in the middle of the long scroll. Sublett had inherited a collection of gold coins from an uncle.

There was nothing more about the collection in any document in the archive.

So what happened to the gold coins when Sublett died?

Jake remembered enough from law school to know all estates over a certain dollar amount had to go through a court-administered probate process. He searched his way to the county probate records and found a listing for Sublett, but the only information provided online were the docket entries describing courtroom events and documents filed. He spent a few minutes on them, but couldn't make much sense out of it all. He wasn't familiar with this area of legal jargon.

But Coogan was a native speaker.

He thought about calling Coogan right then, but his friend was an early-to-bed, early-to-rise kind of guy. Jake would enlist his friend's help tomorrow.

He flipped through his notebook to prepare for updating the murder book, but the vast majority of what he'd learned since his last update pointed at Bull and Bev—and if he put it in the book, he'd be yanked off the case. Then the truth might never come out.

He considered what to do. Leaving out material facts was as bad as filling the murder book with lies. Sure, he'd left out facts already when he didn't report that information was missing from the online incident report—but that was only because he'd thought the omissions were data entry errors. That was defensible. This was different. The facts about Bull were real, material facts. He should report them. But he honestly couldn't believe Bull had killed the three men.

Even as he made the argument to himself, it made his gut burn, and not just because it was a self-serving rationalization, but also because he wasn't sure he believed in his uncle's innocence anymore. And he had to know—for sure—one way or another. He had to know if his uncle was a triple murderer. He had to know if he was right that Bev was only in it to help her dad. So he had to stay on the case.

If the truth was that Bull killed these three men, he'd put it all in there. Until he knew the truth, it would have to stay out.

He picked up the laptop, opened the murder book, and entered the few facts he'd learned that didn't point at his family: what he'd found at the shop, that Graves was little Donny's birth father, the type of fracture in Silva's neck, and the rock and the rosary.

When he was done, he set the laptop on the floor and cracked the window to listen to the sounds of his community. When he first moved back to Weston, it had been more about coming home than about the job as lead Major Crimes detective. About reconnecting with his old friends and with the places where he'd always felt so comfortable. About rejoining his family, the Warrens.

Ten years later, he had to admit that most of what he'd hoped for had failed.

Most of his old friends had moved away. Coogan and Erin and Henry were still here, but all three were busy with their own lives. And the places he remembered were either gone or different. Most of downtown had changed hands as rising real estate prices drove out the old stores for national franchises like Starbucks and Eddie Bauer. Most houses close to downtown had been replaced by lot-bursting mini-mansions.

And his family was still controlled by Bull Warren. Jake had never understood the animosity between his dad and Bull. His dad waved it off when Jake asked, saying Bull was just an ass and there was nothing more to it. Jake could agree Bull was an ass, but he'd always felt there was something more substantial behind the enmity. He considered calling his dad down in Scottsdale, but talking about Bull would just make him angry, and he deserved the peaceful life he'd made for himself down there.

Jake jumped up from the chair, his mental agitation vibrating his muscles into activity. He needed to do something. He'd go for a run.

The night air was clean and refreshing. He took the Riverwalk west, dodging people working off their dinners and walking their dogs. Their numbers dropped as he passed Centennial Beach and were down to nothing once he crossed the river on the Jefferson Avenue bridge and went north on the Paget River Trail. He increased his pace, hoping the exertion would clear his mind: of the case, of his family, and of Callie. He sped under the Burlington Railroad bridge and pounded up the hill into Radar Grove before finally turning around and starting back. His heart was pumping and his mind was almost clear. His pounding pulse drowned out the burbling river. Back under the railroad bridge and down the blacktop path, then across the river again.

As he ducked in front of two men about to enter the Riverwalk from the opposite direction, their German shepherd made a hard lunge for him and came up short against his leash. Jake didn't break stride. But moments later, when the path dropped down closer to the riverbank, Callie came suddenly to mind—and that made his stride falter. Maybe friends with benefits was enough? Maybe she knew he didn't really have more than that in him. She wouldn't be the first woman who knew him better than he knew himself. Mary had often laughed before he even started one of his lame jokes, reading him and the situation so well she knew exactly which joke was coming. After ten years of working together and a life-long friendship, Erin could now read him almost that well.

As the path edged between the bluff and the river Jake caught motion in his peripheral vision. That dog must have gotten loose. He landed hard on his right leg to slow down, and turned toward the motion, hands up, ready to fight off the dog.

"Umph!" Impact to his chest drove Jake sideways, his head whiplashing. He hit the ground with a weight on top of him.

It wasn't the dog.

Jake and his attacker rolled off the brick path and down the slope toward the river, picking up speed. Jake fought his hands between them and pushed, then *whump*—their progress stopped, the attacker yelling with pain. With a creak and a crack, the sapling that had momentarily arrested their plummet snapped, and both men dropped into the river.

Jake shouted, the fall and the water stunning him. He flipped over, hands and knees digging into the mud, and got to his feet, the water just over his knees. He was alone. He spun, his feet dragging in the mud, and was hit again, a shoulder in his back, a hand driving his head underwater. He pushed off the bottom, spinning and torquing his body, and dislodged himself from his attacker.

"Hey!" A voice from the bank.

Splashing. Jake sat up, the water mid-chest.

"He's running away!"

A dog barked in a long angry stream.

Jake followed the sound of splashing and found the attacker. A big man wearing black, taking big loping strides toward the opposite bank, the water spraying off his thrusting feet and sparkling in the illumination from the lights on the bridge.

Jake stood up, wincing at a pain shooting from his lower back down his right leg. He moved to give chase, but almost immediately collapsed into the river, his leg failing him. Instead he lifted his head and watched the man, hoping to identify him. The man passed through a sliver of light—he was big, dressed in all black, thick body.

Hogan.

Or Lace.

The man scrambled up the bank and disappeared into the underbrush, the crack and snap of his movement away from the river clear in the stillness.

"You okay?"

The two men and the German shepherd. The taller man pulled the dog tight up against his leg, and its barks cut off into a hoarse rasp, then stopped. It still strained against the leash though, its hind end quivering.

"I'm fine." Jake stood up, another jolt of pain shooting down his leg.

"You want us to call the police?"

"I am the police."

Jake knew this pain. The nerve along his sacroiliac joint. The worst of it would fade fast, but it would leave behind a debilitating soreness that could last for days or longer. He sloshed toward the bank, one hand rubbing at the sac joint, kneading the flesh all around the knob in his lower back. As he reached the bank, one of the men came down and helped him up the embankment. Jake almost pulled him into the water when he slipped to a knee. A gasp of pain burst from him.

"I can call an ambulance."

"No." Jake stood on the path, water dripping onto the bricks, mud sliding off his knee to pool on his shoe. "I'll handle it. Personal matter."

"You want me to pull my car up and give you a ride home at least?"

"I'm fine, guys."

"You sure?"

"Yes!" Jake turned away from them and hobbled back up toward the road. His place was almost a straight shot down Jefferson, so the sidewalk would save him a quarter mile over the brick path. He moved slowly, slightly hunched, rubbing the knobby joint, wincing and gasping. The cool night air on his wet clothes chilled the pain-induced heat pouring off him.

Within a block he was walking nearly upright. Another block and the pain had pulled back to within a few inches of the joint, shooting down his leg when he took an awkward step on the uneven bricks. He paused and did some stretches, bringing his knee to his chest and holding it there. He was almost home before the pain had subsided enough for him to consider what had happened.

First the car, now this.

Bull was playing hardball.

It wasn't going to stop Jake.

He struggled up the stairs to his apartment, took three over-the-counter naproxen, dropped his muddy clothes in a heap on the bathroom floor, and got in the shower. He took his time there, stretching and flexing and massaging.

The painkiller and heat flushed the tension from him, and he was out almost as soon as he crawled into bed.

* * *

He woke fully at 1:47 a.m., his mind dark with thoughts of Royce Fletcher, his sheets soaked with sweat. He lay awake, trying to focus on what had really happened in that alley, but the reality was still so mixed up with his union rep's suggestions that he couldn't find his way to the truth.

As he got up, pain shot through his right buttock before fading to a pulsing ache. He splashed some cold water on his face, wiped the sweat off with a towel, and put on his robe. He'd be awake for a few hours and might as well use the time. He set his heating pad up at the recliner and settled in with the laptop.

The story Erin had told him about the abduction and murder of Siebert's son made Jake wonder how that experience had affected Siebert. Maybe he had blamed his son for not fighting back against his abductor, and when he himself failed to fight back in that parking lot, that had amplified his shame.

Jake pulled up a search window and googled the abduction. A St. Louis paper reported it first, followed by the daily papers in Champaign and Springfield, before the *Chicago Tribune* finally picked up the story. The family had lived in

Mount Logan. The son, Mark, was an industrious kid delivering penny-savers to earn money to buy a computer. He hauled his papers in a wagon. One day he disappeared halfway through his route.

The local police department started out treating the case as a runaway, probably because they'd never handled a child abduction and couldn't admit what they had. In the early news stories, Paul and Linda were supportive of the Mount Logan police department and stood next to the chief at press conferences where the man asked the community for help finding "the runaway." But within a few days, the chief was alone at the podium, and the Siebert quotes came from ever more distant relatives.

Two months later a vagrant confessed to abducting and killing the boy and hiding his body in the national forest. They never found Mark's body, despite repeated trips to the forest with the confessed killer and thousands of man-hours searching the giant area.

The typical anniversary follow-up articles questioned the confession, but the local authorities never wavered: the vagrant was the right guy. Paul and Linda always refused to be interviewed. Jake didn't blame them for withdrawing into their grief. He'd felt the same when his wife was killed. And he could understand their anger. Anyone who watched cop shows knew the first few days were the most critical. The Mount Logan police wasted those days on a runaway scenario, with nothing to support it except fear of the truth.

Jake shut down his computer and went back to bed.

Wondering, as he drifted off, whether he'd locked the front door.

CHAPTER FIFTY

When Jake's alarm went off, he woke as if rising from the deep, his brain slowly booting up until he could open his eyes and look at the clock: 7:01 a.m. He rolled onto his back, rubbing at a sudden pain at the top of his right buttock.

The river.

The memory pumped angry heat through him. If his attacker thought that would scare him off the case, he was in for a surprise.

But Jake had only until five o'clock—ten short hours—to find the truth. If he didn't, he would forever wonder whether Bull had been involved in killing the three men.

He would make the most of his day.

He swung his legs off the bed and got moving. After downing two more naproxen, he spent twenty minutes stretching and a half hour under a hot shower before he felt loose enough to handle the day ahead of him. He flipped through the *Tribune* while he ate a bowl of microwave oatmeal. He found a short piece on the case by the reporter who had called him, but nothing about the Woodling complaint. The article, *Scouts Find More Than Bargained For*, said three bodies were found in a Paget County park and quoted an unnamed source in the sheriff's office speculating it was a murder-suicide.

Jake equipped himself and descended the stairs, one hand on the railing, his right leg trembling with each step. The cool in the long shadows outside was already losing the battle against the heat from the rising sun. He lumbered off on foot, waiting for a long break in traffic before shuffling across the street. He needed to talk to Coogan. He was sure something in the Sublett probate file would unlock the secret the inventory held, and Coog was the key to understanding the probate file.

As Jake rounded the corner onto Jackson, his phone shuddered in his pocket. Callie.

"What's up?"

"I went to talk to Morgan last night. Lace. He's one of those guys knows his rights. Made me stand on the front stoop. He's a big bastard, too. Stood in the doorway looking down on me. I asked him where he was when we got the big man on video in your alley, and we went back and forth on that for ten minutes before he finally said he was at home. Alone, of course."

"So it could have been him."

"He gave me such a bad feeling I staked him out. All the good it did me."

"What happened?"

"He took off on his motorcycle. He must have spotted me, because he ducked into that park north of his house, rode across the pedestrian bridge over the river, and disappeared up the Paget River Trail. Probably came out on Butterfield."

"What was he wearing?"

"Wearing? All black, like most bikers. Why?"

"Curious. Thanks, Callie." He hung up before she could probe him any deeper.

Big man wearing black. It could have been Lace, both at the river and in the alley cutting the Crown Vic's brakes. Protecting Vicky Silva. He had coveted Donald Silva's life—the business, the wife, and the child. He could have killed Silva, too, to get a clear shot at his wife. But if that were true, why did Lace leave town right after it happened? And he'd been just a boy back then. Silva's mascot.

No. It was Hogan. Jake shot a quick look behind him, but he was alone. Hogan was probably getting ready for their morning meeting and would figure Jake was doing the same. Jake was almost sorry he wouldn't be there to see Callie lay into the man.

He used the side entrance to Coogan's ancient building and took his time climbing the creaking stairs, favoring his right leg. The movement was loosening it, but it was still sore.

Coogan's outer door was unlocked, and Jake pushed through into the reception area.

"Hey, Jake." Jennifer looked up from her desk, a hand keeping her place in a stack of paper. Her eyes shot to the closed door to Coogan's office. "He's in with clients." She lowered her voice. "A will signing. Should only be a few minutes."

"How's Declan?"

Her face lit up. "Perfect."

"And his daddy?"

"Robbie just deployed to South Korea."

"Does he keep asking?"

"Of course," she laughed. "Told him we had to be face-to-face for marriage talk."

She had work to do, so Jake let her get back to it. He sat in a waiting-room chair and tried to distract himself with a golf magazine, but he didn't play golf and was too juiced to read. Jake knew that despite what Jennifer had said, this could take more than a few minutes. Coogan liked to take his time and give each client a personal touch. And Jake's leg was going numb, so he got up and paced the small area, warming the muscles, hoping they'd stay loose enough to keep moving.

He decided there was something he could do with his time—something he should have done already.

"Can I use the conference room?"

"Sure. If you want coffee, there's a pot on in the kitchen."

Jake got himself a cup of the Hawaiian Jenny had brewed and took it to the conference room. The place was classic lawyer—dark paneling, a huge glossy table, a wall of law books in matching covers. Three windows looked across Jackson to the Riverwalk. Jake set his coffee down then stood facing the middle window as he made the call, lifting and lowering his right leg, left hand on the window frame.

"Good morning, Jake."

He couldn't help but smile at the sound of Bev's voice. They'd been tight as kids, playing together at every family function.

"Hey, Bev." He'd called to give her a chance to explain, but now he hesitated.

"What can I do for you?"

"Your Deputy Hogan has me coming up there for a meeting this morning."

"Yes."

"Am I on speaker?" He'd heard an odd echo behind her words.

"Yes, but I'm alone in my car. Why did you call?"

"Are you going to be there? Looking out for your kissing cousin?" They'd shared their first kiss in sixth grade. Nothing romantic about it, just two kids experimenting.

"Jake!" He'd got her with that, but she cut her amusement short. "I'm the reason you're getting the chance to jump on this so quickly and kill it before it gets serious."

"Too quickly," he said.

"What do you mean?"

"Bev…" He didn't want to go any further. "How's your dad doing?"

"He's a fighter. You know Bull."

"Not really." Jake cleared his throat. "I *am* sorry he's going through this, Bev. Before it fell apart between our dads, I liked the old guy."

"Thanks, Jake."

"I am going to solve this case."

"Your mayor would prefer that you didn't."

"Jurisdiction. Statistics. Media." He paused to give her a chance to say something, but she was silent. "The Woodling complaint. You've left nothing out."

"You're out of time."

"So why cut my brake lines? And why last night?"

A long silence, then: "What are you talking about?"

Now Jake paused, not wanting to take his accusation any further. He wanted to believe she'd had nothing to do with it. That it was her dad and Hogan and that she was still, at some level, a friend. He reversed course.

"I've got all day," he said.

"My investigators can handle this case as well as you can."

"But would they get a chance to? Sounds like you've already decided it's a murder-suicide without asking anyone a single question."

"No decision has been made. We will investigate."

"Tell Hogan I'm going to miss seeing him in my rearview mirror when this is over."

He ended the call, then picked up his coffee and sipped. Bev had confirmed she was directing the Woodling complaint—a scheme to delay his investigation. But she couldn't have been involved in the murders herself or the attacks on him. Maybe Bull, but not Bev.

That had to be true.

* * *

Bev sat in her car thinking about what Jake said until the heat of the morning sun forced her to go inside. She deflected a dozen greetings and several people asking about her dad as she walked to her office. She told her assistant to cancel her appointments and hold her calls, then retreated behind her closed door.

Hogan had been so sure Jake hadn't seen him following. Did it matter that Jake had spotted him? What could he do with it? She could claim it was for the investigation into the Woodling complaint. If that failed, she could claim she had Hogan keeping an eye on an investigation she knew she'd be taking over. Both were plausible, and that was good enough to defend herself.

But Jake's remark about cut brake lines, and something that had happened last night... Bev couldn't shake it. It could be unrelated; that was possible. Jake handled all Weston's major cases and was the city's representative on the Paget County Opioid Task Force—lots of bad guys owed him for their time in prison. Any one of them could try for revenge at any time. But that called for too much coincidence. Her stomach flopped, and she clutched her abdominal muscles against it. Had her offhand comment about slowing Jake down incited Hogan into action? Or had her dad ordered Hogan to do it behind her back?

Her eye caught the picture on her credenza, pulling her thoughts back to her dad. She had called Edgar Hospice first thing this morning and learned her dad had had a "good night." The phrase had surprised her after what the doctor said morphine would do to her dad.

She spun her chair to look out the window. Should she be here, or there with him?

Here, she might be able to do something about Jake. *Doing* was one of her dad's mantras—when in doubt, do something. Jake had until end of business, and she had to make sure he wasted the day without finding anything concrete. The meeting with Hogan was a good start. If it flustered Jake badly enough, he'd spend the rest of the day locked up for hitting Woodling or hiring a lawyer to defend him against the complaint.

But she couldn't count on that. She needed to stay at her desk and be available as the day unfolded. She would rein

Hogan in and find ways to keep Jake away from her dad. So far he didn't have enough to prove her dad had done anything, much less murder three men.

She was sure her dad hadn't done *that*. He used favors and debts and coercion, not violence. His secret files proved that. But even if he had stuck to his favorite tools, that might not save him. In Illinois, the criminal code said that if someone put a felony in motion and it resulted in a death, the instigator was guilty of murder, even when he didn't do the killing himself. Even if he wasn't present at the scene. Her dad said he hired Silva to steal the document. If that theft resulted in the three deaths, then her dad could be charged with three murders.

Shit.

CHAPTER FIFTY-ONE

Bull heard the *thwump-thwump* first, pulsing in, fading away, then finally holding steady. Behind its rhythm the hiss rose and expanded until it filled his head with a cloud of fuzz.

That goddamn air machine.

He ground his teeth, then—

His eyes snapped open. Sunlight. Motes floating. Voices in the hall. He flopped his head over to look that way and blinked until he found focus. Orderlies delivering breakfast.

"I'm still alive." His voice was hoarse and scratchy and dull behind the air mask.

One of the orderlies broke away from the group and stepped into the room. "How ya feeling this morning, Bull?"

A wiry little guy who moved in twitches. Lenny. His dad had been a bartender at the VFW for fifty years until he killed himself last year. Lenny was good people.

"Fine," Bull grunted.

"Let's sit you up a little higher."

Lenny powered up the head of the bed, rearranged the pillows, and adjusted the table. Bull reflexively rubbed his stomach where it always hurt when they folded him like this, but there was no pain to rub at.

Lenny pushed the table so it spanned the bed, slid Bull's things to one end, and brought a breakfast tray in from a cart in the hall. Oatmeal, OJ, toast, and yogurt. Too much damn food.

Bull watched, a fog around the edges of his perception. The morphine.

"You probably aren't hungry because of the morphine, but if you can eat you'll be better for it. Want me to help you?"

"I'm good, Lenny." Bull picked up the spoon and got to work on the oatmeal. He'd been eating it every day his entire life. It wasn't easy with the oxygen mask, but he found a rhythm. Pull the mask aside, shovel it in. Put the mask back. Chew.

Lenny watched him eat a few bites, then twitched away.

Bull was struggling with the OJ's foil cover when another figure appeared in his doorway.

"Mr. Warren! Glad to see you eating! How are you feeling?" Nurse Hart. She thought everyone was deaf. She bustled over, took the OJ out of his hands, opened it with a practiced tug, and held it to his lips. He kept his mouth closed. He could feed himself.

"Just a sip, now." She leaned in and lowered her voice. "I heard about the morphine, so I'm glad to see you eating. Keep your strength up. When Bev calls I'll tell her how well you're doing."

He opened his mouth and drank until it was gone.

"Would you like me to ask Bev to come see you?"

"No!" She would end up sitting here waiting for him to die.

"This afternoon, maybe."

She bustled off, leaving him to finish his breakfast. But he left it alone. He didn't have the energy to crunch his way through the toast, and yogurt was nothing but baby food.

He thumbed the button to flatten the bed and closed his eyes. He felt... good. Better than good. Not even an itch in his gut, and his body loose and his brain fuzzy like he'd had a glass of good red wine.

The morphine had been the right call.

Then his breath turned into a gurgle, and a wet lump blocked his windpipe. He coughed it out, his entire body clenching around the effort. When he started breathing again, a trickle of moisture moved up and down his windpipe as he inhaled and exhaled. It accumulated into a blob, and he had another coughing fit.

The head of the bed rose again. The burbling in his lungs quieted.

"You'll do better with the head up, Bull."

Lenny again.

Bull nodded.

Lenny twitched away, leaving him alone, the bed halfway to vertical. He thumbed the button and brought the knees up so he wouldn't slither down under the covers, then sat, held in place by gravity and the fancy bed, and waited.

His cell phone rang.

Hogan. Wanting advice on his meeting with Houser.

He listened to the boy talk, doubting himself like he sometimes did, and encouraged him the best he could.

"Be tough," Bull said. "It's your meeting. And call Bev."

He held off another cough until he hung up. Then he let his head fall back and closed his eyes.

* * *

Jake walked into Coogan's big corner office to find his lanky friend standing behind his desk tapping a handful of manila folders into an even stack.

"Your case made a splash on the internet news." Coogan slipped the folders into an accordion file that he put on his credenza. He sat, his ancient leather high-back giving a prolonged squeak. "But the suicide angle dampened the original enthusiasm."

"Coog, I need your help."

Jake told Coogan about the inventory of coins Siebert had found, the burglary at his house, and the deleted video at the cable station. "The list had Jedidiah Sublett's name on it, and the historical society database says he owned a collection of gold coins."

"Uncle Jed," Coogan said.

"I need help reading the probate file. You're the expert on—"

Jake's phone buzzed in his pocket: the deputy chief.

"I have to take this." Jake moved to the far end of the office and answered.

"Houser, how come you didn't tell me about this interview with the investigator this morning?" The deputy chief yelled at someone in the background, then came back on the line. "Are you ready for it?"

"Sorry, Deputy Chief." He should have texted Erin; she could have covered it with Braff. "I called in Callie Diggs to rep me."

"Ha!" There was nothing the deputy chief liked better than a tough broad. "Take that, you county bastards! Are you meeting with her now? Let me talk to her for a minute."

"We talked last night, and she's taking the meeting for me."

"Well, that ought to get their panties in a bunch." Braff laughed. "What're you chasing this morning?"

"I need to do some follow-up."

"The deadline stands, Houser. You need to wrap it up."

"Then I better get to it."

"No sass, Houser."

"I'll call by five."

Braff hung up without another word.

Jake turned to find Coogan already standing by the door. "Did I mention the DC put me on the clock?"

"Well then, we better get going."

* * *

Jake's hip and leg were looser as they walked to the car, the pain reducing with every step. Coogan was chewing on his lip, a tell that meant his mind was spinning, so Jake let him think.

Coog started talking as soon as they were in the car. "Head up Winfield to the county complex." He slid his seat back, strapped himself in, and placed his hands on his knees. "The Subletts were a founding family, like your mom's family, the Warrens."

Coogan liked to start his explanations at the beginning, always doubting Jake knew the background well enough to skip it. He was usually right. But not this time.

"I've already read the man's biography." Jake flipped on his seat heater, hoping the warmth would soothe his pain.

"I have a point," Coogan said.

As Jake took Mill Street north and then the curve over to Winfield, Coogan fleshed out the first hundred years of family history. Jake's seat got hot, and his glute and hamstring loosened.

"Both families were heavy speculators in real estate. Between them they owned half the lots on the first town plat. The Subletts got into the brewery business, then sold off most of their city lots and bought the land along the Paget that became the gravel pits and now holds Centennial Beach and the Riverwalk. Your family, the Warrens, stayed in real estate. At their land-owning peak there were three brothers—one of them was your great-grandfather. Your granddad was an only child, and your mom was *his* only child, so you ended up with a full third of the legacy wealth. The other two brothers had nine children between them, and these kids all had multiples of their own. More than half of that generation moved away. Some, like Bev, have stayed. Take a right on Roosevelt and a left on County Farm."

"Enough with the Warrens already," Jake said. Coogan had always loved Warren family history. Maybe because there was so much of it, while Coog's own history was a closed book. His mom was a single parent who had moved here from someplace she would only identify as "out west," with a Nevada birth certificate for Coogan that listed his father as unknown.

"A comparison, for background." Coogan didn't like interruptions when expounding. "Jedidiah was the last surviving Sublett and the only one alive after about 1940. Everything the family owned became his, and he never had a wife or kids. Over his lifetime he gifted most of his family's real estate to the city, designating it as open space or parkland, and he dedicated most of his cash wealth to turning the old sanitarium into what we now call Edgar Hospital."

"Why not Sublett Hospital?" Jake flexed his glutes and rocked his hips in the tight bucket seat. Much better.

"James Edgar was his best friend and live-in assistant." Coogan shot a look at Jake. "If you know what I mean."

"They were a closeted couple?"

"Historical society speculation, but it seems likely." Coogan shrugged. "We're going to the county archives on Manchester west of County Farm." He illustrated his directions with hand motions, but Jake knew the way.

"Get to your point," Jake said.

"Although Sublett gave away all the family's real estate and most of its money during his lifetime, he did keep the old house, and he had personal possessions when he died without heirs in 1983."

He went silent.

Jake bit. "Are you going to make your point now?"

"My point is this: in a will, personal property is often listed in an attached *inventory*."

CHAPTER FIFTY-TWO

Hogan set up in the conference room ten minutes early. A cup of coffee for himself and nothing for Houser.

He sat with the two folders in front of him. The manila folder held the written report, and the blue folder held the photos. It was the same color scheme the Weston Police Department used for its case folders. He slid the blue folder to the side and squared it up to the table edge, then sat back. He reached out and tapped it.

"Good."

He slid the blue folder in an arc toward the chair Houser would sit in, then yanked it toward himself. "He won't be able to keep his eyes off it."

He opened it and went through the pictures one more time. The first series showed Woodling's face. The top photo showed the wound puckered open by the swelling on top. He found the one showing the sutures squeezing the flesh closed and the bruising that had already begun. He put it second. Other photos showed Woodling's wrists. The zip cuffs' squared-off edges had chewed the man's wrists to hamburger.

"What an idiot."

The clock on the opposite wall hit ten, and the minute hand slowly edged past the hour. He checked his digital recorder and centered it on the table, then squared the folders once more.

Finally the door swung open, and a curvy black woman in a tight-fitting linen suit burst in.

"I am Callie Diggs. Here representing Detective Houser." Her voice echoed against the bare walls. "I assume *you* are Deputy Hogan."

Hogan slumped in his chair. "Good, uh… morning."

She pulled out the chair across from him and slid into it, hooking her bag over the back and pulling out a legal pad in the same fluid motion. She set the pad in front of her, the top page blank. "I'm here to represent Detective Houser in this inquiry."

"Okay," Hogan said. He licked his lips and wiped his brow.

"I'm here whether it's okay with you or not." She placed her hands on the legal pad and laced her fingers. "My presence is his right and not subject to your approval."

"Where is Detective Houser?"

"He is *not* required to be here." She flashed a smile and pulled a pen out of an inside blazer pocket. "Pursuant to our collective bargaining agreement, Detective Houser is only required to attend disciplinary meetings where his testimony will be taken, and then only on seventy-two hours' written notice." She tapped her pen on the table. "Here, there was no written notice of any kind and barely twelve hours' oral notice. You get to talk with me, or you can read the rules and follow them."

"I see." Hogan cast his gaze around the room, then came back to Diggs. He sat straighter, hands against the table edge. "I'm surprised the detective didn't see the importance of this opportunity to set the record straight. Maybe his priorities aren't in order."

"*His* priorities?" Diggs clicked her pen and wrote a large number 3 on her pad, a vertical line, and another number 3. She held the pad up and pointed at the left 3. "This is the number of murders Detective Houser is trying to solve. Some people are already calling it a mass murder. The first in the city's history."

"My understanding is it's a murder-suicide," Hogan said.

"Oh? I wasn't aware this was your case already. Or did Detective Houser reach a conclusion and forget to tell me?"

Hogan kept his mouth shut.

Diggs pointed to the 3 on the right. "This is the number of Mr. Woodling's felony arrests. All three involve violence." She put down her pad and pen.

"Ms. Diggs," Hogan said, "although discrediting the witness is a favorite tactic of criminal defense attorneys, just because someone has a history of violent behavior doesn't mean he instigated a violent encounter. In court, Mr. Houser's counsel won't be able to bring that up." He smiled and gave a small nod to himself. "None of those arrests are for anything involving dishonesty, so they can't be used to impeach his general credibility."

"Let's get into the complaint itself." Diggs's hand darted across the table and snagged the manila folder. She flipped the cover open and smoothed her fingers over the complaint form.

Hogan just stared. She had moved too fast for him to do anything else.

"I see the date and time of the alleged encounter between Detective Houser and Woodling." She looked up at Hogan and smiled. "But I see blanks where it should say the date and time of the complaint itself." She held up the page and waved it at him. "It doesn't even say how you got the complaint. That box is empty."

"It also isn't signed, Miss Diggs. We were trying to keep this from becoming a formal investigation. That's why I invited Detective Houser here to explain it."

Diggs leaned back and gave him a hard stare. "This is informal, huh?" She pointed at the recorder. "That's why you're recording it and we're meeting in the sheriff's HQ?"

Hogan smiled and stood. "I'm going to refill my coffee. Can I get you anything?"

Diggs smirked and declined.

Hogan grabbed his coffee cup and left her alone. In the hallway, he ducked into the viewing room to watch her on the remote camera. She had pulled out her phone, and the flash of its camera pulsed brightly. That complaint was now written in stone.

He pulled out his cell phone and called the sheriff.

* * *

"I was about to call you," Bev said. She'd been waiting at her desk for something to happen, and it had. "We have a problem."

"Here, too." Hogan sighed.

"What?"

"Houser didn't show. Sent his union rep. You know Diggs? That... one. She's spouting off about wasting Houser's time while he's investigating a mass murder."

"Callie said mass murder?" The media loved Callie Diggs, and she looked amazing on camera. If she gave that sound bite it would light a fire under the press.

"How do you want me to play this?"

"Listen to her. Act like you're taking it all in. Then tell her you'll investigate further and get back to her."

"I'll do what I can. She's... never mind. I'll get it done."

"We have a bigger problem." She told him about the text she'd just received from one of her dad's people, telling her that attorney Bill Coogan had requested the Sublett probate file at the archives. Everyone knew Coogan was Jake's best friend, so he was obviously there for Jake. "Jake's probably with him since he's not with you. Get over there and see what they're up to."

"Will do."

"Jake knows you've been following him," she added. "He called me this morning."

"No shit?" Hogan said it with a little laugh but didn't explain himself.

"He also said someone cut his brake lines."

"That's why he wrecked his cruiser? I saw that happen, but I had nothing to do with it."

"What about last night?"

"Last night? Like we already talked about. The cable station, then Siebert's, then home."

"You didn't do something else to him?"

"Like what?"

She didn't answer. Her dad wanted Hogan involved to do the things she couldn't. Maybe he had already started.

CHAPTER FIFTY-THREE

Jake flicked his thumb over the edge of Jedidiah Sublett's probate file.

"You're up, Coog."

Coogan sat on the lone plastic chair at the small metal table and started through the file. Something in this thick bundle of paper would reveal why the inventory was so important to Bull. Jake watched, rubbing his knobby sac joint.

Legal files are built chronologically, with the originating petition on the bottom and each later document bound on top of it. Coogan read through the final pages, then flipped back to the beginning, an index finger tracing across the pages and tapping on important pieces of information. Jake couldn't follow his moves, so he turned away and paced the room's narrow confines.

Finally, Coogan closed the file with two fingers stuck near the bottom of the paper stack. "Three things," he said. "First, Jedidiah died without any heirs, as we suspected. Two, he did have a will, and it was filed and probated. Three, because Sublett didn't have any heirs and the man he'd named as his executor had died, the public administrator probated the will."

Coogan raised his eyebrows as if to ask if Jake understood what he was getting at. Jake didn't, and shrugged.

"The public administrator is appointed by the governor. The PA collects the estate's assets, liquidates them, pays the deceased's bills, and fulfills the testamentary intent. If there's no will, he distributes the estate according to state law."

"Okay."

Coogan flipped the file open to an early document. "Sublett's will—here—gave his entire estate to the City of Weston to support its parks."

"That makes sense. The Sublett name is on at least one park in town."

"Two, actually. But the land for them was donated during Sublett's lifetime." Coogan stabbed the paper. "The gift to the parks references an inventory. I quote: '... and the proceeds from liquidating the items listed on the inventory held by my attorney and executor, Francis Maloney, as it may read from time to time.'"

"The list Siebert found has to be the missing inventory." It was finally coming together.

Coogan flipped the page up. "But the inventory isn't missing."

Jake took the file from Coogan and looked at the inventory: a single page with less than two dozen entries, all household goods, and Sublett's signature at the bottom. He flipped back to the will. "The paper the inventory is typed on is different from the paper used for the will. Sublett's signature looks different, too."

"I'm no handwriting expert, but I agree."

The signature on the will was carefully written the way people did in the old days when penmanship was an actual school subject. The signature on the inventory, by contrast, was tight and shaky.

"It's possible that Jedidiah signed both, but at different times in his life or under different circumstances," Coogan said. "The inventory wasn't stored with the will and was probably changed now and then when Sublett acquired or liquidated an asset. When he died, the executor—his attorney, Maloney—would have had the current version."

"Did you know Maloney?"

"Not well. He had an office in the old bank building that was torn down five or ten years ago."

"But with Maloney dead—"

"The public administrator took over. He would search for the will, then go through Sublett's belongings looking for heirs and cataloging his assets. Looking at every piece of paper, opening every drawer, looking under every bed."

"He was the first person to see the inventory and the coin collection."

"Exactly."

"I need to talk to that public administrator," Jake said. "Who was it?"

Coogan pulled the file back out of Jake's hands, flipped through to an early document, and held it out, pointing at the signature line.

"Grant Warren, Public Administrator of Paget County."

CHAPTER FIFTY-FOUR

Jake rubbed his sac joint while Coogan used paper clips to mark the pages he wanted copied: the will, the inventory, and the documents Bull Warren had filed as public administrator swearing to the validity of both the will and its inventory. Coogan also marked the final accounting. It listed the PA's fee and every item he sold from the estate.

It did not mention the coin collection.

Coogan took the file to the window and explained what he wanted to the clerk.

While they waited for the copies, Jake rebuilt the narrative he'd been creating. Bull Warren had been public administrator and handled Jedidiah Sublett's estate. He found no heirs, but did find a collection of gold coins. When he realized the coins were listed on a separate inventory and not in the estate documents, he seized the opportunity to substitute a fake inventory and take the coins for himself. Twenty-five years later, the original inventory turned up in Siebert's desk—live on cable television—and… the rest was unclear. Either Bull hired Silva to go get it, and when Silva saw it he recognized its value and demanded more than Bull had offered to pay him… or Silva initiated the theft from Siebert on his own, then blackmailed Bull with it.

Either way, three men ended up dead in the Radar Grove lagoon because Bull didn't get what he wanted.

Even if Bull didn't kill the three men himself, he'd ordered Hogan to do it.

The throb in Jake's back was dulled by a quick flood of nausea.

When the copies were ready, they returned to the car.

"Now that we know the original inventory is what Bull has Hogan looking for, I see why he can't risk it turning up." Coogan flipped through the copies as he talked. "If someone found it and recognized what it meant, the Illinois attorney general, the state auditor, and state inspector general would descend on Paget County in an investigatory shit storm."

"Bull's last days on earth would be hell," Jake said. And for Bev, the pain would go on and on.

Coogan opened the passenger door and folded himself into the car. Jake lowered himself into the driver's seat, and they headed back to Weston.

"Maybe Silva was working for the Warrens that night," Coog said. "But when he saw the inventory he realized its value and held out."

"Or he was working for himself and Bull objected to being blackmailed," Jake said. But there's no way Bev had been involved at that point. He was as sure of that as he'd ever been of anything.

Coogan didn't argue, and they were both silent.

After Jake turned south on Winfield he floated the element he couldn't explain. "Either way, Silva didn't run into Siebert at the liquor store by chance."

"That whole encounter makes no logical sense," Coogan said. "Why would Silva think Siebert had the inventory on him?"

"I've talked with Siebert twice. Graves and Lange took his money and his wine. Classic strong-arm robbery. Simple and quick." Mason's story backed that up, as did the wine bottles found at the lagoon and in the car. "Siebert barely remembered the inventory even when I brought it up. If Silva stole it from him or even asked him about it, Siebert would have remembered. That night is etched into his brain."

"To quote you, not all questions can be answered."

Jake had said that. Many times. Even in solved cases, facts go unexplained. People don't always act rationally, and an investigation attempts to solve a crime by examining it logically.

Jake mulled over the time he had left on Braff's deadline and the holes he had yet to fill. If he could establish a connection between Bull Warren and Silva, that could shake something else loose. He'd drop Coogan off at his office, then drive back up to the Bends and hammer away at Pearl Cassano until she told him the truth.

CHAPTER FIFTY-FIVE

Bull hung on.

His chest crackled and gurgled, and twice he thought, *This is it!* But then his cough cleared his lungs, and he could breathe again.

He spent the time thinking about his family. About Bev and Abby and Daniel. He'd known Abby his entire life. The next-door neighbor. One time one of his aunties showed him a picture of him and Abby playing together on a blanket before they could walk. For a while, Abby was the one who got away when she went off to college—but then she came home, and he won her back.

They were inseparable after that.

Until she and Daniel died.

Daniel would have really been something. So kind and funny and athletic—but with just enough of that Warren cunning that helped navigate the real world.

When Abby and Daniel died, he wanted to join them. But Bev needed him. He'd resented her for that—he could admit that now. He'd barely known his daughter at the time. She did things with her mom, while Bull spent all his free time with Daniel. But it was Bev who held him here in this world; it was Bev who re-awakened him. Without her, these last thirty years would have been empty.

A globule got hung up in his chest, so dense it had weight. His body clenched before he knew it was ready, and he pulled the mask away and coughed until sweat dripped from him.

Better.

His cell phone rang, skittering across the table. Hogan. He put the mask back on and sucked in two deep breaths, then pulled it away to answer.

"Tell me," he said, his voice hoarse from coughing.

"Houser sent his union rep to the meeting. While I was with her, he and Coogan went up to the archive and pulled the Sublett file. They're leaving right now. Coogan's got a thick wad of papers."

"Damn it!" Bull sucked air. "My name's all over that file."

"I'm following them now. Looks like they're headed back to town."

Bull's mind spun, but the morphine still fuzzed him. He kept coming back to what had already failed. Leveraging the coroner hadn't helped. Doctoring the incident report and deleting the video at the cable station hadn't slowed Houser a bit. And now the brutality complaint had worked in the bastard's favor, wasting Hogan's time while Houser and Coogan pulled the Sublett file.

"We need to do something more direct," Hogan said.

"Stop him." Bull put the mask back and sucked in three hard breaths. His mind cleared enough to tell him that wasn't right. "No! Call Bev. This is her deal now."

"Stop him, or let Bev—"

"Call Bev."

Bull dropped the phone on the table. Bev would handle it.

* * *

Bev's stomach churned when Hogan told her Jake now had the Sublett file. It churned even more when Hogan pressed her to let him "finally end this." She ordered him to wait; the case was theirs in a few more hours.

She needed to know what was in that damn file.

She grabbed her purse and stormed out, ignoring her assistant's efforts to hand her a thick stack of messages. It was a short drive through the county complex and across County Farm Road to the archives. The sun burned hot and bright, and she squinted against it and tried not to think about her dad.

She hesitated before going inside. But probate files were public documents, and there was nothing wrong with asking to see one. "You have every right to be here, Bev Warren," she told herself.

She went inside, the cold air chilling her sweaty arms. The door opened to a small room with a service window in the opposite wall.

"Ms. Warren?"

A gray-haired woman with narrow features sat in the cubicle behind the service window. She was so short only the top of her head was visible until she stood up.

"Yes?" Bev's voice wavered with the shame of being caught.

"I thought it was you. You look so much like your dad. I'm the one who texted you earlier. Your dad asked me to keep an eye on, well, a few things." She held up a thick file wrapped with a fat rubber band. "This is the Sublett file. They copied the pages marked with paper clips along the sides." Her hand flicked at the stacked pages.

"Thank you!" That would save her a lot of time.

"I'll buzz you through."

The door buzzed and clicked, and Bev stepped through.

The woman met her on the other side. "It's my pleasure to help," she said, her eyes wet. "Your dad's always been good to me. Got me this job twenty-six years ago after my husband died. Raised my kids on it." She sniffed and handed Bev the file. "I'm praying for him."

"I appreciate that." Bev's own eyes began to tear.

The woman hugged her, the file bulky between them.

Bev took a seat in a tiny cubicle. Thanks to the marked pages, it didn't take her long to understand what her dad had done and which document was the issue. The inventory filed with the will listed nothing of any value, so there was no reason to even have it. It was a fake. The original inventory was the document they were all after. It must have listed Sublett's collection of gold coins. It was a land mine that would tear her dad's work as PA apart, and taint every good thing he had ever done.

She would not let that happen.

CHAPTER FIFTY-SIX

Jake dropped Coogan at the curb outside his office. His friend had been quiet for the rest of the drive back to Weston, flipping through the copies he'd had made at the archives. After he got out of the car he leaned back in through the open door, rolling the copies into a tight tube.

"I'll see what else I can dig up about Sublett and his estate." His hands worked the tube. "Jake... Bull Warren isn't like his daughter."

"And?"

"He's more confrontational."

"From his hospital bed?"

"He's got Hogan, so you can't count him out."

Jake nodded. The attack at the river proved Coogan was right.

Coogan swung the door shut, and Jake started off toward the Bends to interview Mrs. Cassano. After rounding the second corner, he spotted Hogan's car in a stream of minivans and SUVs in his rearview mirror. When had he appeared? Jake considered trying to shake him, but this trip wouldn't give Hogan any new information.

He pulled out his phone and called Callie.

"Diggs."

"How'd it go with Hogan?"

"He was *not* expecting me. Fool brought the incomplete *and unsigned* complaint form with him. I took a picture of it. Pushing a complaint that isn't signed is pure bullshit. He almost imploded when I asked how the complaint got to him so fast."

"How long did the meeting last?"

"Not long. Within five minutes he knew he was screwed and hustled me out of there as fast as he could."

Fast enough that Hogan could have seen them at the archive. But how would he have known to go there?

"I want to hear the rest of this story, Jake."

Jake was silent, thinking about what he wanted—or *had* wanted—from her.

"You hear me, Jake?"

"I hear you. Soon."

He hung up, smiling at getting in the last word, which was hard to do with Callie Diggs.

* * *

Jake struggled into his blazer as he walked up Pearl Cassano's driveway. He threw a quick "How ya doin'" at old man Simari, who once again was out on his porch, a tall sweaty glass of ice water on the railing by his shoulder. Jake was glad to see him there. Simari had known the Cassanos for a long time and had his eye on the neighborhood. Jake might have a few questions for the old man after he was done with Mrs. Cassano.

"She's not out back, Houser." Simari gestured toward the house. "Been holed up inside all day."

Jake thanked him and headed toward the front door. He climbed the concrete steps and dodged his way through the gauntlet of wind chimes hanging on the porch.

The front door was mostly glass, a tall oval with a beveled edge set in dark wood, and Mrs. Cassano, reading on the couch, saw him before he knocked. He waved, and she came to the door, her steps as slow and sure as they had been the first time he visited. Her face was lined and her eyes red, and she clutched a handkerchief in one hand.

She ushered him inside. "Good afternoon, Detective. Please come in."

Her greeting startled Jake, and he checked his watch. It was just after noon. The trip to the archives had eaten up a lot of time.

He followed her into a front room that smelled of a floral air freshener. The air conditioning was turned up just enough to cut the top off the heat. She led him across a deep carpet that still showed vacuum trails to a couch and pair of chairs upholstered in soft colors. The book Mrs. Cassano had been reading was open, spine up, on an ottoman. A Robert Crais mystery.

"Please sit."

He sat where she'd pointed, then asked, "Did Victoria call?"

"Yes." Her eyes squeezed shut and she took a sharp breath. "Donald and his friends."

"I have a few questions I hope you can help me with."

"And I have a few questions for you, Detective." Her tight smile was a statement of distrust. "This time I want the truth." She held up her hand as he opened his mouth. "The *whole* truth."

Jake pulled out his notebook and read from it like he was giving her everything he had. He did tell her a lot—including that he had motives for Silva to kill the other two that he couldn't share, and that Silva might have been upset about police interest in his purported criminal activity. All this to give her the murder-suicide theory so she could attack it from the depth of her Catholic faith and be eager to help him find a different answer.

She bit.

"Nonsense." She pulled her shoulders back, her mouth tight in disbelief. "Donald would never—*could* never—did *not*, do such a thing. Ask me whatever question will help you understand that."

Now that he had her cooperation, he dove into the carpet business. He planned to move from that to her husband's clients and on to the Warren family, but he soon ran into trouble, because she knew nothing about the business. She'd put complete trust in her husband and then in Silva. Jake detected no deception, and after she recommended he talk with her accountant, he moved on to the Warren family.

"Your family—the Cassanos—have lived in Weston for a long time."

"My husband was the native, Detective. I didn't move here until after we married."

"Did your husband talk about the other old families? The Napers or the Subletts?"

"He did, but most of them have died out or moved away. Other than the Warrens, of course."

Perfect. "And the Warrens?"

"Anthony grew up on the same block as Bull." She smiled. "Bull was younger, but proved himself to be a good friend over the years."

Wheels spun and cogs slipped together. "How did he do that?"

"Well, I remember he sent some work Anthony's way." She adjusted herself on the couch and brought a hand to her face. "I wouldn't know the details." She dropped her gaze.

Deception. She knew more. Maybe not everything, but more. Her beloved Anthony had been a fence and had done work for Bull Warren.

"Did Mr. Cassano sell things for Bull Warren? Gold coins, maybe?"

Her chin jerked up at the word *coins*, and she nodded. But her words didn't match her body language. More deception. "My husband didn't sell things for people. He installed carpet."

"Carpet installation was the work Bull Warren sent his way?"

Her gaze shot around the room. "Yes."

"After Mr. Cassano passed, did Bull send any work to Donald?"

"I'm sure I don't know." Mrs. Cassano's lips pulled tight. "I don't like these questions. My husband was a carpet installer, nothing more." She twisted the handkerchief she held. "And please remove my report about the car being taken. I don't want Donald's memory tainted any further."

The missing stolen vehicle report. "When did you make the report?"

Her gaze pulled away, then came back. "I'm not sure, exactly, but it was very soon after Donald took the car. Within a week, I'd say."

"Did you come into the station to report it?"

"No." She shook her head. "A man came here and asked me about it. He made the report."

"Do you remember reading it over? Signing it?"

She was still, searching her memory. "I don't remember signing anything. I'm not sure there was a piece of paper. I think he wrote it in his notebook. Like you do."

"Was he a big man with red hair?"

"Yes. Yes he was."

"He came and asked you if your car had been stolen?"

Her focus faded, then came back. "Well, he asked about the car. And about who I let drive it. He was insistent. I told him I didn't *let* anyone drive it. But I did tell him—he was very pushy—that Donald didn't bring it back."

Hogan had followed the trail in the incident report straight here. And he hadn't come to ask about the car—he already knew where it was. He came to find out what Cassano knew about Silva.

Jake thanked Mrs. Cassano for her time. She didn't walk him to the door.

On his way across the porch Jake brushed against a few wind chimes to make sure Simari heard him. He glanced that way as he stepped off the last stair, and Simari waved him over. As Jake ducked into the shade on Simari's porch, he glanced up the street and spotted Hogan's car parked near the end of the block, slotted between a minivan and a pickup loaded with lawn care equipment.

Jake sat on a milk can across from Simari. The old man opened his mouth, gesturing toward Cassano's house, but Jake cut him off. He was on the clock and didn't have time to hear about the old-timer's crush on Pearl Cassano. "Mrs. Cassano didn't like my questions today."

Simari dropped his hand. "Police have been around to talk to her about Anthony before. She wouldn't ever say, or believe, a bad word about him."

Jake pulled at the front of his shirt. It was hot even here in the shade. "Would you?" He watched Simari carefully.

"Anthony was a good friend. Played checkers with him right here on this porch when weather allowed."

The Cassano house was only a narrow driveway's width away. Simari had to see and hear everything that went on over there. Jake had nothing to lose by confronting Simari. "Cassano was a thief and a fence. He was right under your nose and you didn't know that?"

Simari gave a snort. "If that were true, why didn't he ever do time?" He took a sip from his icy glass.

"Maybe someone was looking out for him."

Simari put his glass down. "Maybe."

"You know the kid he took on? Donald Silva?"

The old man pulled his hands into his lap. "He took care of Pearl after Anthony died. Vicky has taken over since Donald left."

"Silva didn't leave. He died."

Simari blinked in surprise.

"Right here in Weston, five years ago, while working a job for Bull Warren."

Jake's stomach twisted as his brain struggled with the thought of his own uncle being a killer. Even if he had only told Hogan to steal the list, and killing the three men wasn't in the original plan, being guilty of a felony that ended in a murder was the same as murder under Illinois law. Felony murder.

"You okay, Detective?"

Jake pulled himself together, his vision refocusing on Simari. "The heat is getting to me."

Bev couldn't have been involved. No way. But she was involved *now*, even if only to protect her dad. Accessory after the fact was also a stiff felony.

"Well," Simari said, "it never made sense to me that he ran off and left that beautiful woman of his, but I never heard anything about him dying. How'd it happen?"

"It doesn't surprise you that Silva was working a job for Bull?"

Simari gnawed his lower lip, and his gaze faded away into a past that produced a shake of his head. Jake fought an urge to push. Finally Simari came back from wherever he had gone and looked Jake in the eye.

"That would explain your followers. I called you over here to point that out." Simari's eyes darted quickly to the side. "Isn't Bull's daughter the sheriff now? With that big antenna, that one looks like a county car."

"I picked the tail up yesterday. You know the big redhead?"

"Earlier than that. That car was on you the first time you came by."

From the very beginning? "I should have you riding shotgun."

"No thanks, Detective. My fighting days are long behind me." Simari leaned back in his chair and stretched his arm for his glass, taking a long drink before returning it to the railing. Stalling. "Me and Anthony went way back. Grew up together on Benton. Our houses are long gone now. The garages those new houses have are bigger than the houses we lived in."

Jake knew better than to interrupt a man who was already talking, but the clock was ticking. "What are you telling me, Mr. Simari?"

"People in our neighborhood were loyal to each other. Bull Warren lived on that block, too. Back when Anthony was working, the police came around once. Bull put a stop to it."

"But Silva was from Kirwin."

"So no loyalty due or owed. If Silva was doing something for Bull, it was because he needed to do it. Or was paid to do it."

* * *

When Bev returned from the archives, her assistant stopped her at the door to her office with a thick wad of phone messages, but Bev brushed by her and told her to keep holding her calls.

"I've been doing that but..." The pink bundle rattled as the frustrated woman shook it.

Bev slammed her office door and dropped into her chair. Back where she belonged and things made sense. She thumbed the corner of a thick stack of budget reports, then pushed it away and spun her chair to stare out the window. Today—right now—she had to *do* something. Jake had made it to the meat of this mess. He didn't have the inventory itself, or any courtroom-worthy evidence, but now that he knew where to look, and when, he'd find it. He was too good for her to believe—or even to hope—otherwise. Stopping Jake was her only real play.

Stopping him.

She hiccupped and gulped back a sour mouthful of vomit.

The sun edged across her window, and shadows shifted.

She picked up the photo of her and her dad at Wrigley Field. She still remembered that day: perfect weather, riding the El, getting a bunch of her baseball cards autographed. Look at those smiles. They looked so real. This picture was from the early eighties—eighty-three, judging by her braces—while her dad had been robbing the Sublett estate. But he had smiled like his life was perfect.

She held the photo closer. Her smile looked so… dumb. She'd been dumb. She'd totally bought his whole loving father bit.

She slammed the photo on the credenza. The glass shattered, and shards of it sliced through the air. One of them stuck in the weave of her slacks. She plucked it out and examined it, turning it back and forth, admiring the sharp edge. A dark wave of despair washed over her in a hollow swell, and she wallowed in the blackness, the only light a reflection off a facet of the fractured glass.

She closed her eyes and flung the shard away.

So her dad wasn't perfect. On some level she'd always known that. But he'd been a good dad. This was indulgent self-pitying bullshit, and she knew it. But stealing from the dead and killing three men to cover it up?

Her mouth filled with vomit again, and she dropped to her knees, yanked the trash can from under the desk, and spewed in gut-wrenching heaves. She wiped a hand across her mouth. Did she just accept that her dad had killed those men? That couldn't be true.

She pushed herself back into her chair, the sour stench following her.

She had to stop Jake.

It was time to turn Hogan loose.

CHAPTER FIFTY-SEVEN

Jake sat in his Mustang in front of Cassano's house with the engine running and the air conditioning cranked. Pearl Cassano had confirmed Hogan was the cop who took the phantom stolen vehicle report. But there had been no report; the big man had really been there to find out whether she knew anything about Silva's activities that night.

More importantly, Pearl had connected Bull to her husband, which brought the existence of a prior connection between Bull and Silva closer to fact.

Silva's name had gone to the county burglary task force, and as far as Jake could tell it had died there. Bull must have killed the case. He had a lot of county-level influence through his own connections and through his daughter—and he had Hogan. Maybe some record of that event still existed.

Jake dialed Benny Larson at his Chicago law firm. The attorney had given Jake the brush-off the day before, but he wasn't going to let that happen again.

"Law offices. How can I help you?"

The bright, cheery voice didn't soften Jake's mood. "Homicide Detective Jake Houser calling for Benny Larson about a murder I'm investigating. I need to speak to him immediately."

"I'll put you through."

She did it so fast Jake didn't have time to thank her.

"Jake?"

"Ben, I need—"

"Man, I'm sorry about yesterday. My toxic tort case went to shit on me, but I dug up my old planner and have it with me."

Progress. "Can you check it for both names? Nicholas Lange was the guy trying to do the deal, and Donald Silva was the guy he was selling out." The car was cool now. Jake turned the AC down a notch.

"I remember the names you gave me, but it's a planner. Chronological. If you have a date I can check it quick, otherwise I'll have to read through the whole damn thing."

Jake flipped through his notebook and found the date Lange was arrested and the date he was set for trial. He read both off. "Check between those dates."

The sharp snap of pages came over the line.

"Here we go. Yeah, Lange brought us Donald Silva, but nothing with it. He promised to get us something concrete."

More pages snapped. "And here. October twenty-first, a sheriff's deputy told us to drop it. Deputy Hogan. I didn't write down why, but there must have been something else cooking with either Silva or Lange."

Bingo. That confirmed the connection between Bull and Silva. Bull—through Hogan— had stopped an investigation into Silva. And Silva had repaid the favor by robbing Siebert of the inventory—but then held out on Bull and paid the ultimate price for that mistake.

A few more pages snapped. "Yeah, that's it. That enough or do I need to go back through it all?"

"That's enough. All that'll be in a task force file? An official one?"

"Should be."

"Thanks, Benny."

Jake dropped the Mustang into gear and pulled his foot off the brake.

"Hang on, Jake. I had drinks last night with another former ASA." Benny paused, and the lengthening silence drew out Jake's curiosity—exactly as the trial practice trick was meant to do. "Lange's story wasn't the first time Silva's name came up. Our office looked at him once before. Even got a warrant to search his shop. But everything he owned was papered up tight and clean."

Jake stopped the car. "How did you get a warrant?"

"The usual. Confidential informant."

"Who was the CI?"

"You cops protect those names. We never knew it."

"You knew Lange's name."

"He wasn't a CI, just some shit-heel turning in a friend to save himself."

"Did the name Cassano come up?"

"Yeah. Cassano was why they looked at Silva. He had taken over the fencing business."

"Cassano never did time for fencing." Erin had checked, and Simari had said the same thing.

"Sometimes we know things we can't prove. You know how that goes, Houser. I bet most of your cold cases are like that."

"Did you believe Lange's story?"

"Never talked to him. The deal was canceled before I got that far into it."

"Warren Hogan, the deputy sheriff who told you to drop it when Lange coughed up Silva's name? He's Bull's gofer."

"The hell you say!"

"Could Bull have tipped Silva off in time to make his collections look clean?"

"Shit, Jake." Benny gave a short laugh. "I have no evidence of that. But of course anything's possible. Bull Warren had a hand in everything in the county back then."

After the call, Jake thought over Benny's words.

Bull Warren had a hand in everything in the county back then.

And still did.

Jake pulled away from the curb. When he reached the end of the block, Hogan eased out of his spot to follow. Jake didn't care. He was running out of time, but there was only one person left to talk to. And Hogan could follow him the entire way there.

* * *

Hogan dropped back a few car lengths when Houser turned south for downtown Weston. He dropped even farther back when Houser turned east toward the police station. But then Houser passed the police station and took a right on West Street.

"That asshole *can't* be going to see Bull. No way."

Hogan's phone vibrated. The sheriff. He moved his thumb over the green dot to accept the call, but stopped before touching the glass.

"I've had enough of watch and report."

He put the phone away.

He'd fallen a couple hundred yards behind Houser while he considered the sheriff's call. He sped up and pulled into the hospice's parking lot as Houser parked in a handicapped space and hustled up the front walk. Hogan swung his car into the first open space, jumped out, and darted across the lawn. As he ran he pulled out his phone, fumbling and dropping it. He picked it up, brushed off bits of mown grass, and dialed.

"Bull?"

The man wheezed into the phone. "What?"

"Houser's coming to you right now. He'll be in there in a minute, tops."

Hogan stopped in the deep shade at the edge of the woods bordering the grounds. He had a clear view through Bull's window where his boss lay on the blocky hospital bed.

The old man was silent, the hissing air and thunking machine clear through the line. A wet cough carried on in a wave before dying out. "Okay."

* * *

When Bev tried Hogan several times with no answer, she got in her car to go find him.

She went by Siebert's house, then Cassano's, but her fire to have Hogan do something to stop Jake had turned around on her. Her dad was the bad guy here, not Jake.

She gripped the wheel and headed south toward the hospice. No more guessing at what her dad had done. She would pull the truth out of him.

CHAPTER FIFTY-EIGHT

Jake's pace slowed as he approached the hospice's front door. He was in the right place to talk to the right guy, but what if Bull did confess? How could Jake use it without pulling Bev into it? Maybe she deserved it, technically, but…

But what? Was she more important than avenging the three dead men? Just because she was family? The answer could only be no.

He darted a glance at his watch. The minute hand was moving too fast.

"I'm here to see Bull Warren," he told the lady at the desk.

"He's only seeing family."

"He's my uncle."

The nurse narrowed her eyes, then nodded. "Last room at the end." She pointed off to her left.

Jake strode down the hall, slowing as he approached Bull's open door. He paused at the threshold, his body casting a shadow ahead of him into the dim room. A machine against the wall thumped mechanically, and an airy hiss came from the bed. He saw the man lying on the bed. Bull Warren. Or what was left of him after illness had eaten much of him away.

Jake stepped inside and flicked the light switch on the headboard; a soft glow pooled against the ceiling. Bull's eyes opened, bright and blue, peering up from between his knobby skull and the clear plastic mask that covered the lower half of his face.

"Ha!" The old man barked through the mask, one hand pawing at it. "Houser."

"Bull." Jake had never called the old man "Uncle." When studying the rules of inheritance in law school, he'd figured out Bull was actually his second cousin, once removed. "I doubt this is a surprise, since your man followed me here."

The old man grunted, then pushed at the bed and rolled onto his back, a wet cough convulsing him and spraying the mask with cloudy splatter. His hand reached toward Jake and lifted in a request that Jake get to it.

"I figured it out," Jake said.

"Tell. Me."

"You administered the Sublett estate. You found the will and the original inventory that listed the gold coins. You substituted the fake inventory and took the coins for yourself."

Bull's brow furrowed when Jake mentioned the coins.

"And you got away with it. But a couple decades later Siebert found the original inventory, and you decided you had to destroy it to protect yourself. You hired Silva to get it, but he turned on you." And despite the violence they'd done to him that ended with his broken neck, Silva had never given up the inventory. "You did what you could to protect yourself: your man deleted the cable station video and searched Siebert's house and Silva's shop and house and barn. But you never found it; that smoking gun was still out there."

The old man lay motionless, only his bright eyes revealing his interest.

"Now the car comes out of the river, and you panic. What if the inventory is somehow still in there?"

Bull's eyes were hard now, the blue icy.

"Whether you killed them yourself doesn't matter. You put the whole thing in motion, and those men died in the effort. Under Illinois law that's called felony murder."

Bull tensed, his head lifting from the pillow. "You got—"
He shook out another series of wet coughs that splashed against
the plastic. He clawed at the mask, then gave up. His arms fell
back to the bed. "Nothing."

Jake's stomach twisted. A simple denial would have saved
the old man precious air, but instead he'd gone after what Jake
could prove.

The guilty man's favorite defense.

His uncle was a murderer.

"Dragging Bev into your cleanup operation has made her
an accessory after the fact."

"Bev." Bull reached a hand toward Jake, then shook his
knobby head and scrabbled at the mask. "Don't you—!"

"You sign a complete confession and I'll keep Bev out of
it." Jake tried to control his voice, but his anger leaked through.
This old bastard had killed three men to protect himself, and
now he'd dragged his daughter into it.

Bull pawed at his mask.

"I'll take your mask off. That what you want?"

Bull nodded.

Jake gritted his teeth as a shiver ran up his back. He pulled
the mask off and slid it down under Bull's chin. His efforts to
calm his fury failed, and his voice was still filled with anger.
"You have something to say?"

"Don't..." Bull's voice died out into a soggy cough. "...
trust you." He held up a hand for Jake to wait, but then his face
turned red and his mouth opened and squeaked with the effort
to pull in air. His hands grabbed for his mask, trying to push it
back over his mouth—then gave up and pounded the mattress
once, twice. His eyes closed.

Jake reached out to help—but stopped. His hands fell to
his sides.

What am I doing?

He took a short step back. His mind filled with retribu-
tion and punishment and justice.

Bull bucked against the bed, body arching, eyes popping open. A long squeak from his throat. The bed frame banged against the floor. Again. Then his entire body relaxed into the bed, shrinking under Jake's gaze. No alarms went off because none were connected.

Jake waited, watching the second hand on the wall clock sweep around once, twice. After the third time he wiped his fingerprints off the mask with the edge of the sheet and put it back on Bull's face, the eyes wide and blank. Then he walked out quietly, nodding at the woman at the desk as he left. Holding himself tightly together.

His gaze swept the lot for Hogan but he didn't see him. Jake walked to his car, legs wobbling.

* * *

Hogan had watched through the window, the words coming through the cell phone muffled by the rustling sheets and the hissing air machine. Houser's voice suddenly louder, angry. *"… take your mask off. That what you want?"* Bull grunting and gasping. *"… something to say?"* Bull's body bucking on the bed, a bang, then silence. Houser stood still, no sound but the hissing. Then he left the room.

Hogan ran across the lawn toward the parking lot and ducked behind the first set of cars as Houser came out the front door. Hogan watched him through the windows of an SUV. Houser looked around, his face slack and pale, then walked to his car. Staying in a crouch, Hogan darted to his own car, pulled the door open, and slipped into his seat before Houser's car started moving.

Hogan darted his eyes toward the hospice. For a moment, he reached for the handle and put his shoulder against the door, planning to get out and go inside. But he stopped himself.

"Shit!"

He bit his lip and started the car. When Houser had a short lead he followed, taking the turn onto West a few seconds after Houser and dropping into the thin traffic behind him. He still held the cell phone in his hand. He pressed it back to his ear, but the connection had dropped. He redialed Bull's number.

"Come on, Bull." His stomach gurgled and his head went fuzzy as Bull's phone went to voicemail. He scrolled through his contacts and found the hospice's general number.

"I'm calling to see how Mr. Warren is doing."

"We can't discuss a patient's condition without authorization."

"Can you check on him? I've had a… premonition, I guess you would call it. That he's gone."

The line was silent for a few seconds. Then, "I'll check."

The woman put him on hold, and Hogan kept the phone pressed to his ear as he followed Houser. Then the voice returned. "Sir? I didn't get your name."

"Deputy Hogan. I work for Bull's daughter."

"Well, I need to talk with Ms. Warren before I can say any more."

Hogan ended the call.

"Goddamn you, Houser!"

CHAPTER FIFTY-NINE

Jake drove slowly, his sweat-slicked hands slipping on the wheel. He wiped them on his pants as he tried to bring what had happened in Bull's room into focus. Bull was in the hospice to die... and he had died. On his own. Jake hadn't *done* anything, and failure to act is not a crime when you don't have a duty. The rule from law school popped into his mind, and he tried to hold on to it, but the legal technicality didn't make him feel any better. As a cop, and as a relative, his moral and ethical duties exceeded state law.

The air conditioning was chilling his sweat-drenched body, and he shuddered. He flicked off the AC and rolled the windows down to let the summer air flood through the car. Loosening his grip on the wheel, he forced himself to relax, but within a minute he had pulled himself up to strangle the wheel again. *Damn it!*

He pulled into the faculty parking lot at Weston Central, grabbed a fistful of paper napkins from the glove box, and wiped his sweaty face and then his whole head, his hair holding the sweat against his scalp. He wadded up the napkins and stuffed them into the door pocket and got back on the road.

If he hadn't done anything wrong, why did he wipe his fingerprints off the mask and put it back on Bull's face? And why did he slink out of there like a criminal? It was Bull Warren who had done wrong—a triple murder that his daughter would now pay for while he evaded punishment by dying.

As if his agonizing had brought it on, his phone rang. It was Braff. Jake checked the dashboard clock. Two hours and fifty-four minutes left on his deadline.

"This is Houser." He took the corner at River and headed north.

"How's the case looking? The sheriff has had people pestering me all day."

"I need the time I've got left." Jake didn't have another lead to follow or witness to question, but he would think of something.

Then a familiar vehicle in his rearview mirror caught his eye. Hogan.

The last person he could talk to.

"If you've got something, spit it out. If not, we give the case to your cousin, building goodwill and making the mayor happy by keeping the deaths off our stats. Win-win."

"I want all the time you gave me."

"Fine. But I want to hear from you by five, or I call the sheriff and turn it over. In the meantime I won't answer my damn phone."

Jake checked his mirror again. Hogan was still behind him in the thin stream of minivans and SUVs. Jake drove on and entered Radar Grove a few minutes later. Hogan turned in behind him, but Jake lost sight of the county cruiser as he drove the long curving parking lot. He pulled into a spot near the end. A hundred feet beyond his windshield, hard chunks of gray dirt lay where the Buick had come to rest. The drag marks were still visible across the browned-out grass all the way to the riverbank.

He shut the Mustang down and stretched in his seat, arching his back to relieve the tension in his gut, then rubbed at his sac joint. It was feeling a lot better.

The image jumped into his mind before he could stop it. A clear vision of Bev getting the call from the hospice. He squeezed his eyes shut until it passed. He needed to focus. This play was all he had left.

He adjusted his side mirror to get a look down the parking lot. There, in the little square of mirror, was the back end of Hogan's car, edged in behind the Dumpster still mounded with trash.

Good.

* * *

As Hogan followed Houser into Radar Grove, his chest was sending fire out through his limbs, his fingers tingling. He gripped the wheel tight, his lips pressed into a grim line.

The place was deserted apart from Houser, who followed the curve to the end of the lot and parked.

Hogan rolled up behind the giant Dumpster, out of Houser's sight. He opened his glove box, got out his drop gun, and eased out of the car, closing the door silently. He squatted behind the Dumpster, the small revolver nearly hidden in his big hand, and slowly peered around the corner.

CHAPTER SIXTY

Bev pulled into the hospice parking lot going too fast, a rear tire catching the curb and bucking her so hard her teeth clattered.

"Get a grip on yourself."

She parked and pulled her purse onto her lap. She knew what she wanted to achieve here: pull the truth from her dad about Sublett and Silva and Radar Grove. *But how?* She'd have to ask, and press, and insist and pound the table. But he would tell her, that was for damn sure.

She went inside. There was no one at the front desk to have her sign the log, so she powered past it, hustling down the hall.

A cluster of people stood outside her dad's door. Her stride faltered, then stopped.

She was too late.

Her vision clouded, and her breath caught.

"Here's the daughter."

A blurry pink form approached, resolving into a nurse as Bev blinked her vision clear.

"Ms. Warren?"

"Yes?" Bev's voice was so faint she barely heard it.

The nurse took her elbow and led her down the hall. The cluster broke up and drifted away. Bev stopped at the threshold to her dad's room, pulling her shoulders back and straightening her spine. The nurse released her elbow.

Bev's dad lay still, his arms at his sides. She dropped her purse to the floor and stood at his bedside, her anger bleeding away as she gazed at his relaxed face. Minutes passed. Then the quiet intruded, and she realized the air machine was off and they'd removed the mask and air hose. She cupped his cheek, the stubble rough on her palm.

"Hey, Dad." Talking to him felt right. "I'm sorry I wasn't here for you when you passed."

A dark loneliness rose up inside her. Her brother and her mom, and now her dad. Her face bloomed with heat and her shoulders heaved with a sob before she bit it off. She wasn't ready for him to be gone, despite the months in hospice to prepare for it. And especially now that she'd learned he was a fraud, at best, and maybe a killer. The legacy of good works he'd left behind were now tainted by a fog of lies and corruption.

Her shoulders trembled as she fought off another sob. He'd been a great dad, though. The best.

"I'm sorry you were alone."

"He had a visitor."

Bev spun, startled by the voice so close behind her. The nurse in pink stood in the open doorway.

"Who?"

"A man—said he was a relative—visited just before Bull passed."

"Big redhead?"

"No. He was—I don't know, normal height, piercing eyes. Brown buzz cut. A police officer. I saw a badge on his belt when he walked past the front desk."

Jake.

"Can I have a few minutes alone with my dad?"

"Certainly."

The nurse left, and Bev swung the door shut, the latch catching with a clack.

She hadn't expected Jake to visit a dying man to force a confession out of him. Her teeth ground together. What if her dad had said something? He was now past all human punishment—but *she* sure as hell wasn't.

Was she a bitch for thinking about herself?

Maybe.

Probably.

She scrambled over to her purse and pulled out her phone. As the line connected, she laid a hand on her dad's shoulder, a tear running down her face.

* * *

Jake checked the caller ID on his phone's screen. Bev.

Shit.

He adjusted the side mirror to get the Dumpster in view, then answered, his face hot with shame. "This is Jake."

"It's Bev," she said.

Hearing her soft familiar voice made the phone shake in his hand. He pressed it to his cheek to steady it. *I didn't kill him.*

"I'm here with my dad. He's dead." A hiccup of a sob. "I wanted you to know."

"I'm sorry." If she was at the hospice, she hadn't missed him by much. "I was just there."

"Why?" Energy pulsed into her voice. "What did you want from him?"

"Bev… I, uh…" Guilt burned his chest. "I wanted to give him a chance to explain his role in the lagoon murders."

"His ro—never mind that. What happened when you were here?"

"He woke up, and I asked him about the murders. He understood and wanted to talk. I think he was worried about you taking the blame for it." He paused and realized his eyes had drifted away from the mirror. He brought them back to it—still no Hogan. "He had a… fit of some kind. Coughing."

"You didn't call the nurse?"

"My mom was in hospice, remember? So I know the deal." People are supposed to die, and the nurses stand back and let it happen. Wasn't that exactly what Jake had done?

"Then what happened?" Her voice was weak now, barely a whisper.

"Then…" Was he about to confess that he'd pulled off her dad's oxygen mask and then refused to put it back on?

"Then what, Jake? What?"

"He started breathing normally again, but he fell asleep. So I left." The lies burned, a heat that traveled down his throat and spread through his torso. "I'm sorry, Bev."

The line went dead.

* * *

Hogan crouched behind the Dumpster, leaning out to get a clear view. Houser was sitting in his car, talking on his cell, but his voice was too low to make out any words. Finally he pulled the phone from his ear and stared at it while rubbing his face with his other hand.

Hogan looked at his gun, considering, then put the little revolver in the pocket of his blazer. With a smile, he rubbed his hands together and flexed them.

He stayed low as he came out from the behind the Dumpster. Houser sat frozen in his seat, staring blankly ahead of him. Hogan darted behind Houser's car and squatted there, his knees bunched under him, his back pressed to the bumper. He smiled again, his big hands flexing as if wrapped around someone's neck.

CHAPTER SIXTY-ONE

Jake had a lifetime to think about what he'd done. Right now he needed to focus on pulling a confession out of Hogan.

He accessed his phone's voice memo feature, hit record, then stuck it in his shirt pocket. He put a hand on his gun. Hogan would be armed, so it might come to that. He'd pull it if he had to. But he wouldn't pull it first.

A stray cloud drifted overhead, shading the clearing and easing the glare. The shadow turned Jake's mind back to Bull's dimly lit room and the man pounding on his mattress.

He shook his head. He needed his mind to be right here, right now.

He got out of the Mustang and walked toward the water, his feet crunching the dried-out grass. As he walked, his peripheral vision caught movement behind the Dumpster. He stopped and turned that way, tensing up and setting his feet in preparation for Hogan, but there was no one coming. He relaxed, his shoulders dropping, and continued on.

A blur of movement from behind his cruiser now. He turned, but too late.

Hogan's shoulder caught him in the chest, taking him off his feet.

Jake lifted his knees as his back hit the ground then pushed his legs up and into Hogan. The man flew over him, his big hands grabbing at Jake's shoulders but catching only air. Jake flipped onto his hands and knees, then leapt to his feet. Hogan landed hard but scrambled to his knees. The sun broke from behind a cloud and glinted off something on the grass. Jake's cell phone. He stepped toward it, but Hogan was already on his feet and moving forward, flexing his hands.

"I'm going to kill you like you killed Bull."

Shit. What did Hogan know? He hadn't been there.

Jake shook the question away. "Why did Bull send Silva for the inventory and not you?" He circled to keep out of Hogan's reach and to keep the phone between them. Focusing on Hogan's torso, he ignored the man's little feints and jabs. When the big man moved, Jake would see it in his core first.

"He was the burglary expert."

Jake nodded at the admission; it was a start.

Hogan lunged. Jake darted right and shot a left jab at the man's nose. Hogan ducked, and Jake hit solid forehead instead. Pain shot up his arm, but the blow forced Hogan back.

"You didn't deserve an uncle like Bull." Hogan licked his lips, eyes dark and tight on Jake.

"Did Silva deserve to die just to protect Bull?"

Jake circled again, flexing his left hand. The back of it was numb and his fingers tingled, but everything worked. The pain in his lower back had returned—sending a throbbing spike down his right leg on every step—but he knew it was only nerve pain. The muscles weren't damaged; they would do what he told them to.

He needed to get Hogan back on topic. "All this—three dead men—just to protect Bull from that inventory coming out?"

"They got what they deserved."

Jake shot a glance at the grass. He hoped the phone was still recording. "Because Silva held out on you?"

Hogan feinted right, then charged left. Jake spun around him, sending a hard right into his rib cage and a left into his kidneys. Hogan stumbled and fell.

Jake stood over him, releasing his fists and shaking his left hand to relieve the buzzing in his forearm.

Hogan kicked out. Jake jumped away, landing on his right leg and almost collapsing from the spike of pain in his sac joint. He ignored the throbbing and tried for another admission.

"Silva held out on you, so you killed him. All three of them."

"I'm going to crush your throat and rip your head off," Hogan growled, rising slowly to his feet, his eyes locked on Jake. "No. Screw it." He reached into his blazer pocket and pulled out a short-barreled revolver. "I'll just shoot you. Not as much fun, but you'll be just as dead."

Jake stepped back, his hands coming up as the gun barrel rose toward his head.

A form crept from behind the Dumpster, crouched. Someone *had* been there. Jake fought the urge to look that way and focused on distracting Hogan until his savior could act. The sooner the better.

"What's with the gun?" Jake said. "You don't think you can take me without it?"

The figure moved forward at a crouch, picking up speed.

"Shooting you won't be as much fun, but you'll be just as dead."

The approaching form launched itself at Hogan. As Hogan was thrown sideways, the gun discharged, and Jake felt a tug at the fabric on his shoulder.

Hogan landed in a disjointed tangle. Jake's savior landed on top of him, then jumped up to face Jake.

Paul Siebert!

Jake pulled his gun. "What are you doing here?"

"That guy had a gun," Siebert said. "He was going to shoot you."

Jake circled around to keep both men in sight. Hogan groaned and rolled onto his back, his legs spread wide and his hands crossed on his chest. He drew a deep breath that ended in a sharp cry of pain. A hand went to his ribs.

"But why are you here?" Jake asked again.

"I've been following you since you told me about that document."

"What? Why?"

"If those three men were after it, then—"

Hogan rolled onto his stomach with a loud gasping breath and struggled up to his knees and elbows. Siebert jumped back a step, stumbling and dropping to one knee before pushing himself back up. Jake swept his gun back and forth to cover both men. He scanned the burned-out grass for Hogan's gun but didn't spot it.

"Stay down, Hogan." Jake took a step back and directed his next question to Siebert. "You said they never asked you about the inventory."

"I heard this guy say he sent those men after the inventory. That's why—"

"Siebert?" Hogan's voice was hoarse, his breath ragged. He struggled to his feet. "I underestimated you again."

Again?

Siebert stepped toward Hogan. "You sent those men to our house."

"Hold it!" Jake shouted, his gun tracking back and forth between the two men. "Your *house?*"

Siebert's words bounced around Jake's skull like a ricochet through a glass shop, shattering his assumptions and conclusions. And they joined with something Hogan had said just moments ago.

When Hogan admitted that they'd sent Silva to get the inventory, he said it was because Silva was the *burglar*. But the event at the liquor store wasn't a burglary, it was a robbery—theft by force. A burglary was theft from inside a locked building. Hogan was a cop and knew the difference.

They hired Silva to burgle the Sieberts' house.

And Silva had done just that. But not on the night when the desk was damaged. Silva was dead by then. Which meant…

Suddenly, everything clicked. Jake could see it all.

Silva and his crew burgled Siebert's house *on the same night* they accosted him at the liquor store. They were there when Thompson got there to take the victim's report. *That's* why Siebert had refused to let Thompson inside. It wasn't a domestic disturbance at all.

And that was when Silva got the inventory. That's why it wasn't there when Hogan broke open the desk looking for it two weeks later.

A glint in the grass caught Jake's eye. His phone. He side-stepped over to it and picked it up. Was it still recording? He holstered his gun and cupped a hand over the screen to block the glare.

The metallic *ca-lack* of a gun stopped him. He spun around.

Siebert had apparently found Hogan's missing revolver—and now had it pointed at Hogan's head. His hand shook. "For a piece of *paper*?" he shouted. He brought his other hand up and steadied the wavering gun. "You made us… turned us into…"

"Wait!" Jake shouted. The facts finished reshuffling, and a truth bloomed that was so unexpected he had trouble holding on to it.

Paul Siebert killed Silva, and Graves, and Lange.

"Just… wait."

Siebert's hands continued to shake. Rage and pain twisted his face.

"Don't do it," Jake said.

Siebert shook his head. "He deserves to die. For what he turned us into… for what he made us do to those men. We couldn't let them hurt our girl."

"He didn't do it," Jake said. "He worked for someone else. He was just a tool."

"Who?"

"I'll tell you the whole story," Jake said. "I promise you that. But right now you need to give me the gun and go home to your family. I'll take care of this."

Even as he said the words, Jake had no clue how he would do that. Siebert's actions had started as self-defense, but that changed when the car went into the water with Lange still alive in the trunk. No—it had changed even earlier, when Siebert decided to hide the bodies instead of calling 911.

Siebert shook his head, his hands kneading the grip of the little revolver.

"Paul!" Jake said. "You got what you needed. Let me handle this."

Siebert shot Jake a dark look. "What are you talking about?"

"Now you know why those men came to your house. It was to get that document. It wasn't because of your behavior at the liquor store. It wasn't your fault. They were coming no matter what."

Siebert looked from Jake to Hogan and back. The rage left him, and his face went blank in its wake. He paused, then stepped away from Hogan.

"I'll take the gun," Jake said.

Siebert's arms dropped, shaky with adrenaline. Jake took the gun from his hands.

Hogan pressed a hand to the ground and started to leverage himself up. "What are you going to do, Houser?"

Jake kicked the hand out from under Hogan, then grabbed it and twisted it behind his back, forcing him onto his stomach on the hard ground.

"Damn you, Houser!"

Jake flipped up the back of Hogan's suit jacket, revealing the man's handcuffs and a flat black Glock in a belt holster. The revolver must be Hogan's backup. But when Jake frisked his way down Hogan's legs, he didn't find a holster on either ankle. Which meant the little pistol *wasn't* a backup piece. It was a drop gun. Hogan hadn't been bluffing about intending to kill him.

"You were going to use a drop gun on me?"

"You deserve it."

"Shut up." Jake cuffed Hogan's hands behind him, crammed the big Glock in his waistband against his lower back, and slipped the little revolver into his right front pocket.

A cloud blotted out the sun, and the quick drop in temperature helped clear Jake's mind. He stepped back from Hogan, thinking, flexing his left hand, which was still numb from bouncing off Hogan's skull.

Siebert was the killer—killing to protect his family from the threat Hogan and Bull had sent into his home. Self-defense, basically. Jake had gone into both conversations with Siebert thinking of him as a victim, and that bias had colored how he'd read the man, preventing him from seeing what was really there. Paul Siebert had been a victim, sure. First when his son was taken, and then in that parking lot that night. But when the three men entered his home, he'd turned it around on them. He was a survivor.

"Detective?"

Jake looked up and saw Siebert standing by the Dumpster.

He walked over to him, rubbing at the dull ache in his sac joint, keeping an eye on Hogan.

"He almost got you," Paul said. He pointed at Jake's shoulder.

Jake remembered feeling the tug when Hogan's gun discharged. He fingered the hole blasted through the shoulder seam of his blazer. "You can go, Paul."

"I want to explain. About that night."

The man had been holding it in for a long time. If he wanted to talk about it, Jake would listen. He owed him that, at least, for saving his life. "Okay."

As Siebert told his story, there was only a single thought running through Jake's mind: *Now that I know the truth, what am I going to do with it?* The only thing he knew for sure was that he wasn't going to let the justice system get its hands on Paul Siebert for something Bull Warren had forced upon him.

CHAPTER SIXTY-TWO

Jake parked at the end of the lot and lowered the Mustang's windows. A storm had swept through Weston a few days before, lashing the city with a hard rain and leaving behind cooler temperatures. A billow of white clouds softened the light and darkened the greens in the foliage surrounding the lagoon-side picnic area. The Dumpster was gone, and the mud clumps and drag marks across the grass had been washed away.

He took in a lungful of fresh air, rich with the scents of water and earth, and would have smiled if he had one in him. He stripped off the tie he'd worn for Bull's funeral, rolled it carefully, and put it in a cup holder in the console.

The Boy Scout troop, all decked out in their uniforms, were working together arranging picnic tables into a half circle near the water while dozens of family members milled around under the trees. Snippets of conversations and laughter filled the grove. Paul and Linda Siebert walked along the far edge of the grass, holding hands, Linda's long floral print skirt flowing about her legs. She tilted her head back to look up at her husband, then spotted Jake. Her face lost its happy shine. She stopped walking, tugged on Paul's arm, and whispered in his ear. He turned and eyed Jake's Mustang, then released her hand and strode across the grass, eyes locked on Jake. Linda walked toward the Scouts and their families.

Siebert leaned in the passenger window. "What are you doing here?"

"We found your name on the list of people who were here the day the Buick was brought up. Figured you'd be back for the Eagle Scout award ceremony."

"A boy in Steven's troop led the project."

Jake gestured with his head. "Hop in."

Siebert looked off at the Scouts, then opened the door and got in.

"I wanted to say thank you," Jake said. "You saved my life."

Siebert shrugged, his eyes finding Jake's, then pulling away to watch the boys in the clearing. "I saw in the paper that the sheriff and the state's attorney declared it a double murder-suicide."

Jake gritted his teeth and shifted in his seat. He hadn't let himself off the hook just because it had been Bev who had made that decision. She'd only had the opportunity to do so because Jake had called Braff and told him to let her have the case. Making that call had cost Jake a piece of himself—and a lot of sleep. He could catch up on the sleep, but the piece of himself was gone forever.

"This Bull Warren. The old guy that died. He started it all?"

Jake nodded. Paul Siebert had clearly already begun to piece together what Jake had promised to tell him: who had set the whole thing in motion and why. It was important that Paul knew the truth. Important to Paul, and important to Jake. Jake still felt that if only he'd learned who had hired the thief who'd killed Mary... he would have dealt with her death better than he had.

"Did you kill the old man?" Siebert asked.

"Where did you get that idea?"

"I heard everything you and the deputy sheriff said here in the park. I was hiding behind the Dumpster."

So Siebert knew. But that didn't change anything. Siebert would stay silent. He had his own secrets to keep.

"No. I just happened to be there when he died." *Standing over him and judging him guilty. And sentencing him to death.*

Siebert's eyes narrowed with a question, but he didn't ask it.

"Last time we were here—when you saved my life..." Jake said, "I promised to tell you the whole story. I promised to tell you what brought those men to your house."

"They were looking for that list," Siebert said, looking away.

"Yes. It was an inventory, basically part of a will, listing Jedidiah Sublett's assets. Bull Warren was the public administrator when Jedidiah Sublett died; that means he handled Sublett's estate. When he read the will and its inventory of gold coins, he saw an opportunity. He stole the collection and switched out the inventory. But Sublett's lawyer had a copy of the original inventory, and you found it in his old desk."

It was Coogan who had tracked down the auction information and learned who had originally owned the desk.

"When the antique expert found the list and read part of it live on the public access channel, Bull Warren heard about it and feared his theft would be discovered. So he needed to get it from you before you figured out what you had."

"I doubt I ever would have thought of it again," Siebert said.

"Bull couldn't count on that. So he hired Silva to get it back. Silva recruited his two friends to help. They staked out your house and followed you to the liquor store. They confronted you there as a pretext, to explain how they came to be at your house later. Made it look like that was just part of their fun, so you wouldn't connect them to the inventory. Which you never did. You know the rest."

"That old man sent those three goons to our house and turned us into... and he... he gets to die peacefully." Siebert gripped his knees so hard the tendons stood out on his fore-arms. "Gets those nice write-ups in the paper. Gets to keep all that money?" Siebert's voice rose.

"He lost all that money way back then." Coogan had done his research. He'd figured out that Bull had lost the money in failed land speculation out by the mall. "Let's talk about what you get out of how it ended. You and Linda."

"What we get?" Siebert looked at Jake.

"You and Linda get to stay in your nice house and raise your daughter and take care of all those boys who need you. You get away with murder."

"It was self-defense, not murder."

"If you had called 911 when you subdued the men, maybe. But you didn't. At that point two of those men were still alive."

Siebert stared through the windshield at the distant crowd.

Jake let the silence build, his mind filled with the strength and courage Paul and Linda had shown that night. Paul and Linda Siebert were not going to risk losing a second child to violence. When Silva and his crew invaded the Siebert house, they paid the ultimate price.

A price they deserved.

Jake bit his lip as he rolled the word around in his head.

Beyond deserved. The men had earned what happened to them. Vengeance, this time, belonged to the Sieberts for what Bull had forced them to become.

"What about that deputy sheriff, Hogan? He had a part in this, and he tried to kill you."

"I'm not pressing charges." Jake had played the recording back for Hogan. It was enough to convince the man to leave town.

"But he worked for the sheriff, right? And she's the old man's daughter? Was she part of sending those men into my house?"

Jake started shaking his head even before Siebert finished. "She had nothing to do with what happened back then. And she had no idea her deputy was coming after me like that." Hogan had confirmed that Bev hadn't ordered him to cut Jake's brake lines or attack him at the river. And Jake believed him.

Siebert looked off at the Boy Scouts, his hand reaching for the door handle.

"One last thing." Jake tried to look at Siebert, but couldn't. "My mom's grandfather and Bull Warren's grandfather were brothers."

Siebert paused, then waved a hand dismissively. "That makes you and the sheriff, what, second or third cousins? I've got a ton of those back home in Mount Logan, so I know they can be as close as a brother or worse than a stranger. I don't hold that against you."

Paul Siebert offered Jake his hand. Jake took it. And as they shook, the constriction around Jake's chest and lower back released.

* * *

Bev had backed her car into a parking spot so she could keep an eye on Jake. She didn't understand why he'd come back here for the Scout ceremony until the man walked over and climbed into his car. She recognized him immediately. Paul Siebert, the man who'd found the inventory. She'd spent hours poring over Jake's murder book before turning the case over to one of her detectives, and she'd researched every name in it. She'd seen pictures of this man on several different Facebook pages. His foster kids loved him.

While the men talked, she struggled with being here. She should be at her dad's house for the throngs of family and friends and politicians and bureaucrats who were there to pay their respects. But when she saw Jake slip away less than an hour after the funeral, she decided it was time. She needed to know the real truth.

She needed to know it—and to know it would stay buried.

When Siebert left Jake's car and returned to the gathering, Bev got out of her car and slowly walked over. She leaned down to Jake's passenger window. He was staring out the windshield at the families clustered around the picnic tables, his eyes sad. Like he was missing something.

She knew the feeling.

"Jake?"

He jerked in his seat, then turned toward her.

"Bev." His voice was soft. "Thought you'd be tied up at the house all afternoon."

"Can I join you?"

"Sure." He reached across and pushed the door when she lifted the handle.

"Wasn't that Paul Siebert?" She dropped into the seat. The man had been wearing bug spray, and the harsh smell lingered in the close interior.

"Yes."

Despite spending every moment thinking about it, she hadn't come up with how to get the truth from him. She didn't know him well enough anymore.

"You here to ask me about Hogan's story?" Jake looked at her, then away.

Hogan had tried to convince Bev that Jake had killed her dad based on a few words he'd heard over his cell phone. It was nonsense: her dad was at death's door, and Dr. Franklin's autopsy couldn't have been more certain of her dad's cause of death.

But Bev left his question hanging while she asked one of her own. "I want to know the truth about who killed those men."

"What did Hogan tell you?"

Nothing. Hogan had refused to say a word about the dead men. His loyalty to her dad had survived his death. "I want to hear your side of the story."

"You closed the case. Doesn't that mean you know the truth?"

"Your murder book led to only one possible conclusion."

Jake shook his head. "You chose your dad over Victoria Silva. She'll spend the rest of her life thinking her husband was a killer who would rather be dead than with her."

"You would have done the same thing for your dad."

"No!" Jake gritted his teeth. "And Frank Houser is nothing like Bull Warren."

"My dad is dead and buried, Jake. I need to know the truth." Her voice rose so high it sounded almost hysterical. She brought it back down. "He couldn't have killed those men."

"He did and he didn't."

"That's not good enough!" Her voice was a harsh rasp. "Explain."

* * *

Jake saw a bit of his mother in Bev's profile. That Warren family jaw line.

Family.

"You know about the inventory, and that your dad stole the gold coins and—"

"I know everything except how those men died." Her lips pulled thin and her eyes were bright. "Please."

"Bull sent Silva, and Silva brought along his two pals."

Bev's eyes bored into his, waiting.

He kept it short. "They invaded Siebert's house to steal the inventory. They didn't make it out alive."

Her eyes popped wide. "Paul Siebert killed them?"

"Paul and Linda together." Linda Siebert had started it when she slashed Graves's throat with a pair of scissors.

"Jesus." Bev swallowed and looked away. Her eyes squeezed shut and her hands came together. "So where's the inventory now?"

"It wasn't in Siebert's house when Hogan burgled it a couple weeks after the liquor store, so Silva must have had it on him when he went into the river. Siebert didn't check their pockets. Too freaked out by what they'd done. Lange still had Linda Siebert's jewelry on him."

"So my dad didn't…"

"He didn't do it or even order it," Jake said. "But it's still felony murder, Bev."

"No, I know. Technically, but not actually. It was… like an accident."

"It wasn't an accident. Bull sent three men into the Sieberts' home to commit a felony while armed with a deadly weapon. Death was a foreseeable result of the situation he created."

Tears ran down her cheeks, leaving wet trails.

Laughter burst from the crowd around the picnic tables, and Jake looked over. When he turned back to Bev, she had wiped the tears away and her mouth was a hard line.

"Three murders you then covered up, Bev. Making you an accessory after the fact."

Her face went dark. "A fact you are aware of and have now covered up yourself. You're in it with me."

"Family," he said.

"Bullshit. You did this for the Sieberts."

She was right. But it wasn't a question, so he didn't respond.

"You did it for that family, not for ours."

Ours.

"It's been almost thirty years since I've felt like part of the Warren family," Jake said.

She got out of the car without another word and left Jake alone. A state he preferred.

He sat back and watched the ceremony, enjoying the awkward speeches and the parental pride. And most of all, the distance between him and all of it.

THE END

COMING SOON

in the Jake Houser Mystery Series

However Many More
A Jake Houser Mystery (Book #2)
Things get personal for Detective Jake Houser when he investigates the brutal murder of his lifelong friend Henry Fox. He soon learns that the handyman's simple life got a lot more complicated when he sold a silver bar to a local coin dealer.

Everyone who learns about the silver wanted a piece of the action, from the silent partner in Henry's new business, to his always-hard-up-for-cash ex-wife, to the two out-of-towners who have spent decades chasing a lost hoard of silver.

Had Henry found that lost hoard?

Now Jake must find the killer—and the silver—before greed brings more death to his town.

As It Never Was
A Jake Houser Mystery (Book #3)
Years ago, young Mark Siebert was snatched off his paper route. His confessed killer has been rotting in prison ever since. When a man claiming to be Mark shows up at his parents' house—only to disappear again—Mark's parents come to Detective Jake Houser for help. They have one condition: that he keep the cops out of it.

Jake owes the Sieberts his life, so he accepts their terms.

He will wish he hadn't.

Jake's off-the-books investigation digs up the depraved and twisted secrets of powerful men with unlimited resources. Will these dangerous forces erase every link to the past before Jake can find the truth?

ACKNOWLEDGMENTS

This, my first novel, was a long time coming together. It started as a straight noir crime novella I workshopped in a writers group through the College of DuPage. The crime depicted in that story eventually inspired this novel. It then took me many years and dozens of drafts to get to this final product.

Along the way, many people helped. My wife, Diane, and our daughter, Meghan, both read an early draft and helped me with the story's tone and direction. Our son, Jack, was a source of constant encouragement. Peter Thompson, Charlie Knight, and Julia Lightbody read a later draft and provided extremely helpful suggestions.

I also had help from the following professionals:
Ron Edison, Developmental Editor.
David Gatewood, Line Editor.
Kevin Summers, Book Formatting and Design.
Jeroen ten Berge, Cover Design.

I joined the Midwest Chapter of the Mystery Writers of America many years ago and started attending meetings when I became serious about finishing this book. I recommend the organization to anyone interested in writing crime novels. The support and generosity of its members helped propel this book to completion. I would particularly like to acknowledge the support and friendship of the members of my MWA-MW writers group: Allison Baxter, Adam Henkels, Mia P. Manansala, Irene Reed, and Shevon Porter.

ABOUT THE AUTHOR

Bo Thunboe is a suburbanite—born and raised—and still lives in Chicago's western suburbs. When bad eyesight killed his dream to fly helicopters for the Marines, he went to college. It didn't go well, and a few lost years later Bo was out in the world laying bricks and repossessing cars. Then he met his wife, Diane, got his head on straight, and went back to college, where he earned a BA in Economics and a JD from Northern Illinois University. (Go Huskies!) After a couple decades spent lawyering he is now a full-time writer.

Please visit www.thunboe.com to sign up for news and to learn more about Bo and the Jake Houser Mystery Series.

Made in the USA
Lexington, KY
16 September 2018